GREAT
Australian
STORIES

GREAT

Australian

STORIES

LEGENDS, YARNS AND TALL TALES

Graham Seal

ALLEN&UNWIN

First published in 2009

Allen & Unwin
83 Alexander Street
Crows Nest NSW 2065
Australia
Phone: (61 2) 8425 0100
Fax: (61 2) 9906 2218
Email: info@allenandunwin.com
Web: www.allenandunwin.com

Cataloguing-in-Publication details are available
from the National Library of Australia
www.trove.nla.gov.au

ISBN 978 1 74175 847 4

Set in 12.5/17 pt Adobe Caslon Pro by Bookhouse, Sydney

Printed and bound in Australia by The SOS Print + Media Group.

The paper in this book is FSC certified.
FSC promotes environmentally responsible,
socially beneficial and economically viable
management of the world's forests.

10 9

Contents

Foreword

ONCE UPON A time, in a far different Australia, there was no television, no radio and no internet, so families, friends and even strangers entertained each other with stories. Hard to believe but young and old sat around the kitchen table, lounged on verandahs and even around crackling campfires as they swapped tales, recited poetry and maybe sang a song; such poems and songs being part of the storytelling tradition.

As a young country, its people living predominantly in what we now refer to as 'the bush', we were keen to hear stories about the 'old country', usually England, Ireland and Scotland, and be reminded of times gone by. We were also curious to hear stories about the people who lived down the road, even if they were two hundred or two thousand miles away.

The stories played several roles other than just entertainment. They provided an obvious romantic link with the past, fuelled the imagination of their audience, provided a creative outlet for the tellers and, in a country with a dubious past, an opportunity to relax. More often than not, they allowed us to laugh at ourselves—and pomposity in general.

A lot of our stories were born in the bush. It must be remembered that the nineteenth century was a male-dominated society with a definite class-consciousness where the majority of men worked either as shepherds, miners, bullockies or drovers. This is where the campfire ruled as a neutral territory where all men were equal. Over a mug of steaming black China tea men discussed the ways of the world and, as the fire dimmed, talk would often turn to storytelling as an opportunity for escapism. Old tales were told but new ones were also created, in many cases told in the first person and bringing in fellow workmates as members of the cast. Humour has always been a great leveller and there's no denying that Australia developed a unique sense of humour—often described as 'dry'. There are several reasons suggesting why our humour is so laconic, including the immense size and isolation of the country and the reality that Australia was so blatantly different from Europe. It was (and still is) dry, hot, brown and tough as old boots. Many of the stories reinforced our determination to survive against the odds: fighting floods, droughts, bushfires, pestilence and, more often than not, the banks and authorities. In some ways many of the old stories could be described as 'people's history' however, because the folk never let the truth get in the way of a good yarn, they are an unreliable history.

Back in the old days when we entertained each other rather than nowadays where we tend to get entertained, and mainly by the electronic media and fabricated popular culture, most people had a 'party piece'—often a story that they had made their own. We also had the accompanying skills to 'perform' in front of an audience, large or small. We are rapidly losing this ability in proportion to the advancement in technologically delivered entertainment and, sadly, this passivity has a high price resulting in far too many social problems.

This collection is much more than just a bunch of stories retold for the umpteenth dozen time. Graham Seal has provided us with valuable keys to our national identity: why we are unique as a people. He salutes our past, including a good swag of indigenous stories, tales from the back of Bourke, Woop Woop and beyond the Black Stump, stories from our soldiers on the front line and also some ripper yarns from the cities. As a folklorist and fellow 'road's scholar' my old 'China-plate', Graham Seal, has offered insightful observations on why certain stories were created, passed around and also down through the years. *Great Australian Stories* is true to its title as it wanders from bush track to spooky hollow, follows the path of yowies and bunyips, searches for Lasseter's Reef, meets Dad and Dave and, on a different path, Henny-Penny, and then rambles into the cities where just as many entertaining characters are ready to tell *their* stories.

Warren Fahey AM
Folklorist

Acknowledgements

I WOULD LIKE to acknowledge the following people and organisations for providing information, assistance, advice, guidance or permission to publish stories in their care:

Jane Diplock, Warren Fahey, June Factor, Gwenda Davey, Hugh Anderson, Maureen Seal, Peter Sutton, Keith Pabai, Donald Banu, Eric Hayward, Rob Willis, Olya Willis, Phyl Lobl, Chris Woodland, Tim McCabe, Bob Reece, Peter Parkhill, Peter Ellis, Karl Neuenfeldt, the Oral History and Folklore Collection at the National Library of Australia, the Western Australian Folklore Archive in the John Curtin Prime Ministerial Library at Curtin University of Technology, the Battye Library of Western Australian History, the Queensland State Library, La Trobe Library and the New South Wales State Library. I would also like to thank Elizabeth Weiss of Allen & Unwin for taking on this project and the staff at A&U who helped turn manuscript into book. I am grateful to the Faculty of Humanities at Curtin University of Technology for assistance with research and pre-publication work. Finally, I hope this book honours the collectors and conservers of

Australian stories, many of whose names appear in the text and notes. In particular, this book is dedicated to the legacies of Bill Wannan, Bill Scott, Roland Robinson and Ron Edwards.

Introduction:
Telling tales

As FAR AS we know, humans have always told stories. The first inhabitants of Australia created a vast oral archive of myth and legend that explained their origins, the landscape, and its plants, animals and spirits. Before settling the last continent, Europeans swapped fabulous tales about what they imagined it to be like—a land of hermaphrodites, strange winged beasts and people who walked upside down. When they finally did arrive in numbers, they found the reality was sometimes as extraordinary as the fables. As the colonists moved out across the country, they began to make and share new stories about the Australian experience, sometimes blending these with indigenous traditions.

Today, these processes have produced a rich legacy of story that reflects the distinctiveness of Australia's past and present. It is a legacy that includes the ancient stories of the first inhabitants, those tales brought here by settlers from many lands, and those that have developed from the historical experience of modern Australia. There are legends of the Dreaming, yarns of pioneering, the bush, war, work and play, tales of the unexplained, the heroic, the monstrous and the tragic. They reflect the deep beliefs, fears, hopes and humour of those who tell and re-tell them.

The stories in this book are not personal anecdotes, although they may occasionally be told in this way. They are part of a national conversation held by many voices, often over a number of generations and across the country. As a collective cultural possession, they are part of the repertoires of folklore shared between and within social groups. They originate in and spread through the informal interactions of everyday life. As they develop over time and move from place to place, the stories pick up new elements, drop details that are dated or otherwise unintelligible, and adapt to the needs and attitudes of their tellers and hearers. It is these adaptations that keep a story tradition alive from generation to generation and provide its inheritors with a powerful sense of connection with earlier tellers and hearers. These communities of story can be as small as a family or as large as an industry, an army, or spread across a whole nation.

Most tales are the cultural property of their tellers and hearers. The stories of a certain group may be unknown to outsiders. This often surprises those who are familiar with them; they assume that everyone has heard this or that 'old chestnut'. As communities change, so do their reservoirs of story. Some fall silent as their original sources dry up. Others are reshaped to suit new realities. Stories rarely die altogether. Like all forms of folklore, they may hibernate for decades, even centuries, before reappearing—as is the case with a number of ostensibly modern urban legends. Stories old and new are increasingly passed on through audio and video recordings and the internet, which vastly extends their staying power.

When it is possible to trace the evolution of particular tales, we often find out something about their meanings and their relationship to history and folklore. Stories not only tell what has been seen, heard or believed but also connect their hearers with the time, place, events and people about which they speak. They map real and imaginative landscapes, as well as documenting what happened, or is thought to have happened, in them. They help us, in other words, make sense of the world and of our place within it.

Part of the appeal of the stories Australians tell is the colour and vitality of their language. As well as a liberal sprinkling of profanity, there are typically shortened words like 'wharfie', 'bullocky' and 'swaggy', and uniquely Australian ones like 'bushranger', 'digger', 'Speewah', 'bunyip', 'redback' and 'drongo'. Traditional tales also contain many Australian placenames, some of indigenous origin, like Coraki or Min Min, and others which evocatively combine the indigenous and the European, such as Ooldea Soak or Top Bingera. While some tales are versions of those told elsewhere in the world, their local renditions are well and truly Australianised.

While segments of this tradition, particularly indigenous myths and bush yarns, have been collected before, relatively little attention has been given to other types of tales. This book presents, for the first time, a reasonably representative selection of Australian stories in all their variety. The collective tale they tell is one of down-to-earth realism, tragedy and heroism, dry and cutting humour, an unexpectedly wide supernatural streak, a strong sense of place, colourful truths and even the odd lie. It tells us a good deal about what Australians value; what they fear, dislike, laugh at and wonder about.

The stories have been sorted into chapters by theme. The first chapter presents a small selection of tales from the continent's indigenous tradition. These are all translations, of course, though many retain words and phrases from the original languages in which they were recorded. They explain the origins of people, animals and plants in the timeless spirit world usually known as the Dreaming. None of these stories are secret or sacred, so they can be freely told. Some of their themes recur in stories elsewhere in the book.

Pioneering was the central Australian experience of the nineteenth and early twentieth centuries. As settlers spread across the continent from landfalls on the coasts, a frontier was created along whose ever-moving edges Europeans and indigenous people came into often abrasive contact. In some frontier stories Aborigines appear as savage foes; in others they are saviours. Occasionally they appear in both roles in the same story.

Despite, or sometimes because of, these experiences, the story traditions of original occupants and incoming occupiers began to interact, creating such hybrids as the bunyip, the yowie, and other legendary creatures. Aboriginal belief and the actions of settlers merged in the mystery of the Min Min Lights.

The 'Legends on the land' chapter presents stories about particular parts of the country. Some tell how places got their names; others deal with strange events or treasure hunts. There may be different versions of how and when something important began or what happened—and why. Stories of this kind are part of a common fund of local knowledge that reflects the powerful bonds of shared experience.

Also closely linked with locality are Australia's many traditions of ghosts and the supernatural. Considering its small population, the nation has generated a very large number of ghost stories, and continues to do so. The variety of oddities and apparitions involved suggests that Australia is a powerfully haunted land. Its indigenous traditions are rich with spirits of many kinds, and its settler history adds European ghosts and gremlins.

As well as the supernatural, there is plenty of scope for the fantastic. So-called fairy tales were widely told to children by adults and by adults to each other until at least the early twentieth century. In versions mostly derived from British traditions, accounts of giant-killers, pumpkin coaches and magical beanstalks have proved remarkably durable. Although Australian fairy stories generally lack fairies, they do have witches. These come in imported form from the rich storytelling traditions of Ireland. 'The witch's tale', told by Simon McDonald, is a wonderful example of the Australian bush art of spinning tales.

A favourite bush tradition is the tall tale. Australia has giant mozzies (mosquitoes), hoop snakes and split dogs in abundance. Modern urban legends update the tall tale with funny fables that are highly unlikely to be true. Australians have generally taken their leisure at least as seriously as their labour, producing large numbers of leg-puller yarns about sport, pastimes and, of course, sex. They love a good lie, it seems, no matter what the subject might be.

All traditions contain heroes and villains, as well as a few figures who are a little bit of both. Outstanding men and women, mythical and historical, can be found in indigenous and settler lore. The bushranger is an especially ambivalent character, whose crimes—often violent—are cast in folklore as justified defiance of oppression. In this sense, Australia's handful of celebrated bushrangers are its tragic heroes. The digger is a hero of another kind. Originally the volunteer footsoldier of World War I, the digger has become part of the mythology of Anzac. His larrikin ways are balanced by his sense of humour, his sceptical attitude to authority, and his reputation as a fighter.

Colourful, eccentric and plain crazy characters abound in Australian stories. They include numbskulls like the drongo, Dave in the 'Dad and Dave' stories, and the Cornish-descended Cousin Jacks. There are tricksters aplenty, from Jacky Bindi-i to Snuffler Oldfield. These named identities jostle for our affection with stock figures like the three blokes at a bar and the racecourse doper, among many others.

The frontier experience also produced a string of hard cases, such as the notoriously stingy pastoralist Hungry Tyson and the helpful but deep-drinking Wheelbarrow Jack. These were real people, as were the tough Eulo Queen and the sad Eliza Donnithorne. Others, like the tight-fisted cocky farmer and the world's greatest whinger, are archetypes. Genuine or larger than life, their deeds and sayings are remembered and relished.

A sense of shared experience motivates many stories of working life. These are usually humorous, often with a sharp edge of anti-authoritarianism, satire or outright ridicule of those who are supposedly in charge. The examples given here range from the nineteenth-century frontier farm to the present-day office or factory. While the forms of working humour have changed, the values and attitudes that underlie them have remained substantially the same.

Australia's stories are of pioneering, farming, bushranging, war, hardship, triumph, loss and laughter. They are about the unexplained, the mysterious, the lost and the never-was. They tell of origins and endings, heroes and villains, ghosts and monsters. Some are humorous yarns and tall tales of tricksters, nongs and lucky ducks. Others speak of odd but believable things that might have happened to a friend of a friend. There are tales told by railway workers, soldiers, farmers, parents, sporting types, office workers and just about anyone else. We all have tales to tell. Some of them may even be true.

Whether these stories are fact, fiction or a little of both, it is important to note that tradition can preserve both the bad and the good. As well as humour, determination, resilience and healthy scepticism, Australian stories sometimes reflect attitudes—especially towards Aboriginal people and women—that we find distasteful today. As this book reproduces historical as well as more recent texts, readers should be prepared for occasional jarring notes. Understanding something of their context, however, may help us appreciate the role of stories in social change. The fusion between indigenous and settler traditions about bunyips and ghosts, for example, is a sign of positive engagement. On the other hand, the divergence between those traditions in stories about frontier clashes points to ongoing tensions.

In many of the stories here, it is hard to tell where fact ends and fiction begins. But the myths that form in the spaces between history and folklore exert a powerful spell. Many prefer to believe the myths because they speak to cherished ideals like mateship, freedom and the fair go. If these ideals are often dreams rather than deeds, they are no less beguiling for that. In the end, our stories tell us as much as we want them to.

1
Stories in the heart

She's got her stories in the heart, not on the paper.

Emily Munyungka Austin, Kupa Piti (Coober Pedy) elder,
speaking of her grandmother's Dreamtime traditions

THE CULTURES OF Australia's indigenous peoples, Aborigines
and Torres Strait Islanders, are rich in story. Together with song,
dance and art, stories were a principal means of preserving and
transmitting cultural knowledge from generation to generation.
Much indigenous story is related to secret and sacred ritual and
excluded from general circulation. But there is also an extensive
repertoire of legends and stories that may be told freely. The
very small selection of such stories given here demonstrates
the powerful connections between the land and all the living
things upon it that is the foundation of indigenous belief.

Wirreenun the rainmaker

Katherine Langloh-Parker (1856–1940) was the wife of a
settler near Angledool, New South Wales. She developed a
close relationship with the Noongahburrah, a branch of the

11

Yularoi people. Her knowledge of their customs, beliefs and language helped her compile a unique record of the indigenous traditions of the Narran River region, even if filtered through the perceptions of an outsider and through various translations and retellings.

Wirreenun (meaning a priest or doctor) is a rainmaker who uses his magical abilities to help his people, despite the lapse of their belief in his powers. In this story, Wirreenun is also a name.

The country was stricken with a drought. The rivers were all dry except the deepest holes in them. The grass was dead, and even the trees were dying. The bark *dardurr* (humpy) of the blacks were all fallen to the ground and lay there rotting, so long was it since they had been used, for only in wet weather did they use the bark *dardurr*; at other times they used only *whatdooral*, or bough shades.

The young men of the Noongahburrah murmured among themselves, at first secretly, at last openly, saying: 'Did not our fathers always say that the *wirreenun* could make, as we wanted it, the rain to fall? Yet look at our country—the grass blown away, no *doonburr* seed to grind, the kangaroo are dying, and the emu, the duck, and the swan have flown to far countries. We shall have no food soon; then shall we die, and the Noongahburrah be no more seen on the Narran. Then why, if he is able, does not Wirreenun make rain?'

Soon these murmurs reached the ears of the old Wirreenun. He said nothing, but the young fellows noticed that for two or three days in succession he went to the waterhole in the creek and placed in it a *willgoo willgoo*—a long stick, ornamented at the top with white cockatoo feathers—and beside the stick he placed two big *gubberah*, that is, two big, clear pebbles which at other times he always secreted about him, in the folds of his *waywah*, or in the band or net on his head.

Especially was he careful to hide these stones from the women.

At the end of the third day Wirreenun said to the young men: 'Go you, take your *comeboos* and cut bark sufficient to make *dardurr* for all the tribe.'

The young men did as they were bade. When they had the bark cut and brought in, Wirreenun said: 'Go you now and raise with ant-bed a high place, and put thereon logs and wood for a fire, build the ant-bed about a foot from the ground. Then put you a floor of ant-bed a foot high wherever you are going to build a *dardurr.*'

And they did what he told them. When the *dardurr* were finished, having high floors of ant-bed and water-tight roofs of bark, Wirreenun commanded the whole camp to come with him to the waterhole; men, women, and children, all were to come. They all followed him down to the creek, to the waterhole where he had placed the *willgoo willgoo* and *gubberah*. Wirreenun jumped into the water and bade the tribe follow him, which they did. There in the water they all splashed and played about.

After a little time, Wirreenun went up first behind one black fellow and then behind another, until at length he had been round them all, and taken from the back of each one's head lumps of charcoal. When he went up to each he appeared to suck the back or top of their heads, and to draw out lumps of charcoal, which, as he sucked them out, he spat into the water. When he had gone the round of all, he went out of the water.

But just as he got out, a young man caught him up in his arms and threw him back into the water.

This happened several times, until Wirreenun was shivering. That was the signal for all to leave the creek. Wirreenun sent all the young people into a big bough shed, and bade them all go to sleep. He and two old men and two old women stayed outside. They loaded themselves with all their belongings piled up on their backs, *dayoorl* (grinding) stones and all, as if ready for a flitting. These old people walked impatiently around the bough shed as if waiting a signal to start somewhere. Soon a big black cloud appeared on the horizon, first a single cloud, which, however, was soon followed by others rising all round. They rose quickly until they all met just overhead, forming a big black mass of clouds. As soon as this big, heavy, rain-laden looking cloud was stationary overhead, the old people went into the bough shed and bade the young people wake up and come out and look at the sky.

When they were all roused Wirreenun told them to lose no time, but to gather together all their possessions and hasten to gain the shelter of the bark *dardurr*. Scarcely were they all in the *dardurr*s and their spears well hidden when there sounded a terrific clap of thunder, which was quickly followed by a regular cannonade, lightning flashes shooting across the sky, followed by instantaneous claps of deafening thunder. A sudden flash of lightning, which lit a pathway from heaven to earth, was followed by such a terrific clash that the blacks thought their very camps were struck. But it was a tree a little distance off. The blacks huddled together in their *dardurr*s, frightened to move, the children crying with fear, and the dogs crouching towards their owners.

'We shall be killed,' shrieked the women. The men said nothing but looked as frightened.

Only Wirreenun was fearless. 'I will go out,' he said, 'and stop the storm from hurting us. The lightning shall come no nearer.'

So out in front of the *dardurr*s strode Wirreenun, and naked he stood there facing the storm, singing aloud, as the thunder roared and the lightning flashed, the chant which was to keep it away from the camp.

'*Gurreemooray, mooray, durreemooray, mooray, mooray,*' &c.

Soon came a lull in the cannonade, a slight breeze stirred the trees for a few moments, then an oppressive silence, and then the rain in real earnest began, and settled down to a steady downpour, which lasted for some days.

When the old people had been patrolling the bough shed as the clouds rose overhead, Wirreenun had gone to the waterhole and taken out the *willgoo willgoo* and the stones, for he saw by the cloud that their work was done.

When the rain was over and the country all green again, the blacks had a great corroboree and sang of the skill of Wirreenun, rainmaker to the Noongahburrah.

Wirreenun sat calm and heedless of their praise, as he had been of their murmurs. But he determined to show them that his powers were great, so he summoned the rainmaker of a neighbouring tribe, and after some consultation with him, he ordered the tribes to go to the Googoorewon, (a place of trees) which was then a dry plain with solemn, gaunt trees all round it, which had once been blackfellows.

When they were all camped round the edges of this plain, Wirreenun and his fellow rainmaker made a great rain to fall just over the plain and fill it with water.

When the plain was changed into a lake, Wirreenun said to the young men of his tribe: 'Now take your nets and fish.'

'What good?' said they. 'The lake is filled from the rain, not the flood water of rivers, filled but yesterday, how then shall there be fish?'

'Go,' said Wirreenun. 'Go as I bid you; fish. If your nets catch nothing then shall Wirreenun speak no more to the men of his tribe, he will seek only honey and yams with the women.'

More to please the man who had changed their country from a desert to a hunter's paradise, they did as he bade them, took their nets and went into the lake. And the first time they drew their nets, they were heavy with *goodoo*, *murree*, *tucki*, and *bunmillah*. And so many did they catch that all the tribes, and their dogs, had plenty.

Then the elders of the camp said now that there was plenty everywhere, they would have a *borah* that the boys should be made young men. On one of the ridges away from the camp, that the women should not know, they would prepare a ground.

And so was the big *borah* (ceremonial gathering) of the Googoorewon held, the *borah* which was famous as following on the triumph of Wirreenun the rainmaker.

⌒

Mau and Matang

Australia's northernmost extreme is the small island of Boigu, just six kilometres off the coast of Papua New Guinea. The six clans of the island began when a man named Kiba and his brothers settled there. Christian missionaries came to Boigu in 1871, an event commemorated today in the annual 'Coming of the Light' ceremony, which blends Boigu mythology with elements of Christian belief.

This important Boigu tale of impending doom, revenge and warrior honour highlights the importance of reciprocal relationships—even those of revenge and blood—and the high regard in which warrior skills were held by all the people of Torres Strait and beyond.

*L*ong ago there were two warrior brothers of Boigu, Mau and Matang. Mau was the elder brother. They fought for the love of fighting and very often for no reason.

One day they received a message from their friend Mau of Arudaru, which is on the Papuan mainland just across from Boigu. Mau bade them come quickly for yams and taro, which would otherwise be eaten by pigs.

Mau and Matang made ready to go to Arudaru.

Their sister wove the sails for their canoes. At mid-afternoon, just as she had completed them, she noticed a big stain of blood on one mat. She hurried to her brothers to tell them about it and so try to prevent them from setting out on their voyage.

Mau and Matang would not heed the warning sign, and they set off with their wives and children. They reached Daudai and spent the first night at Kudin. During the night Mau's canoe drifted away. The brothers sent the crew to search for it, and they came upon it at Zunal, the sandbank of *markai* (spirits of the dead).

As they drew close, they saw the ghost of Mau appear in front of the canoe. In its hand was a dugong spear decorated with cassowary feathers. The ghost went through the motions of spearing a dugong, then placed the spear in the canoe and vanished.

Next they saw Matang's ghost pick up the spear from the canoe, just as Mau's had done. It too made as if to spear a dugong. Then it replaced the spear in the canoe and faded from sight.

On reaching the canoe, the crew members found the spear in it.

On their return to Kudin they told Mau and Matang what had happened. The brothers refused also to heed this warning. They ordered the party to set out for Arudaru, which they reached after a day's walk.

The head man of Arudaru, whose name also was Mau, greeted them, with his own people and many others, gave them food, and said that he would give them the yams and taro the following day. With that, the Boigu people slept.

In the morning they woke to a deserted village. Only Mau of Arudaru remained. He gave them breakfast and then presented Mau and Matang with a small bunch of green bananas. It was a declaration of war.

Despite the friendship between Mau of Arudaru and the brothers Mau and Matang, the brothers had lightly killed kinsmen and friends of his, and his first duty as Mau of Arudaru was to avenge them. The invitation to come across for yams and taro had been part of a considered plan.

For days past, fighting men from the neighbouring villages had been gathering at Arudaru. There had been endless talking until the whole plan had ripened. With rage in their hearts, Mau and Matang herded their party together and set out on the return journey.

Mau of Arudaru had hidden his fighting men in two rows in the long grass so as to form two rows of unseen men. He allowed the brothers to lead their people back until they were halfway through the lines of fighting men. Then he gave the signal to attack.

The Boigu people were trapped. The women and children and the crew members fled. Mau bade his brother break the first spear thrown at him. He himself with his bow warded off the first spear that was hurled at him, splitting the end and throwing it backward between his legs, thus giving himself good luck in battle.

Matang warded off the first spear received by him, but did not break it as Mau had commanded.

Before long Matang was struck in the ankle by an arrow with a poisoned tip. 'I have been bitten by a snake,' he cried, and fell dead.

Mau continued to fight and kept backing towards his brother's body until he stood astride it. He fought until nearly all his assailants lay dead. The rest would have fled, but Mau signalled to them to put an end to him, so that he might join his brother. And this they did.

Mau and Matang did not have their heads cut off as would have been done were they ordinary men. Their courage and skill in battle were honoured by their opponents. They sat the brothers against two trees. They tied their bodies to the tree trunks, facing them south towards Boigu. On their heads they placed the warrior's headdress of black cassowary feathers and eagles' wings, so that when the wind blew from the south the eagles' wings were fanned backward and when it dropped, they fell forward.

Ungulla Robunbun

The anthropologist Baldwin Spencer (1860–1929) documented the complex oral traditions about ancestral beings and totemic relationships among the Kakadu people, publishing these in 1914 as *The Native Tribes of the Northern Territory of Australia*. The female entity in this story from Spencer's book creates birds, insects and human beings, giving male and female their physical characteristics. She is also the bringer of language. Pundamunga and Maramma, mentioned at the end of the story, are descended from the one great female ancestor of the Kakadu, Imberombera. Imberombera travelled all over the region, leaving her spirit children wherever she went and eventually sending them forth to take the different languages to the countries of Pundamunga and Maramma. Ungalla's naming of Pundamunga and Maramma's children confirms that this is the country of these two beings and their descendants. Once again, the story highlights the spiritual connections between country, ancestors, totems and language that are the basis of indigenous culture. Spencer recounts the following tale, including a reference to the tale being told to him.

A woman named Ungulla Robunbun came from a place called Palientoi, which lies between two rivers that are now known as the McKinlay and the Mary. She spoke the language of the Noenmil people and had many children. She started off to walk to Kraigpan, a place at the head of the Wildman Creek. Some of her children she carried on her shoulders, others on her hips, and one or two of them walked. At Kraigpan she left one boy and one girl and told them to speak the Quiratari (or

Quiradari) language. Then she walked on to Koarnbo Creek, near the salt water at Murungaraiyu, where she left a boy and a girl and told them to speak Koarnbut. Travelling on to Kupalu, she left the Koarnbut language behind her and crossed over what is now called the East Alligator River, to its west side. She came on to Nimbaku and left a boy and a girl there and told them to speak the Wijirk language. From here she journeyed on across the plains stretching between the Alligator rivers to Koreingen, the place to which Imberombera had previously sent out two individuals named Pundamunga and Maramma. Ungulla Robunbun saw them and said to her children, 'There are blackfellows here; they are talking Kakadu; that is very good talk; this is Kakadu country that we are now in.'

Ungulla went on until she came near enough for them to hear her speaking. She said, 'I am Kakadu like you; I will belong to this country; you and I will talk the same language.' Ungulla then told them to come close up, which they did, and then she saw that the young woman was quite naked. Ungulla herself was completely clothed in sheets of *ranken*, or paper bark, and she took one off, folded it up, and showed the *lubra* how to make an apron such as the Kakadu women always wear now. She told the *lubra* that she did not wish to see her going about naked. Then they all sat down. Ungulla said, 'Are you a *lubra*?' and she replied, 'Yes, I am *ungordiwa*.' Then Ungulla said, 'I have seen Koreingen a long way off; I am going there. Where is your camp?' The Kakadu woman said, 'I shall go back to my camp if you go to Munganillida.' Ungulla then rose and walked on with her children. On the road some of them began to cry, and she said, '*Bialilla waji kobali*, many children are crying; *ameina waji kobali*, why are many children crying?' She was angry and killed

21

two of them, a boy and a girl, and left them behind. Going on, she came near to Koreingung and saw a number of men and women in camp and made her own camp some little distance from theirs. She then walked on to Koreingung and said, 'Here is a blackfellows' camp; I will make mine here also.'

She set to work to make a shelter, saying '*Kunjerogabi ngoinbu kobonji*, I build a grass shelter; *mornia balgi*, there is a big mob of mosquitoes.' As yet the natives had not seen Ungulla or her children. There were plenty of fires in the natives' camps but no mosquitoes. They did not have any of these before Ungulla came, bringing them with her. She went into her shelter with her children and slept. After a time she came out again and then the other natives caught sight of her. Some of the younger Numulakirri determined to go to her camp. When she saw them coming she went into her *kobonji* and armed herself with a strong stick. She was Markogo, that is, elder sister, to the men, and, as they came up, she shouted out from her bush wurley, saying, 'What are you all coming for? You are my *illaberri* (younger brothers). I am *kumali* to you.'

They said nothing but came on with their hands behind their backs. As soon as they were close to the entrance to her shelter she suddenly jumped up, scattering the grass and boughs in all directions. She yelled loudly and, with her great stick, hit them all on their private parts. She was so powerful that she killed them all and their bodies tumbled into the waterhole close by. Then she went to the camp where the women and children had remained behind and drove them ahead of her into the water. The bones of all these natives are still there in the form of stones with which also their spirit parts are associated. When all was over the woman stood in her camp. First of all she pulled out her *kumara* (vagina) and threw it away, saying, 'This belongs to the *lubras.*' Then she threw her breasts away and a *wairbi*, or woman's fighting stick, saying that they all belonged to the *lubras*. From her dilly bag she took a *paliarti*, or flat spear-thrower, and a light reed spear, called *kunjolio*, and, throwing them away, shouted out, 'These are for the men.'

She then took a sharp-pointed blade of grass called *karani*, caught a mosquito (*mornia*) and fixed it on to his head (*reri*), so that it could 'bite' and said, 'Your name is *mornia*.' She also gave him instructions, saying, '*Yapo mapolio, jirongadda mitjerijoro*, go to the plains, close to the mangroves; *manungel jereini jauo*, eat men's blood; *kumanga kaio mornia*, (in) the bush no mosquitoes.' That is why mosquitoes are always so abundant amongst the mangroves. When she had done this Ungalla gathered her remaining children together and, with them, went into the waterhole.

There were a great many natives, and, after they were dead, their skins became transformed into different kinds of birds. Some of them changed into small owls, called *irre-idill*, which catch fish. When they hear the bird calling out at night they say 'dodo', which means wait, or, later on; 'tomorrow morning we will put a net in and catch some fish for you'. Others turned into *kurra-liji-liji*, a bird that keeps a look out to see if any strange natives are about. If a man wants to find out if any strangers are coming, he says to the bird, '*Umbordera jereini einji*? Are men coming to-day?' If they are, the bird answers, '*Pitjit, pitjit.*' Others changed into *jidikera-jidikera*, or willy wagtails, which keep a look out for buffaloes and crocodiles. Others, again, changed into dark-coloured kites, called *daigonora*, which keep a look out to see if any hostile natives are coming up to 'growl'. A man will say to one of these *daigonora*, if he sees it in a tree, '*Breikul jereini jeri?'* that is, 'Far away, are there men coming to growl?' If the bird replies to him he knows that they are coming, but if it makes no sound, then he knows there are no strangers about. Others changed into *moaka*, or crows, that show natives where geese are to be found; others into *tidji-tidji*, a little bird that shows them where the sugar-bags may be secured; others into *mundoro*, a bird that warns them when natives are coming up to steal a *lubra*. Some, again, changed into *murara*, the 'mopoke', which warns them if enemies are coming up in strong numbers. They ask the bird, and if it answers with a loud 'mopoke' they know that there are none about and that they have no need to be anxious, but if it answers with a low call, then they know that hostile natives are somewhere in the neighbourhood, and a man will remain on watch all night. Some of the women changed into laughing jackasses.

All these birds are supposed to understand what the blackfellows say, though they cannot themselves speak. While the men were explaining matters to us they spoke to two or three wagtails that came close up and twittered. The men said that the birds wanted to know what we were talking about, but they told them that they must go away and not listen, which they did.

Before finally going into the waterhole, Ungulla called out the names of the natives to whom she said the country belonged. They were all the children of Pundamunga and Maramma.

Ooldea Water

The colourful and enigmatic Daisy Bates (1863–1951) spent many years living with Aboriginal people in southwestern Australia. She claimed a special relationship with them that gave her unique access to indigenous traditions and insights into their significance. While these claims and many of her interpretations of the anthropological evidence she gathered have been strongly challenged, the stories she collected and preserved are of great value as records of traditions that have since fragmented or been completely lost.

In her book *The Passing of the Aborigines* Daisy Bates dramatically introduces the story of how the small marsupial Karrbiji brought water to Ooldea, in South Australia. The explorer Earnest Giles in 1875 was one of the first Europeans to discover this permanent water source, over 800 kilometres west of Port Augusta, on the eastern edge of the Nullarbor Plain. Bates lived at Ooldea from 1919 to 1934 and gave this description of the place:

> Nothing more than one of the many depressions in the never-ending sandhills that run waveringly from the Bight for nearly a thousand miles, Ooldea Water is one of Nature's miracles in barren Central Australia. No white man coming to this place would ever guess that that dreary hollow with the sand blowing across it was an unfailing fountain, yet a mere scratch and the magic waters welled in sight. Even in the cruellest droughts, it had never failed. Here the tribes gathered in their hundreds for initiation and other ceremonies.

In 1917 the Transcontinental Railway opened and the small settlement became a watering point for the railway line. By 1926 the water had been drained off in a process well described by Bates:

> In the building of the transcontinental line, the water of Ooldea passed out of its own people's hands forever. Pipelines and pumping plants reduced it at the rate of 10,000 gallons a day for locomotives. The natives were forbidden the soak, and permitted to obtain their water only from taps at the siding. In a few years the engineering plant apparently perforated the blue clay bed, twenty feet below surface. Ooldea, already an orphan water, was a thing of the past.

Despite these events, Ooldea retained its special significance for local Aborigines, though access to the area was restricted during the 1950s in response to the atomic testing at Maralinga. By 1988, Ooldea was again Aboriginal land thanks to the *Maralinga Tjarutja Land Rights Act*.

This is the legend of Ooldea Water.

A long, long time ago in *dhoogoor* times, Karrbiji, a little marsupial, came from the west carrying a skin bag of water on his back, and as he travelled east and east there was no water anywhere, and Karrbiji said, 'I will put water in the ground so that the men can have good water always.'

He came to a shallow place like a dried lake. He went into the middle of it, and was just going to empty his water bag when he heard someone whistling. Presently he saw Ngabbula, the spike-backed lizard, coming threateningly towards him, whistling.

As he watched Ngabbula coming along, Karrbiji was very frightened, and he said, 'I can only leave a little water here. I shall call this place Yooldil-Beena—the swamp where I stood to pour out the water,' and he tried to hide the water from Ngabbula by covering it with sand, but Ngabbula came along quickly and Karrbiji took up his skin bag and ran and ran because Ngabbula would take all his water from him.

By and by he had run quite away from Ngabbula, and soon he came to a deep sandy hollow among high hills, and he said, 'This is a good place, I can hide all the water here, and Ngabbula won't be able to find it. He can't smell water.'

Karrbiji went down into the hollow and emptied all the water out of his bag into the sand. He covered up the water so that it could not be seen, and he said, 'This is Yooldil Gabbi, and I shall sit beside this water and watch my friends finding it and drinking it.' Karrbiji was feeling very glad that he had put the water in such a safe place.

All at once, he again heard loud whistling and he looked and saw Ngabbula coming along towards him. Karrbiji was very frightened of Ngabbula, and he quickly picked up his empty skin bag and ran away; but fast as he ran, Ngabbula ran faster.

Now, Giniga, the native cat, and Kallaia, the emu, were great friends of Karrbiji, and they had watched him putting the water under the sand where they could easily scratch for it and drink cool nice water always, and they said, 'We must not let Ngabbula kill our friend', and when Ngabbula chased Karrbiji, Kallaia and Giniga chased Ngabbula, and Ngabbula threw his spears at Giniga and made white spots all over Giniga where the spears had hit him. Giniga hit Ngabbula on the head with his club, and now

27

all *ngabbulas'* heads are flat, because of the great hit that Giniga had given Ngabbula.

Then they ran on again and Ngabbula began to get frightened and he stopped chasing Karrbiji, but Kallaia and Giniga said, 'We must kill Ngabbula, and so stop him from killing Karrbiji,' and a long, long way north they came up to Ngabbula, and Kallaia, the emu, speared him, and he died.

Then they went to Karrbiji's place, and Kallaia, Giniga and Karrbiji made a corroboree, and Beera, the moon, played with them, and by and by he took them up into the sky where they are now *kattang-ga* ('heads', stars).

Karrbiji sat down beside his northern water. When men came to drink of his water, Karrbiji made them his friends, and they said, 'Karrbiji is our Dreamtime totem,' and all the men who lived beside that water were Karrbiji totem men. They made a stone emblem of Karrbiji and they put it in hiding near the water, and no woman has ever walked near the place where the stone emblem sits down.

Kallaia, the emu, 'sat down' beside Yooldil Water, and when the first men came there they saw Kallaia scraping the sand for the water, and they said 'Kallaia shall be our totem. This is his water, but he has shown us how to get it.' Giniga, the native cat, went between the two great waters, Karrbiji's Water and Kallaia's Water, and was always the friend of both. Ngabbula was killed north of Yooldil Gabbi, but he also had his water, and men came there and made him their totem, but Kallaia totem men always fought with Ngabbula totem men and killed them and ate them.

Karrbiji, after his work was done, went north, and 'sat down' among the Mardudharra Wong-ga (*wonga-ga*-speech, talk), not far from the Arrunda, beside his friends Giniga, the native cat, and Kallaia, the emu. And he made plenty of water come to the Mardudharra men, and by and by the men said, 'Karrbiji has brought his good water to us all. We will be brothers of Karrbiji.'

~

The woolgrum

This story is from the Weelman people of Australia's far southwest, now known broadly as Nyungar. It was told to Ethel Hassell, the wife of an early settler in the area during the 1870s. The woolgrum is half woman, half frog. This story, in one variation or another, was widely told. The possibility of winning a non-human wife is widespread in global tale tradition.

Far, far away in the west toward the setting sun there are three big rivers. The waters are fresh and flow down to the sea. Long, long ago, a *jannock* (spirit) lived between these rivers who had neither companions nor wives. He was very lonesome in this region but had to remain there for a certain time. To help overcome his loneliness he tamed all the animals in the region and they became fast friends with him. In the evening they used to sit around his fire. The *chudic* (wildcat) sat with the *coomal* (opossum), they told him stories of what was going on in the forest and on the plains.

In times of flood the rivers used to expand over a great expanse of territory, making many marshes, and, since the water was fresh, these became the breeding grounds for all kinds of *gilgie* (crayfish), fish and frogs [and] the *jannock* became friends with them too. There was one kind of frog, however, that he had difficulty in taming. This was *plomp*, the bullfrog. He coaxed the *plomp* to visit him and finally was able to persuade them to sleep under his cloak with him. He also tamed the *youan*, or bobtailed iguana. The *youan* made love to the *plomp* and this became very annoying to the *jannock*. He told the *plomp* that the *youan* made friends only that they might eat the young *plomp*. The *plomp* were grateful to him for this warning and showed their appreciation by surrounding his hut every night and singing him to sleep.

This kept up for some time, but finally it was time for the *jannock* to return to the other *jannock*. Just before he left, he breathed on the frogs and told them that in time they would be like himself.

The *jannock* had no business to say this, however, for he had not the power to cause them to change into beings like himself. The result was that every now and again the *plomp* brought forth a creature which is called a *woolgrum*. It is always half woman and half frog and never like a man. The *woolgrum*, being of *jannock* blood, were able also to make themselves invisible.

Now, when a man is an outcast from his tribe, no woman will live with him, even though the ostracism is not due to any fault of his own. As a last recourse to find a wife, he must travel towards the setting sun until he comes to the three great rivers which roll widely down to the sea through the broad marshes and between banks covered with thick-growing scrub. When he reaches this land he will hear the frogs croaking and on still nights he will hear the *woolgrum* calling. He will not be able to see them, however, because of their *jannock* blood, except on starlight nights in the winter when there is no moon. At that time the *woolgrum* come on shore and build a hut and a fire to warm themselves. On those occasions, men can sometimes see the figures of women camped by the fire. If they go too near to the fire or make a rush and try to grab the women, however, they find nothing but bushes, and the *woolgrum* disappear, never again to return to that camp. They make camp in another region where they may be seen again under the same conditions, but it is impossible to catch them in such a bold manner.

The only way by which a man can get a *woolgrum* for a wife is by following these directions. He must camp alone near the big marshy flats and live only on fish and *gilgie*. He must not tell anyone where he has gone or for what purpose. He must camp there until the marshes begin to dry up, at which time he must search for the *youan* and catch a female in the act of giving birth to her young. Just as the sun sets, but before it is dark, he must throw the newly born *youan* on the fire and watch until it bursts. As it burst, he must turn to the river marshes, and then he will see the *woolgrum*. As soon as he sees them he must seize the remains of the infant *youan*, throw it at the *woolgrum*, and run as fast as he can to the river.

If a portion of the *youan* touches a *woolgrum*, the lower or frog part disappears and a naked woman stands in the marsh. If he acts quickly he can catch her for his wife, but if he does not move hastily she will sink into the water and float down toward the sea. If this happens, there is nothing he can do to save her. He must commence his operations all over again in another region, for the *woolgrum* will never return to that part of the river. He will also have to wait until the next winter, when the *woolgrum* come to camp on the shore again.

However, should he be successful in catching the woman, he must take her to his camp and roll her up in his cloak and keep her warm by the fire all that night. The next day he can take her as his wife but must hurry away from the locality and remain constantly by her side until the moon is again in the same quarter. By that time she will have lost her power to make herself invisible and, once this is gone, she will never leave him no matter what his faults may be. She will bear him many children and they will be stronger and much more clever than any of the men or women of his tribe. They soon become bad men and women, however, and can never have any children, though the men take many wives and the women many husbands. Thus a man who gets a *woolgrum* for a wife knows that, although he may have many children, he will never have any grandchildren and his race will disappear completely. No *jannock* can harm his children because of their *jannock* blood, and they are always able to tell when the *jannock* are about.

The *woolgrum* herself is very beautiful, but her children are decidedly ugly, with big heads and wide mouths. They are capable of travelling very quickly, however, especially in the river beds and over marshy land, and they have a most highly developed sense of hearing. No native woman likes to think that her son would like to seek a *woolgrum* for a wife, for this is done only as a last recourse. No man likes to be told that his mother was a *woolgrum*, for that reflects on his father's character and implies that he will never have any children to fight for him in his old age.

The *woolgrum* are said not to belong to either moiety; hence, whether a man is a Nunnich or a Wording, he can take as a wife any *woolgrum* he can catch without questioning her relationship.

~

LOST IN THE BUSH.—[Drawn by Chevalier.]

2
Pioneer traditions

WHITE WOMAN! — There are fourteen armed men,
partly White and partly Black, in search of you …

Message to the 'captured white woman of Gippsland', 1846

THE EUROPEAN OCCUPATION of Australia brought mainly British settlers into a world for which they were totally unprepared. The trees and plants, animals, land forms and climate were difficult for them to comprehend, as were the original inhabitants. As settlement pushed into the interior from various parts of the continent's coastline, the frontier took on an increasingly colonial character that mingled the imported traditions of the newcomers with their sometimes dangerous and violent experiences in Australia. The consequences of the frontier's steady encroachment on indigenous lands were devastating for Aborigines and often confronting for settlers.

The uncertainties and fears of the colonists in this strange and harsh new land sometimes led to brutal acts and dark obsessions, even delusions. In many areas, people seized on stories that reflected common nightmares: the woman carried off by 'savages'; the children lost in the bush. And harking back to the fables, there were even stranger stories of Europeans stumbling onto Australian shores long before the arrival of the First Fleet.

The lost colony

The land we now call Australia was known from earliest times as 'the great south land' or 'the unknown southland'. It was the subject of wild speculations, rumours and fantasies about the people who might live in it, the beasts that might prowl across it and the wondrous riches that it might hold. Even before the official first settlement at Botany Bay in 1788, it is said, there was a mysterious Dutch colony deep in the Outback.

The tradition of lost or wandering peoples goes back to at least the Old Testament era with its stories of the lost tribes of Israel. Such tales are often linked with legends of lost or hidden riches or of utopias to be found in undiscovered or little-explored continents. A well-known late mediaeval example is the legend of Prester John, which involved a kingdom of lost Christians somewhere in the Muslim East. Rider Haggard made use of the it in his novel *King Solomon's Mines*, which popularised the idea of a lost white tribe of Africa for nineteenth-century British readers. There are also white Eskimo legends swirling around the tragic story of the ill-fated quest of Lord Franklin, one-time lieutenant-governor of Van Diemen's Land (Tasmania), for a northwest passage through Canada.

Australia also has traditions of secret or unrecorded colonies in the wilderness. For example, there is a well-documented story of a lost colony descended from Dutch mariners, ship-wrecked generations before 1788. On 25 January 1834, an article appeared in the English *Leeds Mercury* newspaper under the headline, DISCOVERY OF A WHITE COLONY ON THE NORTHERN SHORE OF NEW HOLLAND. When it was reprinted in Australian papers, the unsigned item caused amazement and consternation.

A Correspondent living near Halifax has favoured us with the following interesting communication:—

TO THE EDITORS OF THE LEEDS MERCURY.

GENTLEMEN,—A friend of mine lately arrived from Singapore, via India overland, having been one of a party who landed at Raffles Bay, on the north coast of New Holland, on the 10th of April, 1832, and made a two months' excursion into the interior, has permitted me to copy the following extract out of his private journal, which I think contains some particulars of a highly interesting nature, and not generally known.

The exploring party was promoted by a scientific Society at Singapore, aided and patronized by the Local Government, and its object was both commercial and geographical; but it was got up with the greatest secrecy, and remained secret to all except the parties concerned. (For what good purpose it is impossible to conceive.)

Extract from an unpublished manuscript journal of an exploring party in Northern Australia, by Lieutenant Nixon:

M ay 15th, 1832—On reaching the summit of the hill, no words can express the astonishment, delight, and wonder I felt at the magical change of scenery, after having travelled for so many days over nothing but barren hills and rocks, and sands and parching plains, without seeing a single tribe of aborigines excepting those on the sea coast, and having to dig for water every day.

Looking to the southwards, I saw below me, at the distance of about three or four miles, a low and level country, laid out as it were in plantations, with straight rows of trees, through which a broad sheet of smooth water extended in nearly a direct line from east to west, as far as the eye could reach to the westward, but apparently sweeping to the southward at its eastern extremity like a river; and near its banks, at one particular spot on the south side, there appeared to be a group of habitations, embosomed in a grove of tall trees like palms. The water I guessed to be about half a mile wide, and although the stream was clearly open for two thirds of the distance from the southern bank, the remainder of it was studded by thousands of little islands stretching along its northern shores: and what fixed me to the spot with indescribable sensations of rapture and admiration was the number of small boats or canoes with one or two persons in each, gliding along the narrow channels between the little islands in every direction, some of which appeared to be fishing or drawing nets. None of them had a sail, but one that was floating down the body of the stream without wind, which seemed to denote that a current ran from east to west. It seemed as if enchantment had brought me into a civilized country, and I could scarcely resolve to leave the spot I stood upon, had it not been for the overpowering rays of a mid day sun, affecting my bowels, as it frequently had done, during all the journey.

On reaching the bottom of the hill in my return to our party at the tents, I was just turning round a low rock, when I came suddenly upon a human being whose face was so fair and dress so white, that I was for a moment staggered with terror, and thought that I was looking upon an apparition. I had naturally expected to meet an Indian as black or brown as the rest of the natives, and not a white man in these unexplored regions. Still quaking with doubts about the integrity of my eyes, I proceeded on, and saw the apparition advancing upon me with the most perfect indifference: in another minute he was quite near, and I now perceived that he had not yet seen me, for he was walking slowly and pensively with his eyes fixed on the ground, and he appeared to be a young man of a handsome and interesting countenance. We were got within four paces of each other when he heaved a deep and tremulous sigh, raised his eyes, and in an instant uttered a loud exclamation and fell insensible on the ground. My fears had now given place to sympathy, and I hastened to assist the unknown, who, I felt convinced, had been struck with the idea of seeing a supernatural being. It was a considerable time before he recovered and was assured of my mortality; and from a few expressions in old Dutch, which he uttered, I was luckily enabled to hold some conversation with him; for I had been at school in Holland in my youth and not quite forgotten the language. Badly as he spoke Dutch, yet I gathered from him a few particulars of a most extraordinary nature; namely, that he belonged to a small community, all as white as himself, he said about three hundred; that they lived in houses enclosed all together within a great wall to defend them from black men; that their fathers came there about one hundred and seventy years ago, as they said, from a distant land across the great sea;

and that their ship broke, and eighty men and ten of their sisters (female passengers?) with many things were saved on shore. I prevailed on him to accompany me to my party, who I knew would be glad to be introduced to his friends before we set out on our return to our ship at Port Raffles, from which place we were now distant nearly five hundred miles, and our time was limited to a fixed period so as to enable the ship to carry us back to Singapore before the change of the monsoon. The young man's dress consisted of a round jacket and large breeches, both made of skins, divested of the hair and bleached as white as linen; and on his head he wore a tall white skin cap with a brim covered over with white down or the small feathers of the white cocatoo [*sic*]. The latitude of this mountain was eighteen degrees thirty minutes fourteen seconds south; and longitude one hundred and thirty-two degrees twenty-five minutes thirty seconds east. It was christened Mount Singapore, after the name and in honour of the settlement to which the expedition belonged.

A subsequent part of the journal states further, 'that on our party visiting the white village, the joy of the simple inhabitants was quite extravagant. The descendant of an officer is looked up to as chief, and with him (whose name is Van Baerle), the party remained eight days. Their traditional history is, that their fathers were compelled by famine, after the loss of their great vessel, to travel towards the rising sun, carrying with them as much of the stores as they could, during which many died; and by the wise advice of their ten sisters they crossed a ridge of land, and meeting with a rivulet on the other side, followed its course and were led to the spot they now inhabit, where they have continued ever since. They have no animals of the domestic kind, either cows, sheep, pigs or any thing else; their plantations consist only of maize and yams, and these with fresh and dried fish constitute their principal food, which is changed occasionally for Kangaroo and other game; but it appears that they frequently experience a scarcity and shortness of provisions, most probably owing to ignorance and mismanagement; and had little or nothing to offer us now except skins. They are nominal Christians: their marriages are performed without any ceremony: all the elders sit in council to manage their affairs; all the young, from ten up to a certain age, are considered a standing militia, and are armed with long pikes; they have no books or paper, nor any schools; they retain a certain observance of the Sabbath by refraining from their daily labours, and perform a short superstitious ceremony on that day all together; and they may be considered almost a new race of beings.'

While the story seems to have passed out of the colonial newspapers, it never quite faded away in folk tradition. Recent researchers have been unable to identify a likely Lieutenant Nixon, nor have any other verifiable facts about the claimed expedition or lost colony been found. The man who sent the report to the *Leeds Mercury* was Thomas J. Maslen, an Australia enthusiast who, like many others at that time, had never actually visited the place. This did not stop him publishing a book on the subject, titled *The Friend of Australia*, in 1827. The book included a map that, in accord with one of the persistent nineteenth-century delusions about Australia, showed an inland sea at the continent's centre. Much of the book, like the story of the lost colony, must be considered another one of the fables about the great south land.

The battle that was a massacre

Australia's colonial history produced many stories of violence between indigenous people and settlers. Controversial and elusive though the details may be, it is undeniable that there were numerous confrontations, sometimes followed by massacres. Such events are known, or believed, to have taken place at Myall Creek, New South Wales, in 1838, at Mundrabilla Run, on the Nullarbor Plain, in the 1870s, and in dozens of other places on the edge of the frontier. As late as 1928, a massacre of Walpiri people took place at Coniston, 300 kilometres northwest of Alice Springs. Many of these events are remembered in stories told among both black and white people. Not surprisingly, these accounts often reflect very different points of view. On the settler side, they emphasise the fear that pervaded isolated outposts, and just retribution for Aboriginal misdeeds. On the indigenous side they reflect anger over settlers' violence and their invasion of traditional lands.

Events on the Murray River, Western Australia, in late 1834 remain the subject of intense local controversy: direct descendants of participants in the battle—or massacre—still live near the town of Pinjarra, where it took place. One of the earliest sources for what happened that day is the diary of a local settler, George Fletcher Moore, writing just a few days after the chilling events he describes.

THURSDAY—A strange rumour has reached us here that the party who went to the Murray River have fallen in with the natives there, and killed 35 of them. Captain Ellis being slightly wounded, and another soldier grazed by a spear. This is important if true . . .

Saturday, Nov. 1—Went to Perth yesterday, and got from the Governor an account of the battle of Pinjarra. They came upon the offending tribe in a position which I dare say the natives thought was most favourable for their manoeuvres, but which turned into a complete trap for them. In the first onset, three out of five of the small party which went to reconnoitre were unhorsed, two being wounded. The Governor himself came up with a reinforcement just in time to prevent the natives rushing in upon and slaughtering that party. The natives then fled to cross a ford, but were met and driven back by a party which had been detached for the purpose. They tried to cross at another ford, but were met there also, when they took to the river, lying hid under the overhanging banks, and seeking opportunities of casting their spears, but they were soon placed between two fires and punished severely. The women and children were protected, and it is consolatory to know that none suffered but the daring fighting men of the very tribe that had been most hostile. The destruction of European lives and property committed by that tribe was such that they considered themselves quite our masters, and had become so emboldened that either that part of the settlement must have been abandoned or a severe example made of them. It was a painful but urgent necessity, and likely to be the most humane policy [in] the end. The Governor narrowly escaped a spear. Captain Ellis was struck in the temple and unhorsed. Being stunned by the blow he fell.

Tuesday night—Poor Captain Ellis has died in consequence of the injury he received at the time of the conflict with the natives; but it is supposed that it was from the concussion of the brain by the fall from his horse, rather than by the wound from the spear (which was very trifling), that he died. The natives here are uneasy, thinking that we mean to take more lives in revenge.

Appended is a more detailed report of the encounter with the natives in the Pinjarra District, to which I briefly referred the other day. I was not one of that party.

The party consisted of His Excellency Sir Jas. Stirling, Mr. Roe, Cap. Meares and his son (Seymour), Mr Peel, Capt. Ellis, Mr Norcott with five of his mounted police (one sick), Mr Surveyor Smythe, a soldier to lead a pack horse, Mr Peel's servant, two corporals and eight privates of H.M.'s 21st Regiment (to leave at Pinjarra)—in all, 25 persons. On the night of October 27, the party bivouacked at a place called by the natives 'Jimjam', about ten or eleven miles in the direct line E.N.E. from the mouth of the Murray, where is abundance of most luxurious feed for cattle, at a broad and deep reach of the river flowing to the N.W., and at this time perfectly fresh. After an early breakfast, the whole encampment was in motion at ten minutes before six the next morning. Steered South Eastward for Pinjarra—another place of resort for the natives of the district, and situated a little below the first ford across the river, where it was intended to establish a town on a site reserved for the purpose, and to leave half of the party including the military, for the protection of Mr Peel and such other settlers as that gentleman might induce to resort thither.

Crossing the ford, where the river had an average depth of 2 ½ feet, and was running about 1 ½ miles an hour to the north, an Easterly course was taken for the purpose of looking at the adjoining country, but the party had not proceeded more than a quarter of a mile over the undulating surface of the richest description, covered with nutritious food for cattle, when the voices of many natives were heard on the left. This being a neighbourhood much frequented by the native tribe of Kalyute, which had long been indulging in almost unchecked commission of numerous outrages and atrocious murders on the white people resident in the district, and which had hitherto succeeded in eluding the pursuit of the parties that had been searching for them since their treacherous murder of Private Nesbitt of the 21st Regiment, and the spearing of Mr Barron only a few weeks ago—the moment was considered propitiously favourable for punishing the perpetrators of such and other diabolical acts of a similar nature, should this prove to be the offending tribe. For the purposes of ascertaining that point, His Excellency rode forward 200 or 300 yards with Messrs. Peel and Norcott, who were acquainted both with the persons of the natives and their language, and commenced calling out and talking to them for the purpose of bringing on an interview. Their own noise was, however, so loud and clamorous, that all other sounds appeared lost on them, or as mere echoes.

No answer being returned, Captain Ellis, in charge of the mounted police, with Mr. Norcott, his assistant, and the remaining available men of his party, amounting to three in number, were dispatched across the ford again to the left bank, where the natives were posted, to bring on the interview required. The instant the police were observed approaching at about 200 yards distance, the natives, to the number of about 70, started on their feet, the men seized their numerous and recently made spears, and showed a formidable front, but, finding their visitors still approached, they seemed unable to stand a charge, and sullenly retreated, gradually quickening their pace until the word 'forward' from the leader of the gallant little party brought the horsemen in about half a minute dashing into the midst of them, the same moment having discovered the well-known features of some of the most atrocious offenders of the obnoxious tribe. One of these, celebrated for his audacity and outrage, was the first to be recognized at the distance of five or six yards from Mr. Norcott, who knew him well and immediately called out, 'These are the fellows we want, for here's the old rascal Noonar,' on which the savage turned round and cried with peculiar ferocity and emphasis, 'Yes, Noonar me,' and was in the act of hurling his spear at Norcott, in token of requital for the recognition, when the latter shot him dead.

The identity of the tribe being now clearly established, and the natives turning to assail their pursuers, the firing continued, and was returned by the former with spears as they retreated to the river. The first shot, and the loud shouts and yells of the natives, were sufficient signal to the party who had halted a quarter of a mile above, who immediately followed Sir James Stirling, at full speed and arrived opposite Captain Ellis' party just as some of the natives had crossed and others were in the river. It was just the critical moment for them. Five or six rushed up the right bank, but were utterly confounded at meeting a second party of assailants, who immediately drove back those who escaped the firing. Being thus exposed to a cross fire, and having no time to rally their forces, they adopted the alternative of taking to the river and secreting themselves amongst the roots and branches and holes on the banks, or by immersing themselves with the face only uncovered and ready with a spear under water, to take advantage of any one who appeared within reach. Those who were sufficiently hardy or desperate to expose themselves on the offensive, or to attempt breaking through the assailants, were soon cleared off, and the remainder were gradually picked out of the concealments by the cross fire from both banks, until between 25 and 30 were left dead on the field and in the river. The others had either escaped up and down the river, or had secreted themselves too closely to be discovered except in the persons of eight women and some children, who emerged from their hiding places (where, in fact, the creatures were not concealed), on being assured of their personal safety, and were detained prisoners until the determination of the fray. It is, however, very probable that more men were killed in the river, and floated down with the stream.

Notwithstanding the care which was taken not to injure the women during the skirmish, it cannot appear surprising that one and several children were killed, and one woman amongst the prisoners had received a ball through the thigh. On finding the women were spared, and understanding the orders repeatedly issued to that effect, many of the men cried out they were of their sex; but evidence to the contrary was too strong to admit the plea. As it appeared by this time that sufficient punishment had been inflicted on this warlike and sanguinary tribe by the destruction of about half its population, and amongst whom were recognised, on personal examination, fifteen very old and desperate offenders, the bugle sounded to cease firing, and the divided party reassembled at the ford, where the baggage had been left in charge of four soldiers, who were also to maintain the post. Here Captain Ellis had arrived, badly wounded in the right temple, by a spear at three or four yards distance, which knocked him off his horse, and P. Heffron, a constable of the police, had received a bad spear wound above the right elbow. No surgical aid being at hand, it was not without some little difficulty the spear was extracted, and it then proved to be barbed at the distance of five inches from the point.

Having recrossed the river in good order with the baggage on three horses the whole party formed a junction on the left bank, fully expecting the natives would return in stronger force, but in this were disappointed. After a consultation over the prisoners, it was resolved to set them free, for the purpose of fully explaining to the remnant of the tribe the cause of the chastisement which had been inflicted, and to bear a message to the effect that, if they again offered to spear white men or their cattle, or to revenge in any way the punishment which had just been inflicted on these for their numerous murders and outrages, four times the present number of men would proceed amongst them and destroy every man, woman and child. This was perfectly understood by the captives, and they were glad to depart even under such an assurance; nor did several of their number, who were the widows, mothers and daughters of notorious offenders shot that day, evince any stronger feeling on the occasion than what arose out of their anxiety to keep themselves warm.

Nyungar tradition tells a substantially similar tale as far as the details of the encounter are concerned, though the numbers killed are often said to have been much larger. Descendants of the Pinjarra settlers continue to believe that Stirling and his men were reacting to the justifiable fears of their ancestors about the threat of a concerted Aboriginal attack. In settler tradition it was a battle. In Nyungar belief, what happened in 1834 was a massacre. The discrepancy between these views is poignantly reflected in a memorial of the incident in the park just south of Pinjarra township. Never completed, it is the victim of warring stories about the past.

The White Woman of Gippsland

The White Woman of Gippsland legend was widely circulated in Australia and beyond during the nineteenth century. It is part of a class of stories in which settlers are captured by the people they are displacing. Frequently the captives are women. While there were certainly well-authenticated instances of European women living with indigenous groups in America and Australia, many other such stories are folklore rather than fact. And like much folklore, they reveal deep truths about fear and prejudice.

The first mention of the white woman was in a letter published in the *Sydney Herald* in October 1840. A Scots settler in Gippsland named Augustus McMillan claimed that he and a small group of colonists had frightened a band of twenty-five Kurnai people, mostly women, into the bush. The settlers found European clothes, weapons, medicines and a range of other goods in their hastily abandoned camp, even newspapers, dated 1837. They also discovered, in a kangaroo-skin bag, the corpse of a two-year-old boy who was later identified as European.

While the pioneers of this only recently settled region were rummaging through this cache, they noticed that one of the women being herded to safety by the Kurnai men seemed unusually curious about them and what they were doing. Putting together their puzzling find and her interest, McMillan and his companions came to the conclusion 'that the unfortunate female is a European—a captive of these ruthless savages'. They thought the woman, perhaps with a small child, might be a survivor, probably the only one, of a 'dreadful massacre' of settlers. Two years later there surfaced in the newspapers another—anonymous—account of a sighting of Aborigines driving a white person, probably female, before them as they fled from a surveying party. The surveyors found a pile of European objects in the abandoned camp, as well as a giant heart shape drawn in the ground with a sharp object. The letter claimed that other settlers had also seen Aboriginal groups with white captives.

By 1845, these rumours had developed into a storyline in which the white captive was always female. Sightings were reported frequently throughout Gippsland and beyond. In every case, the white woman was supposedly being herded away from the Europeans but looking desperately to them for rescue. By the following year, claimed sightings were so common that people began demanding government intervention. A settler with the pen-name Humanitas wrote a windy letter to the editor of the *Port Phillip Herald* on 10 March 1846, concerning the alleged fate of a missing white woman known as Miss Lord.

> Sir: About twelve months ago, I addressed a letter to one of the newspapers shewing that this lady was a captive of a tribe of blacks in the Portland Bay district, and although that letter was calculated to call forth all the sympathies and at the same time the energies of man on her behalf, yet what has been done?

The letter berated Governor La Trobe for his failure to act and pointed out that a £1000 reward had been offered by the public. Nonetheless, 'The blood of every true Briton boils with indignation at witnessing the utter indifference, the utter barbarity in respect of this lady . . .'

Although the government had been making inquiries into the stories, it took no further official action. Instead, in October that year a private expedition was mounted under the command of Christian De Villiers and James Warman. They carried white handkerchiefs printed with a message of rescue:

WHITE WOMAN! — There are fourteen armed men, partly White and partly Black, in search of you. Be cautious and rush to them when you see them near you. Be particularly on the lookout every dawn of morning, for it is then the party are in hopes of rescuing you. The white settlement is towards the setting sun.

The message was printed in both English and Scots Gaelic, as many of the early Scots settlers spoke only that tongue.

Although the expedition failed to locate the lost woman, it did add a new slant to the story. Dispatches published in the *Port Phillip Herald* suggested that the white woman was a shipwreck survivor, a theory bolstered by the discovery that the Aborigines possessed a wooden ship's figurehead around which they reportedly performed corroborees.

Finally the government mounted its own rescue expedition, led by the head of the Port Phillip Native Police, Henry Dana. There were now two expeditions roaming the same area in search of the elusive white woman. Both focused on capturing a Kurnai chieftain named Bunjaleene, suspected of being the woman's abductor. But after Dana's party murdered a large number of Kurnai people in the Gippsland lakes district, it was recalled. The De Villiers/Warman party's supplies were withheld, forcing it too to return.

Rumour and speculation continued to run wild, however, and the government felt it wise to dispatch another expedition in March 1847. It captured Bunjaleene and held members of his family hostage while he led the would-be rescuers to the Snowy Mountains, where most of the Kurnai had retreated. It was now thought that Bunjaleene's brother was holding the white woman. Winter forced the abandonment of the search, and Bunjaleene and his family were (illegally) detained pending the white woman's return. Mumbalk, one of Bunjaleene's two wives, died in captivity, and the old chieftain, having been told that he and his people would be shot and hanged, died the following year.

Late in 1847, the bodies of a European woman and a part-Aboriginal child were discovered at Jemmy's Point. It was widely speculated that Bunjaleene's brother had murdered them, and the local newspaper concluded that the remains were indeed those of the lost white woman and her child. The sightings, then, had been real, or so the paper declared:

> Death though regarded as a mishap by others, must have descended as a blessing upon this poor woman, who has undergone a trial far more harrowing and terrible than even Death's worst moments.
>
> She is now no more—and it is a melancholy gratification that the public suspense has been at length relieved, by her discovery even in death.

While this should have marked the demise of the White Woman legend, some people still persisted in the belief that at least one white woman was in the hands of the Kurnai. The story, reinforced by persistent Kurnai traditions of the massacres and related injustices that took place as a result of the search for the white woman, lived on, finding its way into artworks and even local histories.

Was there a White Woman of Gippsland? It is possible that there were several. Kurnai tradition holds that there were at least two European women living among them at this period, including one, known as Lohan-tuka, who had long red hair—a feature that appeared in several of the early settler accounts. A number of European women did live with indigenous people, often after surviving shipwrecks. Eliza Fraser, who spent several months with Aborigines on and near what is now Fraser Island in 1836, is the best known of these enforced cultural crossovers. True or not, these stories owed their longevity to their theme's strong hold on the popular imagination.

The lost children of the Wimmera

On the morning of 12 August 1864, seven-year-old Jane Duff and her brothers Frank and Isaac went searching for broom in the bush near their home at Spring Hill Station. Spring Hill was about fifty kilometres from Horsham, Victoria, in the maze of scrub known as the Wimmera. Jane and Frank were the children of Hannah Duff by her previous husband. Isaac was the child of Hannah and her second husband, John Duff, a shepherd. The family lived in a slab hut, and one of the children's chores was to collect twigs for their mother's brooms.

On this Friday, though, the children strayed too far into the bush. When they did not come home, Hannah went looking for them. She found no trace, nor could her husband when he joined the search. On Saturday morning, the Duffs contacted their neighbours and thirty men hunted all through that day and into the next two. At last, on Tuesday, the children's tracks were sighted. Searchers followed them until a storm washed away all traces on the Thursday night.

Now desperate, the searchers made a wise decision. They called on an Aboriginal elder named Wooral, also known as Dick-a-Dick, a noted tracker. (He was destined to be a member of the Aboriginal cricket side that toured England a few years later.) By the time Wooral and two other Aboriginal men arrived, the searchers had found the children's tracks again. The Aborigines were able to follow them much more quickly than the settlers, and soon detected signs that the children had become very weak.

Eventually, however, they were found—huddled together beneath a tree with Jane's dress covering them all for warmth. Fearing the worst, their father rushed to the children and was overjoyed to find them still alive, though only just. The children were returned home and nursed back to health, having miraculously survived eight winter nights in the open with few clothes and hardly any food. They had eaten a few quandong berries but feared that these might be poisonous. 'We used to suck the dew off the leaves at night to ease our thirst and dry throats,' Jane Duff recalled in later life.

The news of their rescue and Jane's heroism—she had helped carry the younger boy as well as sharing her clothing— spread fast through Victoria and beyond. Aside from its local significance, the story resonated with British tales of lost babes in the woods, which had been popular since at least the sixteenth century, and with European fairy tales like that of 'Hansel and Gretel'. General rejoicing over the children's survival combined with these echoes of history and legend to infuse the story with great emotional power. Large donations were made to assist the rescued children and reward the Aboriginal trackers. Jane became a celebrity, and a local squatter later paid for her education. At the age of nineteen she married and settled in Horsham, eventually having eleven children. She died in 1932, still a heroine. Showing how she is remembered in local tradition, the inscription on her gravestone reads:

> In sacred memory
> of
> Jane Duff
> Bush Heroine
> who succoured her brothers
> Isaac and Frank
> nine days and eight nights
> in Nurcoung Scrub in August 1864
> died 20th Jan. 1932 aged 75 years

The story of the lost children became a staple in Victorian school readers and was continuously updated for new generations, still appearing in these books as late as the 1980s. The following version comes from a Victorian school reader from the 1960s. It uses some inaccurate terms—there were no Aboriginal 'monarchs' or 'subjects', for example—and some unrealistic quotations of Aboriginal English, as well as mixing up some minor details of the rescue. But it is a good example of how the story of the Duff children was reworked as a moral tale, at first emphasising Christian virtues and later highlighting self-sacrifice and strength of character. Through all these adaptations, Jane's heroism remained pivotal.

*T*hree children—Isaac, nine years old; Jane, seven and a half; and Frank, a toddler, not four—helped their mother, and filled in the long day as best they could, playing about the hut, for there was no school for them to attend.

Well, one day, their mother called them, and said, 'Now, children, run away to the scrub, and get me some broom to sweep the floor and make it nice for father when he comes home.'

It was a fine day in August—spring was early that year—and the children, who had been to the scrub on the same errand before, liked going: so they set off merrily.

They had a fine time. Isaac amused himself by climbing trees, and cutting down saplings with his tomahawk; he found a possum in a hollow in the trunk of a tree, and poked at the little creature with a stick, but without doing it much harm. Jane chased butterflies, picked flowers, and tried to catch the lizards that Frank wanted so much. When they felt hungry, they all had, in addition to their lunch of bread and treacle, quite a feast of gum from a clump of wattle-trees.

In laughter and play the time passed pleasantly and quickly; and, when half a dozen kangaroos bounded away from them through the bush, their delight knew no bounds. But, by and by, Jane thought of going home; so they gathered each a bundle of broom for Mother, and turned, as they thought, homewards.

After they had walked some distance, Isaac began to think it was farther to the edge of the scrub than he had expected, so he urged his sister and little brother to go faster. In an hour or two the scrub grew thicker, and it looked strange to him. He thought that he might have taken a wrong turn, and started off in another direction, and then tried another, and another; but no remembered spot met his straining eyes.

Then deep dread seized them all. They stopped, and cooeed, and shouted—'Father! Mother!' but there was no answer—only the sad 'caw! caw!' of a crow, winging its homeward flight, came to their ears.

On they pressed once more. Soon little Frank began to cry; and his sister said, 'Don't cry, Frankie dear; don't cry. We'll soon be home, and you shall have a nice supper. Let me carry your broom, it's too heavy for you.'

She took the bundle of tea-tree twigs; and forward again they went with wildly beating hearts, sometimes stopping to cooee and look about; and then on, on till the sun set, and the bush, except for the dismal howl, now and then, of a dingo in the distance, grew gloomy and still.

Tired out and hungry, they huddled together at the foot of a big tree, and said the prayers their mother had taught them. Then they talked of home, wondering if Father would be vexed, and if Mother knew that they were lost. Frank soon cried himself to sleep; and his sister put some of the broom under his head for a pillow. Poor, dear little things! They little thought how glad Mother would be to see them, even without their broom.

As the night went on, it grew cold; and Jane, who was awake, took off her frock to wrap around her little brother, and crept close to him to keep him warm. For hours, she lay listening to the cry of the curlew, and the rush of the possum as it ran, from tree to tree, over the dead leaves and bark. At last, she fell asleep, and slept till the loud, mocking, 'Ha, ha! ho, ho! hoo, hoo!' of the laughing-jackass roused her at dawn. What a waking it was! Tired and cold, hungry and thirsty, and lost.

The mother had grown anxious as the day wore on, and the children did not return; and so, late in the afternoon, she went into the scrub, and cooeed for them till she was hoarse. As she got no answer, she became really alarmed, and, at length, hurried back to tell her husband, who, she expected, would return home from his work just before nightfall. He also searched through the scrub, and cooeed till long after dark, but in vain.

Before daybreak next morning, they were up, and, as soon as it was light enough, were hurrying to tell their nearest neighbours what happened, and ask their help in the search. Before dinner-time, a score of willing people—men and women—were scouring the scrub in various directions.

All that day, and the next, and the next, they searched, but found nothing; and the poor mother began to lose hope of ever seeing her darlings again. A messenger had been sent to a station some distance off to bring two or three blackfellows, who were employed there as boundary-riders.

The Australian blacks can find and follow a trail with wonderful skill. They have sharp eyes; and their training in searching for the tracks of the game they hunt causes them to note signs to guide them in places where a white man, even with good eyesight, sees nothing.

The children had been lost on Saturday; and the black trackers—a monarch, King Richard (better known as Dicky), and two subjects, Jerry and Fred—arrived on Wednesday. The three, taking positions some distance apart, began to look about for the trail of small footsteps. They had worked for some hours, when a yell from Dicky brought them to his side. 'What is it?' asked the father.

'There! there!' exclaimed the black, with a broad smile, pointing to a faint mark of a little boot.

Forward now they went, with the father and some of his neighbours. Sometimes the blacks ran; sometimes they walked; and sometimes they had even to crawl. In rocky places, they had to search carefully for traces, working from one point to another. Whenever this happened, it was a trying time for the poor father, as he felt that every minute's delay lessened the small chance there was of finding his children alive.

The blacks led on so many miles into the bush that the white men began to think their tracking was all a sham. At last, however, they stopped at the foot of a big gum-tree; and, pointing to three bundles of broom, Dicky said, 'Him been sleep there, fus night.'

The father was astonished to find that the children had travelled so far in a day, and much troubled at the thought of the long distance they might yet be from him; but he was comforted, too, for he felt that he could trust his guides.

There was no time to stop; but onward the party pressed still faster, till night came and put an end to their efforts for some hours, in spite of their wishes. How the father must have suffered through those hours, and how eagerly he must have watched for the first streaks of the coming dawn!

We can fancy how anxious the poor mother was, also, as day by day passed without any news of the finding of her children. Her fears slowly grew into the belief that they were dead; and her only hope was that their bodies would not be torn to pieces by dingoes, or eaten by ants.

As Dicky was leading next day at a trot, he was seen to halt, and begin looking around him. An anxious 'What is the matter?'

from the father caused only a sad shake of the head from Dicky; and two fingers held up showed too well what was in his mind. Making a sign to his mates to look about for the dead body, he cast himself on his hands and knees to study the ground. A cry from him soon brought the party together. 'Here three,' he said, 'here two. Big one carry little one'; and he went through the motions of one child taking another on its back.

When the next sleeping-place of the little wanderers was found, the blacks pointed out that the smallest had lain in the middle. 'Him not get cold,' they said.

Their third day's tramp had not been so long as the others had been; and the blacks said again and again. 'Him plenty tired; not go much longer.' The tired little feet could not get over the ground so quickly now.

Another camping-place was reached, and 'Here yesterday!' exclaimed Dicky. On that fourth day's journey, the children had been passing through a patch of broom like that near their home; and the blacks, pointing to some broken twigs, showed that some branches had been broken off. Had they been gathered for a bed? No, there was no sign of that. Dicky turned to the father, and said, 'Him t'ink it him near home.' Yes; the children had supposed that they knew where they were when they reached that spot, and their first thought was of mother's broom. They were weary and starving; but they had been sent for the broom, and they would not go home without it.

'Him run now,' said the blacks; 'Him t'ink it all right'; and they pointed to the signs of haste. But, alas! what a blow to their hopes! By and by a bundle of broom was found. It had been thrown away—a sure sign of despair. 'Him been lose him. Him been sit down. Mine t'ink it him plenty cry.' Thus ran Dicky's history of the event.

Another camping-place was passed; and the blacks became doubly earnest, and kept saying, 'Him walk slow, slow, slow.' Soon Dicky whispered, 'Him close up.' And then he stopped and pointed before him in silence at something stretched on the ground.

'They must be dead,' groaned the father, and rushed forward with drawn face and straining eyes. Though all were living, only one was able to greet him, and that was little Frank, who raised himself slightly, held out his feeble arms, and cried in a weak, husky, voice, 'Daddy, Daddy, we cooeed for you, but you didn't come.' Jane had wrapped her frock around her little brother whenever they lay down to rest; and she and Isaac had carried him for miles, so that he had not suffered so much as they had. All alive, but very near death! Think of it: eight days and eight nights in the bush without food to eat or water to drink!

When they were found, the blacks laughed and cried, and rolled on the ground for joy; and Dicky (we may well call him King Richard now), springing on a horse that belonged to one of the party, gave his last order, 'Me tak gal home'; and Jane was handed up to him.

For some weeks, the children were between life and death, but kind attention and loving care brought them back to health. The story of their suffering and heroism spread far and wide. Jane's motherly attention to her little brother has won for her a place among the world's noble girls.

~

The theme of the child missing in the bush has lost none of its power, and real disappearances periodically recharge it. Henry Lawson wrote poems and short stories on the subject; country singer Johnny Ashcroft had a national and international hit in 1960 with a song titled 'Little Boy Lost' in the wake of another search and rescue drama involving a four-year-old boy in northern New South Wales. And the disappearance of baby Azaria Chamberlain in 1980—and the now notorious trial of her parents—gripped the public imagination and led to a best-selling book and a Hollywood movie.

J.Macfarlane

ABORIGINAL MYTHS.—THE BUNYIP.

3
Making monsters

The old world has her tales of ghoul and vampire, of
Lorelei, spook and pixie, but Australia has ... her bunyip.

Mrs Campbell Praed on the bunyip, 1891

EUROPEAN STORIES BEGAN mingling with Aboriginal ones
within a few years of the first settlement. Just as towns, rivers
and mountains were given often-mangled indigenous names,
so new hybrid legends arose, including that of the fearsome
bunyip, the human-like yowie and the Min Min lights.

The bunyip

Bunyips are creatures of Aboriginal mythology; a few groups
called them something like *banib*. They were usually said to
be hairy, though sometimes feathered, and to live in deep water
holes and ponds from where they attacked unwary passing
humans. The figure of the bunyip quickly merged with stories
of European water monsters such as the northern English
Jenny (or Ginny) Greenteeth.

The earliest substantial description of a bunyip was provided in 1852 in the reminiscences of William Buckley, an escaped convict who lived with Victorian Aborigines from 1803 to 1835:

> I could never see any part [of the bunyip] except the back, which appeared to be covered with feathers of a dusky-grey colour. It seemed to be about the size of a full-grown calf. When alone, I several times attempted to spear a Bun-yip; but had the natives seen me do so it would have caused great displeasure. And again, had I succeeded in killing, or even wounding one, my own life would probably have paid the forfeit; they considering the animal something supernatural.

But accounts of water-dwelling monsters had surfaced some thirty years earlier in the Sydney press. Perhaps the earliest serious appearance of the bunyip in European records is found in the 1821 minutes of the Philosophical Society of Australasia. Three years before, the explorer Hamilton Hume had found bones of apparently amphibious animals near Lake Bathurst, in New South Wales. The society resolved to give Hume a grant 'for the purpose of procuring a specimen of the head, skin or bones'.

The *Melbourne Morning Herald* of 29 October 1849 reported a bunyip at Phillip Island. One was also reported in a lagoon near Melrose, South Australia, in the early 1850s. It was described as 'a large blackish substance advancing towards the bank, which as I approached raised itself out of the water. I crept towards it ... It had a large head and a neck something like that of a horse with thick bristly hair ... Its actual length would be from 15 to 18 feet.' There were several alleged sightings in the 1870s, from Tasmania to central Queensland. In the 1890s a bunyip was seen in the Warra Warra Waterhole near Crystal Brook, South Australia. The newspaper report of this incident neatly sums up the ongoing problem with bunyip sightings: 'Although seen during the last ten days by no less than six different persons, none of them can give an intelligent description of what the bunyip is like.'

In New South Wales, Katherine Langloh-Parker documented stories of water-dwelling monsters among the Euahlayi: 'Several waterholes are taboo as bathing-places. They are said to be haunted by Kurreah, which swallow their victims whole, or by Gowargay, the featherless emu, who sucks down in a whirlpool any one who dares to bathe in his holes.'

In his *Bunjil's Cave: myths, legends and superstitions of the Aborigines of south-east Australia*, Aldo Massola recorded stories of bunyips and many other monsters and bad spirits, including the mindie, which was 'greatly feared by all the tribes in north-western and central Victoria', and was described as 'a huge snake, very, very long, very thick and very powerful. He was visible, yet not visible.'

This story of a bunyip causing a deluge or great flood was probably collected in Victoria in the 1890s:

> ... a party of men were once fishing in a lake, when one man baited his hook with a piece of flesh and soon felt a tremendous bite. Hauling in his line, he found that he had caught a young *bunyip*, a water monster of which the people were much afraid; but though his companions begged him to let it go, because the water monsters would be angry if it were

killed, he refused to listen to them and started to carry the young *bunyip* away. The mother, however, flew into a great rage and caused the waters of the lake to rise and follow the man who had dared to rob her of her young. The deluge mounted higher and higher, until all the country was covered, and the people, fleeing in terror, took refuge upon a high hill; but as the flood increased, gradually surmounting it and touching the people's feet, they were all turned into black swans and have remained so ever since.

The Ngarrindjerie people of South Australia preserve stories of bunyip-like mulgewongks. These creatures live in rivers and drag unsuspecting swimmers down to their caves. Dangerous as mulgewongks are, it is unlucky to kill one. In a story told by Ngarrindjerie man Henry Rankine in 1990, a riverboat captain unwise enough to kill such a creature sickened and died two weeks later. 'He did not listen to the old people who said to him, "Don't do that",' Rankine said, adding that his people still warn their children not to swim in the river at night.

Similar tales of water-dwelling monsters were told by the Nyungar people of southwestern Australia. The marghett, a male figure, was round but very long, with a large head and a great many teeth. It travelled by night, so was rarely seen. If an unwary Nyungar ventured into a marghett's waterhole, the creature would softly seize its victim's legs and drag him or her to a watery death.

So widespread and common were such stories that by 1891 it was possible for Mrs Campbell Praed to write: 'Everyone who has lived in Australia has heard of the bunyip. It is the one respectable flesh-curdling horror of which Australia can boast. The old world has her tales of ghoul and vampire, of Lorelei, spook and pixie, but Australia has ... her bunyip.'

By this time the bunyip had become routinely used by white Australians to discipline their children. In his *Life in the Australian Backblocks* (1911), E.S. Sorenson wrote:

> The average youngster has a horror of darkness, and talks in awe-struck whispers of hairy men, ghosts and bunyips. This fear is inculcated from babyhood. The mother can't always be watching in a playground that is boundless, and she knows the horror that waits the bushed youngster. So she tells them there is a bunyip in the lagoon, and gigantic eels in the creek; and beyond that hill there, and in yonder scrub, there is a 'bogey-man'. Those fairy tales keep the children within bounds—until they are old enough to know better.

Aboriginal parents also used monster stories to warn and control their children.

The figure of the bunyip became deeply embedded in Australian popular culture—it has found its way into children's stories, art, plays and verse. It also travelled to Britain, from where it was reimported in new versions, such as this one from Andrew Lang's *The Brown Fairy Book* (1904), elaborating on the tradition collected in Victoria a decade or so earlier:

*L*ong, long ago, far, far away on the other side of the world, some young men left the camp where they lived to get some food for their wives and children. The sun was hot, but they liked heat, and as they went they ran races and tried who could hurl his spear the farthest, or was cleverest in throwing a strange weapon called a boomerang, which always returns to the thrower.

They did not get on very fast at this rate, but presently they reached a flat place that in time of flood was full of water, but was now, in the height of summer, only a set of pools, each surrounded with a fringe of plants, with bulrushes standing in the inside of all. In that country the people are fond of the roots of bulrushes, which they think as good as onions, and one of the young men said that they had better collect some of the roots and carry them back to the camp. It did not take them long to weave the tops of the willows into a basket, and they were just going to wade into the water and pull up the bulrush roots when a youth suddenly called out: 'After all, why should we waste our time in doing work that is only fit for women and children? Let them come and get the roots for themselves; but we will fish for eels and anything else we can get.'

This delighted the rest of the party, and they all began to arrange their fishing lines, made from the bark of the yellow mimosa, and to search for bait for their hooks. Most of them used worms, but one, who had put a piece of raw meat for dinner into his skin wallet, cut off a little bit and baited his line with it, unseen by his companions.

For a long time they cast patiently, without receiving a single bite; the sun had grown low in the sky, and it seemed as if they would have to go home empty-handed, not even with a basket of roots to show; when the youth, who had baited his hook with raw meat, suddenly saw his line disappear under the water. Something, a very heavy fish he supposed, was pulling so hard that he could hardly keep his feet, and for a few minutes it seemed either as if he must let go or be dragged into the pool. He cried to his friends to help him, and at last, trembling with fright at what they were going to see, they managed between them to land on the bank a creature that was neither a calf nor a seal, but something of both, with a long, broad tail. They looked at each other with horror, cold shivers running down their spines; for though they had never beheld it, there was not a man amongst them who did not know what it was—the cub of the awful bunyip!

All of a sudden the silence was broken by a low wail, answered by another from the other side of the pool, as the mother rose up from her den and came towards them, rage flashing from her horrible yellow eyes. 'Let it go! Let it go!' whispered the young men to each other; but the captor declared that he had caught it, and was going to keep it. 'He had promised his sweetheart,' he said, 'that he would bring back enough meat for her father's house to feast on for three days, and though they could not eat the little bunyip, her brothers and sisters should have it to play with.' So, flinging his spear at the mother to keep her back, he threw the little bunyip on to his shoulders, and set out for the camp, never heeding the poor mother's cries of distress.

By this time it was getting near sunset, and the plain was in shadow, though the tops of the mountains were still quite bright. The youths had all ceased to be afraid, when they were startled by a low rushing sound behind them, and, looking round, saw that the pool was slowly rising, and the spot where they had landed the bunyip was quite covered. 'What could it be?' they asked one of another; there was not a cloud in the sky, yet the water had risen higher already than they had ever known it do before. For an instant they stood watching as if they were frozen, then they turned and ran with all their might, the man with the bunyip running faster than all. When he reached a high peak over-looking all the plain he stopped to take breath, and turned to see if he was safe yet. Safe! Why, only the tops of the trees remained above that sea of water, and these were fast disappearing. They must run fast indeed if they were to escape.

So on they flew, scarcely feeling the ground as they went, till they flung themselves on the ground before the holes scooped out of the earth where they had all been born. The old men were sitting in front, the children were playing, and the women chattering together, when the little bunyip fell into their midst, and there was scarcely a child among them who did not know that something terrible was upon them. 'The water! The water!' gasped one of the young men; and there it was, slowly but steadily mounting the ridge itself. Parents and children clung together, as if by that means they could drive back the advancing flood; and the youth who had caused all this terrible catastrophe, seized his sweetheart, and cried: 'I will climb with you to the top of that tree, and there no waters can reach us.'

But, as he spoke, something cold touched him, and quickly he glanced down at his feet. Then with a shudder he saw that they were feet no longer, but bird's claws. He looked at the girl he was clasping, and beheld a great black bird standing at his side; he turned to his friends, but a flock of great awkward flapping creatures stood in their place. He put up his hands to cover his face, but they were no more hands, only the ends of wings; and when he tried to speak, a noise such as he had never heard before seemed to come from his throat, which had suddenly become narrow and slender. Already the water had risen to his waist, and he found himself sitting easily upon it, while its surface reflected back the image of a black swan, one of many.

Never again did the swans become men; but they are still different from other swans, for in the night-time those who listen can hear them talk in a language that is certainly not swan's language; and there are even sounds of laughing and talking, unlike any noise made by the swans whom we know.

The little bunyip was carried home by its mother, and after that the waters sank back to their own channels. The side of the pool where she lives is always shunned by everyone, as nobody knows when she may suddenly put out her head and draw him into her mighty jaws. But people say that underneath the black waters of the pool she has a house filled with beautiful things, such as mortals who dwell on the earth have no idea of. Though how they know I cannot tell you, as nobody has ever seen it.

⌒

Lang's version of the bunyip story represents the children's end of the tradition. The other end focuses on the creature as killer. According to a version told to author Roland Robinson by an Aboriginal man named Percy Mumbulla, a 'clever man' or sorcerer of his acquaintance who once had a bunyip in his power; the creature was 'high in the front and low at the back, like a hyena, like a lion. It had a terrible bull head and it was milk white. This bunyip could go down into the ground and take the old man with him. They could travel under the ground. They could come out anywhere.' But for ordinary men, Mumbulla said, there was no making friends with a bunyip. 'When he bites you, you die.'

Yaramas, jarnbahs, jannocks and yowies

Indigenous mythology is full of spirits, monsters and usually loathsome creatures, some of which, like the bunyip, have also fused with monsters of European legend.

The yarama (or yaroma) is tall, hairy and has very sharp teeth in a large and hungry mouth, as in this early twentieth-century account:

*O*n one occasion a blackfellow went under a large fig-tree to pick up ripe figs, which had fallen to the ground, when a Yaroma, who was hidden in a hollow place in the base of a tree, rushed out, and catching hold of the man swallowed him head first. It happened that the man was of unusual length, measuring more than a foot taller than the majority of his countrymen. Owing to this circumstance, the Yaroma was not able to gulp him farther than the calves of his legs, leaving his feet protruding from the monster's mouth, thus keeping it open and allowing air to descend to the man's nostrils, which saved him from suffocation. The Yaroma soon began to feel a nausea similar to what occurs when a piece of fishbone or other substance gets stuck in one's throat. He went to the bank of the river close by, and took a drink of water to moisten his throat, thinking by this means to suck into his stomach the remainder of his prey, and complete his repast. This was all to no purpose, however, for, becoming sick, the Yaroma vomited the man out on the dry land, just as the whale got rid of Jonah. He was still alive, but feigned to be dead, in order that he might perhaps have a chance of escape. The Yaroma then started away to bring his mates to assist him to carry the dead man to their camp. He wished, however, to make quite sure that the man was dead before he left him, and after going but a short distance he jumped back suddenly; but the man lay quite still. The Yaroma got a piece of grass and tickled the man's feet and then his nose, but he did not move a muscle. The Yaroma, thinking he was certainly dead, again started away for help, and when he got a good distance off, the man, seeing his opportunity, got up and ran with all his speed into the water close by, and swam to the opposite shore, and so escaped.

In his description of the yarama, under the name *Yara ma tha who*, the Aboriginal writer David Unaipon suggests that the creatures were common along the east coast and explains: 'This is one of the stories told to bad children: that if they do not behave themselves the *Yara ma tha who* will come and take them and make them to become one of their own.'

In his memoir *Wyndham Yella Fella*, Reg Birch tells of his terrifying encounters with the jarnbah, 'an ugly, hairy, smelly little muscular dark man' who invaded dreams and sleep to torment and degrade boys and men. He was not the only Aboriginal male in the district to suffer this way.

The Nyungar of the southwest speak of jannocks, small, evil beings that lurk after dark. Often manifested in puffs of wind, they are especially dangerous to humans—all the more so because they are easily offended. Even referring to them the wrong way can bring trouble.

More widely known and feared is the yowie, a fierce animal of uncertain shape and features. An army officer in 1832 recorded hearing about a wawee, as it was called by the

Eurambone people of the Liverpool Plains, west of Sydney. This was a tortoise-like creature that lived in rivers and fed on unwary humans. The officer, a Captain Forbes of the 39th Regiment of Foot, thought the story might be an indigenous joke at the settlers' expense. Others thought it and similar tales were concocted by the Aborigines to frighten settlers away. Some colonists used 'yowie' interchangeably with 'Yahoos', the fantastical savages invented by Jonathan Swift in his 1726 book *Gulliver's Travels*. Yahoo also sounds like the term for 'dream spirit' in the Yuwaalaraay language of northeastern New South Wales. Whatever its origins, the term has stuck, and yahoo is frequently used as a variation on yowie.

The earliest documented mention of this creature, referred to as both a 'Yahoo' and a 'Devil-Devil', seems to have been in 1835. The *Australian and New Zealand Monthly Magazine* provided this description in 1842:

The natives of Australia have, properly speaking, no idea of any supernatural being; they believe in the imaginary existence of a class which, in the singular number, they call Yahoo, or, when they wish to be anglified, Devil-Devil. This being they describe as resembling a man, of nearly the same height, but more slender, with long white straight hair hanging down from the head over the features, so as almost entirely to conceal them; the arms are extraordinarily long, furnished at the extremities with great talons, and the 'feet turned backwards', so that, on flying from man, the imprint of the foot appears as if the being had travelled in the opposite direction. Altogether, they describe it as a hideous monster, of an unearthly character and ape-like appearance. On the other hand, a contested point has long existed among

Australian naturalists whether or not such an animal as the Yahoo existed, one party contending that it does, and that from its scarceness, slyness, and solitary habits, man has not succeeded in obtaining a specimen, and that it is most likely one of the monkey tribe.

Long before the term yowie came into general use, variants of it were used by indigenous Australians to denote what David Unaipon described as 'the most dreadful animal in existence'. He was referring to the Riverina whowie, a large reptile or goanna with six legs, a tail and an enormous frog-like head. The whowie would devour whatever creatures it came across, including humans—and in large numbers. It lived in a cave on the river bank and its footprints were said to have formed the sandhills along the river. Unaipon retells a story in which the whowie is eventually killed by the animals, birds and reptiles. As with the yarama and bunyip, fearsome tales of the whowie's doings were used to caution disobedient children.

About 1903, William Telfer, a stockman who spent his life around Tamworth, New South Wales, wrote down his memories. These included, from the 1840s, a graphic description of his encounter with a man-like beast on the Liverpool Plains, said in local Aboriginal tradition to have once been a vast lake or inland sea.

*T*he Aborigines have a tradition that it is three hundred miles long, a large lot of islands in the middle of it. One Aboriginal told me his grandfather told him big fellow water all about the plains. He said they used to have canoes and go fishing from one island to the other making a stay at each place as they went across from one side to the other. His story must have some truth in it as Mr Oxley, Surveyor General, when he came over Liverpool Plains had to cross large marshes or swamps . . . I said [to the Aboriginal man] at the time there was the river. He said no river, all water and ridges and mountains all round the outside . . . There came a very wet season and his people shifted away to the mountains. He said they heard great noise at different times, like thunder. He said they were very frightened. When they came back all the big water was gone. Nothing but mud and swamps where the Plains are now, plenty of fish in different waterholes . . . he said the ridges about Gunnedah were swept away by the great rush of water in its course down the Namoi . . .

Then they have a tradition about the yahoo. They say he is a hairy man like a monkey. Plenty at one time, not many now. But the best opinion of the kind I heard from old Bungaree, a Gunnedah Aboriginal. He said at one time there were tribes of them and they were the original inhabitants of the country. He said they were the old race of blacks. He was of Darwin's theory that the original race had a tail on them like a monkey. He said the Aboriginals would camp in one place and those people in a place of their own, telling about how them and the blacks used to fight and the blacks always beat them but the yahoo always made away from the blacks, being a faster runner, mostly escaped. The blacks were frightened of them. When a lot of those were together the blacks would not go near them as the yahoo would make a great noise and frighten them with sticks. He said very strong fellow, very stupid. The blacks were more cunning, getting behind trees, spearing any chance one that came near them. This was his story about those people.

I have seen several stockmen in the old times said they had seen this hairy man. His feet [were] reversed—when you thought he was coming towards you he was going away. I had an experience myself of this gorilla or hairy man. In the year 1883 I was making a short cut across the bush from Keera to Cobedah via Top Bingera. It was a very hot day. I was on foot when, after crossing those steep hills, being tired, camped for about two hours. This left me late. The sun was only an hour high. Having to go about ten miles [I] went about five miles. Getting dark, [I] came on a creek of running water. Had to camp for the night. Made a camp on a high bank of the creek, lit a fire and made myself comfortable, my dog laying down at the fire alongside me. I sat smoking my pipe. The moon rose about an hour after, when you could discern objects two hundred yards away from the camp. I heard a curious noise coming up the creek opposite the camp. Over the creek I went to see what it was about one hundred yards away. He seemed the same as a man only larger. The animal was something like the gorilla in the Sydney Museum, of a darkish colour and made a roaring noise going away towards Top Bingera, the noise getting fainter as he went along in the distance.

I started at daylight, getting to Bell's Mountain about 9 o'clock. Mr Bridger lived there; stopped and had breakfast. I was telling them about the night before. They said several people has seen the gorilla about there. He was often seen in the mountains towards the Gwyder and about Mt Lyndsay. I was thinking how easily this animal could elude pursuit, travelling by night, camping in rocks or caves in the daytime. After those blacks, the Governors [brothers, who murdered five white people in July 1900], so many out after them I do not think it wonderful those wild animals should escape being caught, as they are faster than the

Aboriginal by his own account. Some people think they are only a myth, but how is it they were seen by so many people in the old times fifty years ago?

⌒

In referring to the search for the Governor brothers, Telfer was making the point that a yahoo could hide away in the bush as easily as they could.

The doolagarl, or hairy man, was also well known and feared in southeastern New South Wales. Percy Mumbulla, who told Roland Robinson about the bunyip and the 'clever man', described this creature as 'a man like a gorilla. He has long spindly legs. He has a big chest and long swinging arms. His forehead goes back from his eyebrows. His head goes into his shoulders. He has no neck.'

In 1989, folklore collectors in Queensland recorded fading rumours of a 'wowey-wowey', a creature 'that is supposed to run around the bushes'. Nor was that the end of the yowie legend's career. In September 2000, a bushwalker claimed to have filmed a large creature he believed could be a yowie in the Brindabella ranges near Canberra. The Brindabellas have long been a favourite yowie lair, with reported sightings dating back to pioneer days (one claimed an eyewitness spoke of 'a man-like thing whose coat was as hairy as that of a gorilla'). News reports quoted the bushwalker as saying, 'I was filming what I thought was a large kangaroo in a gully, when I realised it was far too big for a roo.' People who viewed the film, including 'hominid researcher' Tim the Yowie Man, said it seemed to show a large, hairy creature walking upright through the bush but that the footage was too dark to draw any conclusions.

Alien cats

The study and pursuit of mythical animals, including yaramas and bunyips, is known as cryptozoology. Australian folklore is rich in what cryptozoologists call 'Alien Big Cats' or 'ABCs'. One of the best-known of these is the Tantanoola Tiger, said to have been attacking stock in that region of South Australia since the early 1890s. Scant though the evidence is, many people genuinely believe in ABCs and spend a great deal of time and money looking for them.

In an extended study of weird animal traditions in Australia, folklorist Bill Scott noted: 'There is certainly a very strong folk belief in this country of the existence of such an animal, which is usually described by witnesses as a "panther" or a "big cat".' Scott went on to identify a number of these beasts from his own fieldwork and reports by others. These included the Emmaville Panther and the Kangaroo Valley Panther (New South Wales), the Waterford Panther (Queensland), the Dromana Mountain Lion (Victoria), the Marulan Tiger (New South Wales), and the Guyra Cat (New South Wales). To these could be added the Tasmanian Tiger, the Nannup Tiger (Western Australia), and the Kyneton Cat (Victoria), among many others. In Queensland, there are said to be cougars around Townsville, Mount Spec and Charters Towers. In September 2008, a leopard was reported on the northwestern edge of Sydney, the latest of many similar sightings in the Blue Mountains and along the Hawkesbury River.

Most reports of this type involve, as well as descriptions of some variety of 'big cat', an explanation, often venerable, of how such a creature came to be prowling the Australian bush. Often, the animals are said to have escaped from a circus. Another common theme is that a pair of panthers (or cougars, or mountain lions) were brought to Australia as mascots for American troops during World War II and released into the bush after the war. Convincing documentation of such animals, however, has yet to be produced. Big cat sightings nowadays are often 'irrefutably proven' by a photograph or video footage. As with the yowie video of 2000, these invariably turn out to be murky snaps that could show almost any animal at all.

Another feature of big cat (and yowie) lore is outsized, backward-pointing or otherwise odd tracks. Plaster casts are often made of these prints for examination by 'experts' whose task seems to be to vindicate the claims of the cat seekers. The experts' findings, however, rarely see the light of day.

Naturally, farmers who find their stock mauled to death want to know what did it. Reports of big-cat attacks on sheep and cattle have surfaced regularly since the nineteenth century. Around Busselton, south of Perth, for example, a series of unexplained sheep losses in 1997 and 1998 were blamed by some locals on a wild cougar. A cast of a suspected paw print was given to Perth Zoo for inspection. Its specialist was 'unable to determine what had left the print, but said it was not large enough to be a cougar', according to a report in Perth's *Sunday Times*. 'The claws have the characteristics of a cat,' the specialist said. 'But I would not like to put my money on it being a big cat, it could even be a large dog.'

In the mid 1970s, reports of pumas in Victoria's Grampian Ranges were investigated by environmental science students at Deakin University, who collected casts of footprints, fur, bone, and even faeces. Puma experts in Colorado who examined the specimens found them consistent with pumas. The outcome 'was tantalising but not conclusive', Professor John Henry, who had been in charge of the investigation, later said.

Henry decided to probe further. He had heard the story that the US Air Force had released big cats into the Grampians during World War II. Now he tracked down six former members and quizzed them about it in writing. Some of the ex-servicemen recalled hearing stories along those lines, but that is as far as any of them would go. Henry's final (2001) report on the case for pumas found there was 'sufficient evidence from a number of intersecting sources to affirm beyond reasonable doubt the presence of a big-cat population in western Victoria'.

In 2000, there was another sighting of a mysterious creature in the area, and this time video 'evidence' was screened on television. Officials in Victoria's Department of Natural Resources thought the animal was probably a feral cat. A spokesman told *The Weekend Australian*: 'We remain sceptical of the exotic cat theory until field evidence comes along rather than hearsay of sightings.'

The Tasmanian Tiger, *Thylacinus cynocephalus* (pouched animal with a dog's head), became extinct in 1936, but many have hunted in vain for it since. A descendent of the carnivorous marsupial is widely believed to roam the mainland's far south-west and is still pursued in Tasmania. Reports of the beast, known as the Nannup Tiger (or some variant of that name), seem to date back almost to the earliest European settlement of Western Australia, but were especially frequent in the late 1960s and early 1970s, when wet winters supposedly forced it into the wooded areas around Nannup. Various attempts were made to capture the Nannup Tiger, without success. As with the bunyip and the yowie lack of evidence has not prevented this and other Alien Big Cats from taking up residence in Australia's monster menagerie.

The Min Min lights

The Min Min lights are a Queensland version of an eerie phenomenon reported elsewhere in Australia and around the world. Ghost lights were reported by explorers in southeastern Australia from the 1830s. The Wongagai people of Australia's northwest believe the night lights they sometimes observe on the plains are spirits luring humans into the desert with evil intent. Several of these apparitions, as they were often called in the nineteenth century, are associated with tales of haunting. People in Hay, New South Wales, for example, used to see a light that appeared to be on a mail coach travelling across One Tree Plain. No matter how fast men rode after the light, no one was ever able to catch up with it. But while the Phantom Mail is a legend known mainly to locals, the story of the Min Min lights has become widely told.

Min Min was the Aboriginal-derived name of an inn built in the late nineteenth century, about 100 kilometres east of the town of Boulia, in the channel country of north-central Queensland. The pub thrived as the Queensland frontier expanded, and a small township grew up around it, but the population gradually dwindled, and during World War I the pub burned down. Since at least the time the hotel was built, however, there have been reports of strange lights dancing through the night skies in the area. The lights are described in a bewildering variety of ways: as small, large, single, numerous, of one colour, changing in colour, standing still, moving slowly, moving fast, or sometimes following startled travellers.

There are many scientific and pseudo-scientific explanations for the Min Min lights. Probably the most frequent is that they are a form of marsh light, or *ignis fatuus* (Latin for foolish fire). Also known as will o' the wisps, these are caused by phosphorescent gases rising from swampy ground. Min Min lights have also been attributed to mirages, weather effects, the ghosts of massacred Aborigines and, inevitably, UFOs. One sceptical scientist has even managed to reproduce the lights in his laboratory in a probably futile attempt to quash the notion that they are somehow supernatural. The legend of the Min Min lights arose from a mingling of Aboriginal, British and Australian settler traditions, with a romantic gloss provided mostly by the press.

Even before European settlement, Aborigines seem to have witnessed the lights; a number of the local Pitta Pitta people averred that they were or of unearthly origin, in some cases associated with the spirits of stillborn children. They have also been said to be linked to an Aboriginal burial ground. A variation on this theme is that the lights first appeared after a number of Aborigines were killed by settlers. This is possibly a reference to the incident at Battle Mountain near Mount Isa in 1884, when as many as several hundred Kalkadoon people may have been killed; or it may refer to other reprisal killings of Kalkadoons by settlers. Queensland oral tradition contains many massacre stories that have never been historically confirmed.

When settlers first saw the lights, they generally interpreted them as marsh lights. These are often explained in British folklore as ghosts or disembodied souls, sometimes referred to as 'corpse candles'. Similar phenomena around the world are also widely associated with ill luck, evil and death.

The earliest accounts of the Min Min lights generally have them arising from the cemetery behind the hotel. This establishment apparently gained a bad reputation for encouraging bush workers to 'lamb down', or drink down, their pay cheques, giving no change and plying them with rotgut alcohol. In some versions of the Min Min tale, patrons of the hotel were sometimes drugged and robbed or murdered. This embellishment added an extra dimension of spookiness to the legend; perhaps the lights were the vengeful ghosts of murdered men.

The first coherent account of the lights comes from Henry Lamond, a station manager, who saw them in 1912:

*D*uring the middle of winter—June or July—I had to go to Slasher's Creek to start the lamb-marking. I did not leave the head station until about 2 a.m., expecting to get to Slasher's well before daylight . . .

After crossing the Hamilton River, 5 miles wide with 45 channels, I was out on the high downs . . . 5 or 6, or 8 or 10, miles out on the downs I saw the headlight of a car coming straight for me . . . Cars, though they were not common, were not rare. I took note of the thing, singing and trotting as I rode, and I even estimated the strength of the approaching light by the way it picked out individual hairs in the mare's mane.

Suddenly I realised it was not a car light—it remained in one bulbous ball instead of dividing into the 2 headlights, which it should have done as it came closer; it was too green-glary for an acetylene light; it floated too high for any car; there was something eerie about it. I ceased to sing, though I kept the mare at the trot. She stopped that: she propped her four legs wide, lifted her head, pricked her ears, and she snorted her challenge to the unknown!

The light came on, floating as airily as a bubble, moving with comparative slowness—though I did not at the time check its rate of progression. I should estimate now that it was moving at about 10 m.p.h. and anything from 5 to 10 feet above the ground . . . Its size, I would say, at an approximate guess, would be about that of a new-risen moon. That light and I passed each other, going in opposite directions. I kept an eye on it while it was passing, and I'd say it was about 200 yards off when suddenly it just faded and died away. It did not go out with a snap—its vanishing was more like the gradual fading of the wires in an electric bulb. The mare acknowledged the dowsing of the glim by another snorting whistle: it must have been at least five miles or so ere I lifted up my voice again in song.

Lamond's recollection of this incident was not published until twenty-five years later, on 1 April 1937—not a date to engender confidence in the veracity of the story. But many other people also reported seeing a similar light, or lights.

In May 1981, Detective Sergeant Lyall Booth, of the Police Stock Investigation Squad at Cloncurry, was camped at a waterhole about 60 kilometres east of Boulia. Waking at around 11 p.m., he saw what looked like a car's headlight on the road. Police Commissioner Norriv Bauer later published a report of Booth's statement on the sighting. He quoted Booth as saying the light 'appeared to be moving but it did not seem to get any closer (I know that's hard to grasp, but that is how it appeared)'. He described the light as 'white in colour, similar to the light thrown by a quartz iodide headlight'. He went back to sleep but woke about 1 a.m., and saw another light about 1000 metres southwest of where he'd seen the earlier one.

It was not as bright as the first light and had a slightly yellow colour to it. It was about the colour of a gas light which is turned down very low and is about to go out, but it was of much greater intensity than that type of light.

It appeared to be slightly bigger than the gas light used in the cook's camp. It seemed to be from 3 to 6 feet from the ground, and moved only several yards from west to east and then remained stationary. It illuminated the ground around it, but I was too far away from it to see any detail. I could, however, see the cook's camp.

Booth watched it for another five or six minutes, 'and then it suddenly dived towards the ground and went out. It may even have gone out on contact with the ground. I did not see it again.' Bauer quoted Booth as saying he was 'at a loss to explain in physical terms the lights that I saw. My enquiries lead me to believe that they were not caused by man.'

Despite the inconsistencies among (and within) reported sightings, the scepticism of scientists and the existence of a number of possible natural explanations, the notion that the Min Min lights are supernatural in origin lives on. Tourism promoters refer to them, and UFOlogists investigate them. Whatever their origin, the lights have become one of Australia's most persistent tales of the unexplained.

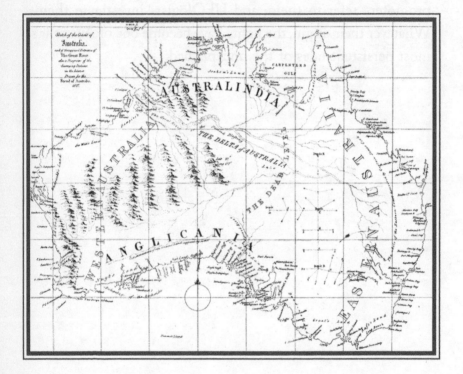

4
Legends on the land

These stories belong to us.

Bob Turnbull

MUCH LORE AND legend is closely tied to places. Such stories often help to forge and maintain a common sense of identity. They may not be widely known outside the locality where they arose, though some are local variants of tales told around the world. A few, however—like that of the Min Min lights—manage to spread widely without losing their links with the places of their birth.

Place-specific stories often contain explanations for the names of local landmarks or for local customs. A large group of these type of legends concerns buried, or otherwise lost, treasure.

The man who sold his Dreaming

Australia's earliest local tales are, of course, those of the first Australians. And as this next one shows, they are not necessarily set in the mythological world before European settlement. Collected by Roland Robinson from an Aboriginal man named Bob Turnbull, it is a good example of the way indigenous and settler traditions often coalesce. As well as explaining how the local town got its name, it is a cautionary tale about giving up what is most important to you. The term jurraveel, introduced near the end of the story, means 'a sacred place', to which Frank Jock was connected by his totem, a bird similar to a bantam rooster.

You know that water-hen with the red beak? He sings out 'Kerk', and 'Kerk', well, that bird is my totem. Every dark feller has a totem. It's his spirit. It looks after him and warns him of any danger. In my tribe, the Bunjalung tribe of the Richmond River, his name is *geeyarng*. And our native name for a totem is *barnyunbee*.

I want to tell you about a totem that belonged to a dark feller named Frank Jock. Frank Jock had a totem that was something like a little bantam rooster. Everyone would hear this bird singing out. They'd go to look for him, but they could never find him.

Away on the mountain in the lantana, he'd be singing out. He was sort of minding that place, looking after it, you'd say.

Well, the mayor of Coraki wanted to make a quarry in that mountain. There was the best kind of blue metal there. He sent the men of the council to that place. They put three charges, one after another, into the rock. But not one of those charges would go off.

There was a dark feller in the gang by the name of Andrew Henry. He told the mayor of Coraki that he'd have to go and have a talk to Frank Jock. The mayor would have to ask Frank if he could do something so that they could blow up this mountain and make a quarry in it.

The mayor sent for Frank Jock, he said he wanted to see him. 'Look,' the mayor said to Frank, 'can you let us blow this mountain up?'

'All right,' Frank said, 'but you'll have to pay me.'

So the mayor gave Frank five gold sovereigns and two bottles of rum to let the council blow up the mountain.

The council men went back to the mountain and they put in one big charge. When it went off, it blew the side right out of the mountain. The explosion shook Coraki. A big spout of black water rushed up out of the mountainside. The council had to wait a long time until all the water cleared away before they could work the quarry.

The little bantam rooster, he disappeared. He didn't sing out any more. *Jurraveel* I can see you know all about this black-feller business.

Well, after the mountain was blown up, Frank Jock, the owner of that *jurraveel*, began to get sick. In three weeks he was dead. You see, like it says in the Bible, he'd sold his birthright. It was the same as killing him. He sold his *jurraveel* to the mayor of the town.

That's why we call it in our language Gurrigai, meaning 'blowing up the mountain'. That's how Coraki got its name.

～

After Bob Turnbull had finished telling the story, he said to Roland Robinson, 'You know, I've been looking for years for a feller like you to write these stories down. These stories are dying out. They're lost to the young people. I'd like to think that one day the young people will read these stories and say, "These stories belong to us."'

Naming places

The American humorist and travel writer Mark Twain visited Australia in the late 1890s. A master yarn spinner and teller of tall tales himself, Twain was mildly sceptical when told by a local liar that the Blue Mountains of New South Wales had been thrown up by the rabbits then plaguing the country. Tongue in cheek, Twain wrote that the rabbit plague 'could account for one mountain, but not for a mountain range, it seems to me. It is too large an order.' Whether this was the origin of the long-running joke about Australians outdoing Americans in the size of their lies, the rabbit-pile theory certainly fits into it.

In 1989, folklorists collected at least six different stories about the origins of the Queensland town of Ravenshoe. These included the suggestion that someone had once seen some ravens or crows playing with an old shoe on the creek bank—despite the fact that the name is pronounced Ravens-hoe. (Hoe, or Hoo, is the name of a place in Norfolk). There was also an elaborate story about how local streams, when viewed from the air, meet in the shape of a crow's foot. Many of the people who supplied these stories thought the town's original name, Cedar Creek, was a much better choice.

Locals say Crows Nest, Queensland, is so named because Aborigines called the place something like 'home of the crows'. A more colourful version of this story holds that during the early days of settlement, an Aboriginal man lived in a hollow tree in the town, from which vantage point he provided directions to bullock drivers and cedar getters as well as acting as an unofficial post office. It is said that the settlers called him Jimmy Crow and his tree Jimmy Crow's Nest, a contraction of which became the town's name.

Whipstick, near Bendigo in Victoria, is an area of mallee scrub first encountered by gold diggers. As some locals told folklorist Peter Ellis, the scrub was almost impenetrable, twisted about with creepers that whipped back into men's faces as they struggled through it or tried to cut it down. Other people claimed that Whipstick was named after the whip handles made from the scrub by bullock drivers.

Another story from the goldfields explained how Dunolly got its name. A couple were driving their horse-drawn cart along a track. The woman, whose name was Olive, asked her husband to stop and went to squat behind a bush. After a while, her husband became impatient and called out, 'Are you done, Ollie?'

Leatherass Gully is another goldfields name that cries out for a foundation legend. In this case, it's based on an old fossicker who had a leather patch on the seat of his worn-out trousers. The original spelling was Leatherarse, but that was deemed vulgar, so it was replaced by Leatherass.

Walkaway, near Geraldton, Western Australia, was established in the 1850s and now has a population of 612. Some say its name is derived from *waggawah*, an Aboriginal word meaning either camping place, a break in the hills, or the hill of the dogs. One tradition has it that some of the earliest settlers in the district left when their wheat crop failed. When the Aborigines were asked what happened to them, they replied: 'Him walk away.' Another version that alludes to these early farmers' struggles is heartbreakingly succinct: 'If you saw the place, you'd walk away too!' Yet another version involves the railway line that for a time terminated near Walkaway: passengers who wanted to go further north were told they would have to walk a way.

The dramatic legend of Govetts Leap, in the Blue Mountains of New South Wales, tells of an escaped convict turned bush-ranger named Govett who, pursued by troopers, found himself trapped on the edge of a 300-metre cliff. Preferring death to capture, he wheeled his horse around and rode it over the edge. In fact, the place was named after a colonial assistant surveyor, William Govett, who discovered the site in 1831. It is possible that the more romantic version originated from the observations of the English novelist Anthony Trollope, who travelled through Australia during the early 1870s. In his sometimes abrasive account of that trip, *Australia and New Zealand,* Trollope wrote:

> . . . there is a ravine called Govett's Leap. Mr. Govett was, I believe, simply a government surveyor, who never made a leap into the place at all. Had he done so, it would certainly have been effectual for putting an end to his earthly sorrows. I had hoped, when I heard the name, to find that some interesting but murderous bushranger had on that spot baffled his pursuers and braved eternity—but I was informed that a government surveyor had visited the spot, had named it, and had gone home again. No one seeing it could fail to expect better things from such a spot and such a name.

The Lone Pine seedlings

The heroism and slaughter of the Gallipoli campaign in World War I gave rise to one of Australia's most enduring national stories: the legend of Anzac. Closely bound up with it are tales related to Lone Pine. This was, on the day of the landings at Gallipoli, part of a ridge officially named 400 Plateau. Australian troops called it Lonesome (later Lone) Pine for a single, stunted tree that rose above the scrub. In August 1915, Lone Pine was seared into Australian memory when a terrible battle took place there. More than 2000 Australians were killed or wounded, and seven won the Victoria Cross. Each Anzac Day, Lone Pine cemetery is the site of the official Australian memorial service at Gallipoli.

Today, Australia is dotted with trees said to be descended from the original lone pine. There are various stories about the origins of these symbolic trees. According to one of these, a Lance Corporal Benjamin Smith witnessed the death of his brother at Lone Pine and later pocketed a cone from the by-then felled pine tree that the Turks had used to cover their trenches. He sent it home to his mother who kept the cone for some years, eventually growing two seedlings from it. One of these was sent to Inverell, New South Wales, the place where her dead son had enlisted. Here it was planted and grew until it had to be cut down in 2007. In 1929, Smith's mother sent another seedling to Canberra, where it was planted in the Yarralumla nursery. In 1934, the visiting Duke of Gloucester planted this tree in the grounds of the Australian War Memorial.

Although the War Memorial's Lone Pine is not often featured in official ceremonies, its existence is well known in the Australian community. When the tree was damaged by a storm in December 2008, the incident received nationwide media coverage. Memorial staff also report that 'small wreaths, home-made posies and the occasional red poppy are sometimes seen resting at its base'.

Another story has it that a Sergeant Keith McDowell of the 24th Battalion also souvenired a Lone Pine cone and kept it with him until the war's end when he returned safely to Victoria, giving the cone to his aunt, Mrs Emma Gray, who lived near Warrnambool. Mrs Gray kept the cone for a decade or so until she too propagated four seedlings. These were planted variously throughout Victoria from 1933, in Wattle Park and the Shrine of Rememberance in Melbourne, and the Soldiers Memorial Hall, The Sisters, and at Warrnambool Botanic Gardens. However, researchers say they have found no such digger as Sergeant Keith McDowell and the battalion to which he supposedly belonged did not reach Gallipoli until a month after Lone Pine. Nor, it seems, were any Smiths involved in the Lone Pine battle. Nonetheless, the legend of the Lone Pine seedlings is now deeply rooted, and the trees so widely distributed (two seedlings were planted at Gallipoli for the 75th anniversary of the battle) that no amount of historical fact will weaken it.

Like most such legends, the Lone Pine story arises from a powerful national desire for tangible connections to long-ago tragedies. If the connections are incomplete, explanatory tales are spun to bridge the gaps. While the Lone Pines are an unusually stark example of the process, similar needs underlie many national traditions, including the Anzac dawn service.

The first dawn service

Australia's single most important national ritual is Anzac Day. Before sunrise each 25 April, people gather at memorials all over the country to begin the day with prayers for the fallen of all wars. This dawn service varies in form from place to place and has evolved over time to suit a variety of local needs and traditions. Its basic meaning, however, remains the same. In the years immediately after World War I, the services were relatively simple, spontaneous ceremonies. Over time they have become more elaborate as Anzac Day has developed into what is arguably a more consensual expression of national identity than Australia Day, the anniversary of the first settlement. Given its significance and its emotional resonance, it is not surprising that there are a number of different versions of the dawn service's origins.

The military version is that the ceremony is derived from the 'stand-to', in which soldiers were put on full alert to guard against a pre-dawn (or post-sunset) attack. Great War veterans are said to have remembered stand-to as a peaceful moment of the day in which the bonds of comradeship were keenly felt. Some began to hold informal stand-to ceremonies on Anzac Day, their significance increased by the dawn timing of the first Gallipoli landings. The order to stand-to would be given. Then there would be two minutes' silence, after which a lone bugler would play the Last Post call and finally the Reveille. It is unlikely that these events were referred to as services, as there were no clergy present and no sermons or speeches. These elements of formality crept in from 1927, when the first official dawn service was held at the Cenotaph in central Sydney.

This event has its own foundation legend. According to the story, five members of the Australian Legion of Ex-Service Clubs were on their unsteady way home in the early hours of Anzac Day after a celebratory evening. As they rolled past the Cenotaph they saw an elderly woman laying a wreath in memory of a lost soldier. The roisterers were so shamed and sobered by this dignified act of commemoration that they joined the woman in silent tribute and prayer. Inspired by this experience, the men decided to conduct a wreath-laying ceremony at the Cenotaph at dawn the following year, 1927. More and more people began to join them, including government dignitaries and representatives of the clergy and the military.

In Albany, Western Australia, the first dawn service took a different form. At 4 a.m. on the day the first Anzac convoy left the town, the Anglican reverend Arthur Ernest White conducted a service for members of the 44th Battalion, AIF. After serving in the war, White returned to Albany. There, at dawn on 25 April 1923, he led a small group of parishioners up nearby Mount Clarence. As they watched the sun rise over King George Sound, a man in a boat threw a wreath onto the water. White recited the lines: 'As the sun rises and goeth down, we will remember them'—a fusion of a Biblical verse and poet Laurence Binyon's 'At the going down of the sun and in the morning/We will remember them.' News of this simple but moving observance—again with no strong religious overtones, despite a clergyman's presence—is said to have spread rapidly, and the ritual was adapted and adopted in many other communities.

Though well attested, this version does have a rival in Queensland. There, it is said that the first dawn service took place at 4 a.m. on Anzac Day, 1919. A small party led by a Captain Harrington placed flowers on the graves and memorials of World War I soldiers in Toowoomba, then drank to the memory of their fallen comrades. The observance was repeated, the Last Post and Reveille bugle calls were added, and other communities followed suit.

These different accounts of the origins of the dawn service have many features in common, but each is adapted to its own locality. Like the dawn service itself, they have become part of the edifice of legend that has formed around the Anzac tradition.

Lasseter's Reef

Many of Australia's wilder places have a tale of lost treasure. It may be in a reef, a cave, a river or under the ground; sometimes it involves secret maps, indigenous custodians or even pirates. Despite varying details, these legends are suspiciously similar—suggesting that they are more likely to be rooted in folklore than fact. The best known of all is the legend of the ill-fated Lasseter.

In Billy Marshall-Stoneking's book *Lasseter: the making of a legend*, he quotes the observation of a Papunya man named Shorty Lungkarta that Australians' obsession with Lasseter's 'lost' gold reef is just 'a whitefella dreaming'. It's a perceptive judgement. Marshall-Stoneking said he was inspired to investigate Lasseter's story by memories of the 1956 movie *Green Fire*—about a 'lost' South American emerald mine—in which Stewart Granger's character mentions 'Lasseter's Reef'. *Green Fire* is only one of innumerable films and novels that deal with the El Dorado get-rich-quick theme of the quest for a fabulous treasure.

The 'mystery', the history and the folklore of Lasseter's Reef have been kicking around Australia for over a century. They—and the numerous books, articles and fruitless expeditions the legend has spawned—are a revealing insight into human acquisitiveness.

In 1929 a man named Lewis Harold Bell Lasseter claimed that, years before, he had become lost in central Australia. During his wanderings, he said, he had discovered a reef of gold with nuggets 'as thick as plums in a pudding', but had been unable to mark or otherwise document its location. He said he had been saved from certain death by an Afghan cameleer. He claimed that three years later, in partnership with another man, he had managed to locate the reef. Because their watches were slow, however, the bearings they took were wrong and the reef was lost again.

In 1930, with backing from a trade union leader and other investors, Lasseter formed the Central Australian Gold Company, which mounted a large expedition. It was plagued with mishaps almost from the first. Eventually, after considerable strife and bickering, the party split up. Lasseter was stranded in the desert, and died in the Petermann Ranges, southwest of Alice Springs, probably in January 1931. The famous bushman Bob Buck was commissioned by the company to find Lasseter. After considerable hardship and danger, he found and, allegedly, buried Lasseter's remains, and retrieved the dead prospector's diary and some letters.

These papers, which included a map of the supposed location of the reef, triggered a futher series of expeditions. The fact that these ended in failure did nothing to quash the legend. At least eight books have been written about Lasseter and his treasure, the best known of which is Ion Idriess's semi-fictional and often-reprinted *Lasseter's Last Ride* (1931).

In 1957, the American explorer Lowell Thomas made a television documentary on the story that included interviews with the ageing Bob Buck and the opening of Lasseter's grave. This was intended to settle speculation that the remains Buck buried were not those of Lasseter and that the prospector had made his way to safety, only to disappear into either an obscure but wealthy life or anonymous shame. Whatever the truth, a number of people claimed to have seen or met Lasseter in Australia or overseas after the date of his death.

And there is a curse. One of the expedition members took a *churinga*, a sacred Aboriginal artefact, back to England. Almost immediately, he was plagued by misfortune; there were deaths in the family and he fell into a depression. Finally, he destroyed the precious but cursed object.

In some ways a uniquely Australian legend, the story of Lasseter's Reef neatly fits the template common to 'lost treasure' folklore around the world: an intrepid male explorer stumbles on a fabulous trove but loses its location in his struggle to return to civilisation alive. Perhaps he has a sample of the find. Invariably he has a map or a diary, or some other clue, either too cryptic to be useful or itself mislaid. These scant signs and indications entice others to embark on vain—even fatal— searches. Disturbing the treasure or coming too close to it may arouse its native guardians or trigger some dreadful curse. The treasure remains lost.

Yet the story lives on. We don't want to let go of Lasseter and his reef. The story is a variant on El Dorado, a universal beacon for the greedy. But it also stirs specifically Australian feelings: the awe and fear that, even in the jet age, the 'dead heart' still provokes.

The carpet of silver

On 5 July 1834, the *Perth Gazette* carried an intriguing report of a shipwreck.

A strange report has just reached us, communicated to Parker, of Guildford, by some natives, that a vessel had been seen wrecked on the beach, a considerable distance to the northward. The story has been handed from tribe to tribe until it has reached our natives and runs as follows. We give it of course without implicitly relying on its accuracy, but the account is sufficiently authenticated to excite well-founded suspicions that some accident has happened. It appears the wreck has been lying on shore for 6 moons, or months, and the distance from this is said to be 30 day's journey, or about 400 miles. When the water is low, the natives are said to go on board, and bring from the wreck 'white money'; on money being shown to the native who brought the report, he picked out a dollar, as a similar piece to the money he had seen. Some steps should be immediately taken to establish or refute this statement: the native can soon be found. He is said to be importunate that soldier man, and white man, with horse, should go to the wreck, volunteering to escort them. We shall look with anxiety for further information upon this point.

This news was met with some scepticism, but the following Saturday the paper published a fresh version of the story. In this rendition, the wreck, or 'broke boat', as the Aborigines called it, also had survivors.

The report we gave publicity to last week respecting the supposed wreck of a vessel to the northward, has met with some farther confirmation, and has attracted the attention of the local Government. A Council was held on Wednesday last (we believe) expressly for the purpose of taking this subject into consideration, and, after a diligent inquiry, it was thought expedient to make arrangements for despatching an expedition to the northward, which will be immediately carried into effect. This, the winter season, rendering a land expedition both dangerous, and, in every probability, futile, it has been determined to charter the *Monkey* (a small vessel, now lying in our harbour) to proceed immediately to Shark's Bay, somewhere about the distance described at which the wreck may be expected to be fallen in with, where Mr. H. M. Ommanney, of the Survey Department, and a party under his directions, will be landed to traverse the coast north and south, the *Monkey* remaining as a depot from whence they will draw their supplies, to enable them to extend their search in either direction . . .

. . . The following we believe to be the substance of the information conveyed to the Government: about a week or ten days since, Tonguin and Weenat came to Parker's and gave him and his sons to understand, that they (Tonguin and Weenat) had recently learned from some of the northern tribes (who appear to be indiscriminately referred to under the name of Waylo men, or Weelmen) that a ship was wrecked ('boat broke') on the coast to the northward, about 30 (native) days walk from the Swan—that there was white money plenty lying on the beach for several yards, as thick as seed vessels under a red gum tree. On some article of brass being shewn, they said that was not like the colour of the money; but on a dollar being shewn, they recognized it immediately as the kind of money they meant: but laid the dollar on the ground and drawing a somewhat larger circle round it with the finger, said 'the money was like that'. They represented that the wreck had been seen six moons ago, and that all the white men were dead: none, as it is supposed, having been then seen by their informants, the Weelmen. They added that, at low water, the natives could reach the wreck, which had blankets (sails) flying about it: from which it is presumed that the supposed vessel may not have entirely lost her masts on first striking, and they stuck up three sticks in a manner which led Parker's sons to understand that the wreck they were attempting to describe had three masts, but Parker himself did not infer the same meaning.

A day or two after Tonguin's visit, Moiley Dibbin called at Parker's with further information on the same subject, but derived from the same distant source; namely, the Weelmen. Moiley had been informed by some of the latter that there were several white men, represented to be of very large stature, ladies and 'plenty piccaninnie'—that they were living in houses made of canvas and wood (pointing out these materials, among several shewn to him)—that there are five such houses, two large and three small—that they are not on a river but on the open sea ('Gabby England come')—that the sea coast, at the site of the wreck, takes a bend easterly into an apparent bay (as described by Moiley on the ground)—that the spot where the white money is strewed on the beach is some (indefinite) distance from the spot where the houses are and more within the bay—that the gabby (surf) breaks with very great noise where the money is, and as it runs back, the Weelmen run forward and pick it up—that the white men gave the Weelmen some gentlemen's (white) biscuit, and the latter gave in return spears, shields, &c.—that they, Moiley, Tonguin, and Weenat, had never seen the wreck or the white men, and were afraid to go through the territories of the Weelmen, who are cannibals: but that they intend to go as far as the Waylo country, and then coo-ee to the Weelmen, who will come to meet them and give them some of the white money—and that the white men then could walk to the houses at the wreck in ten days—but though the word walk be used, there can be little doubt that Moiley alludes to a 'walk—on horseback'.

The prospect of rescuing white people from the aftermath of shipwreck and perhaps the depredations of the 'natives', together with the lure of money, electrified the small settlement. A few months before, some other Aborigines from the north had brought a few British coins into Perth, claiming that they had received them from the fearsome 'Wayl men'. This only increased people's eagerness to find out more, and plans were made for a boat to sail north in search of the wreck.

At this point, a local Aboriginal leader named Weeip enters the story. He had recently been outlawed for his resistance to colonial rule, and his son had been taken as, in effect, a hostage by the administration of Governor James Stirling. Hoping to win his son back, Weeip volunteered to travel north to see what he could discover. He returned in early August, claiming he had been told by the northern people that there were definitely no survivors of the mysterious wreck, but that there was plenty of 'white money'. The settlers were sceptical, but the Governor released Weeip's son all the same in return for Weeip's promise of good behaviour. The *Monkey* returned in October, having found nothing but some worm-eaten teak and fir wreckage on reefs off Dirk Hartog Island.

Meanwhile, however, other odd stories had begun to circulate. In July, soon after the *Perth Gazette*'s first story on the 'wreck', some Aborigines reported that they had contact with a party of whites living about eighty kilometres inland from the Perth colony. As there was no known settlement at that distance from the colony, this was astounding news. Who these people might have been, if they ever existed, is a mystery. Although highly unlikely, it is conceivable that a group had landed unnoticed and trekked inland to settle in the wilds.

It was eventually determined that the shipwreck stories were old. They had been passed from one generation to the next for perhaps a century or more. Stories passed on in this way tend to compress time spans. In this case, the 'broke boat' and the 'white money' did have a basis in fact, but that did not become clear until 1927, when the wreck of the Dutch East Indiaman *Zuytdorp* was first located. She had foundered in 1712, and perhaps thirty survivors had mysteriously disappeared into the continent's vast emptiness. The only evidence of their coming was the wreckage of their craft and a sandy bottom carpeted in silver coins—a scene that bore out the Aboriginal story of 1834.

FISHER'S
GHOST
POOL
CAMPBELLTOWN

1768. K & C°

5

The haunted land

She'll cross the moonlit road in haste
And vanish down the track;
Her long black hair hangs to her waist
And she is dressed in black . . .

Henry Lawson, 'The Black Lady of Mount Victoria'

MORE PEOPLE BELIEVE in ghosts than don't, according to researchers. Certainly, stories of hauntings and other ghostly visitations are no less widely told in Australia than anywhere else, and they appear in both European and indigenous traditions.

In Aboriginal lore, as in European, spirits caught between this world and the next are said to trouble the living. Some groups believe ghosts can move between worlds for a time, but must finally separate from the living. Some believe that ghosts have certain places where they await the right moment to leave the living and join their ancestors. Aboriginal people often treat ghosts as everyday realities rather than as unusual or frightening ones.

Stories of European-style ghosts also tend to be associated with particular places. Famous apparitions include the headless ghost of Berrima, New South Wales, and a blue nun who is said to disturb locals from time to time in the monastic town of New Norcia, Western Australia. Haunted houses can be found at Bungaribee, New South Wales; Drysdale, Victoria; and on the River Esk, near Fingal, Tasmania.

Other favoured ghost haunts include shipwrecks, hotels, theatres, jails and other old buildings. A headless diver is said to lurk beneath the Sydney Harbour Bridge—the ghost of a worker who died there. The explorer Robert O'Hara Burke, bushranger Johnny Gilbert and navigator William Dampier are all said to linger in ghostly form.

Fisher's ghost

Australian ghost stories, like many others, often involve violent or unusual deaths. The first such death to produce a ghost in Australia seems to have been that of ex-convict Frederick Fisher, who was murdered and secretly buried at what is now Fishers Creek, New South Wales.

On 17 June 1826, Fred Fisher, the proprietor of the Horse and Groom Hotel near Campbelltown, west of Sydney, was released from prison. He had knifed a customer in a fight at the hotel and been jailed for six months. Fisher had been transported in 1816, at the age of twenty-two, for possessing forged banknotes. He had worked hard in the colony, obtained a ticket-of-leave, and now owned considerable property. After his release, Fisher returned to his hotel—and almost immediately disappeared.

Fisher's neighbour, George Worrall, said he'd returned to England. Since Fisher had expressed no interest in leaving the colony where he was doing so well, locals found this unconvincing. Then Worrall, to whom Fisher had given power of attorney over his farm while serving his sentence, began selling the vanished man's belongings. Documents he produced to prove ownership were shown to be forged, and Worrall was arrested on suspicion of murder. No body, however, was found.

At this point the legend begins. Here is one of its earliest versions, from 1863. The writer has mistakenly named a Mr Hurley as the sighter of the ghost; it was actually a man named Farley.

*A*bout six weeks after Fisher's disappearance, Mr Hurley, a respectable settler in the vicinity of Campbelltown, was returning thence to his residence; he had long been acquainted with Fisher, and it is by no means improbable that his mind reverted to his sudden disappearance, when passing the place where he had so long resided; be that as it may, however, no doubt as to Worrall's statement ever entered his mind.

It was about ten o'clock at night when he left Campbelltown; the moon had risen, but her brilliance was obscured by clouds. After he had passed the late residence of Fisher, about from five to eight hundred yards, he observed the figure of a man sitting on the top of the fence on the same side of the road as the house. On approaching nearer, what was his surprise to recognize distinctly, the features of Fisher, whom he had supposed then far on his way to England. He approached the figure with the intention of assuring himself that he had not been deceived by a fancied resemblance.

The ghastly appearance which the features presented to his view on his nearer approach, struck such a chill of terror to his heart, as chained him motionless to the spot. The figure, as he gazed, rose from the fence, and waving its arm pointed in the direction of a small creek, which crosses the paddock at the place, and disappeared gradually from his view, apparently following the windings of the creek. The terror which overpowered the faculties of Hurley at this sight, defies all powers of description; in a state of stupefaction he left the spot, and endeavoured to obtain an entrance into the nearest house. How he managed to find his way to the house he has no recollection, but just as he approached it, his senses totally forsook him. The noise caused by his head striking the door as he fell, alarmed the inmates, who on opening it found him lying in a death-like swoon; he was carried into the house, where he lay for a whole week in the delirium of a brain fever.

The frequent mention of the name of Fisher in his ravings, attracted the attention of those who attended him, and conjecture was soon busy at work to ascertain what had driven him into such a state; his known character for sobriety, as well as the testimony of those who had parted from him only a few minutes before, forbade the supposition that he had been caused by drunkenness; and rumour, with her thousand tongues, turned the villagers' heads with vain conjectures as to its probable cause.

On the morning of the ninth day of Hurley's illness, he awoke after a long and refreshing sleep, in full possession of his senses, and expressed a wish to those around him that the Police Magistrate should be sent for.

William Howe, Esq., of Glenlee, who then filled the situation of Superintendent of Police for Campbelltown and the surrounding districts, was sent for, and came immediately on being made aware of the circumstances. To him Hurley disclosed what he had seen, and the suspicion of Fisher's having met with foul play, which that sight had impressed on his mind. As soon as Hurley was able to leave his bed, Mr. Howe, accompanied by a few constables, among whom was a native black man named Gilbert, went, conducted by Hurley, to the place where the apparition had been seen. On closely examining the panel of fencing pointed out, Mr Howe discovered spots of blood. An active search was commenced to discover further traces of the supposed murder, but nothing more was observed.

It was thought advisable to trace the course of the creek, in the direction to which the apparition had pointed, and in which it had disappeared. Some small ponds of water still remained in the creek, and these Black Gilbert was directed to explore with his spear; he carefully examined each as he approached it, but the shake of his head denoted his want of success. On approaching a larger pond than any of those he had before searched, the standers by observed his eyes sparkle, as he exclaimed in a tone of triumph, while yet at some distance from the pool, 'white man's fat sit down here'; as soon as he reached the bank of the pond he thrust his spear into the water, and after some search, he pointed to a particular spot in the water, saying 'white man there'. The constables were immediately set to work to clear away the water, which was soon effected—and on digging among the sand the remains of a human being in advanced stage of decomposition were discovered.

It became now obvious to all that Fisher (if the remains which had been found were really his) had met with an untimely end. Suspicion alighted on Worrall, who was the only person who had reaped any benefit from Fisher's death; and it was remembered also that he it was who had first propagated the story of Fisher's return to England. Many circumstances, corroborative of this suspicion, flashed on the minds of the neighbours, which until now had escaped their notice. Mr Howe caused Worrall to be arrested, and the suspicion being confirmed by the body of circumstantial evidence, he was committed to take his trial before the Supreme Court for the murder.

The conviction that retributive justice was now about to overtake him, had such an effect on his mind that he confessed his guilt. His reason for so barbarous a proceeding arose from the transaction mentioned in the former part of the narrative. Fisher, overjoyed at the success of the scheme by which he had defrauded his creditors, forgot to regain possession of the deed of conveyance by which he had made over his property to Worrall. The thought occurred to Worrall, that if he could only get Fisher quietly out of the way, he would be able to claim possession of the property in right of that conveyance; this project had repeatedly occurred to him while Fisher was in jail: and he had resolved even then, either to regain possession of the private agreement which compelled him to restore the property whenever it might be required, or to get rid of him entirely. Foiled in his scheme to obtain possession of this document by Fisher's unexpected liberation, he formed the diabolical scheme, which he ultimately accomplished.

Under the mask of friendship, he was Fisher's companion during the day—and night after night he watched Fisher's motions from the time of this return from jail, but had accidentally been foiled in every attempt he made, until the one on which the murder was committed. On that night he was as usual prowling about Fisher's cottage, looking out for an opportunity to attain his ends, when Fisher, tempted by the beauty of the evening, left his house to take a walk, followed at some distance by Worrall. At the place where the blood was afterwards discovered, Fisher stopped and leant against the fence, apparently wrapped in deep thought. The assassin had now before him the opportunity he had so long waited for, and taking up a broken panel of fence, he stole quietly behind him, and with one blow of his weapon stretched him lifeless on the ground; he carried the body from the scene of the murder to the place where it was afterwards discovered, and buried it deep in the sand. A few weeks after he had made the confession he expiated his crime on the scaffold, imploring with his last breath the forgiveness of his Maker.

No mention of the ghost was made at Worrall's trial, but the story had already gained its own momentum. While there was considerable speculation about whether the helpful ghost had really appeared, the story quickly escaped the confines of local gossip to become one of the nineteenth century's best-known tales. An anonymous ballad version appeared as early as 1832 in a colonial guidebook, quickly followed by articles in colonial periodicals, and even an early history. The story soon made the British and French newspapers, and in 1879 a play based on it was performed at the Sydney School of Arts.

The Scots folklorist Andrew Lang made an exhaustive investigation of the evidence in the early twentieth century, by which time, he wrote 'Everybody has heard about "Fisher's

Ghost". It is one of the stock "yarns" of the world . . .' Through some impressively researched comparisons between the Fisher's Ghost tales (whose origins had by then been lost in time), and a number of similar British cases, Lang convincingly argued that the story of the ghost developed rapidly in the locality of the murder. The tale was probably included in the initial evidence put before local magistrates but suppressed, for sound legal reasons, when the case was tried in the Sydney criminal courts. Despite this official silencing (for which Lang also provides some interesting British parallels), the story of the ghost leading authorities to its own murdered body continued to enthral common folk and scholars alike, chiming as it did with other tales and ballads involving ghostly messengers. Campbelltown hosts an annual Fisher's Ghost Festival and enthusiastically promotes the area's connections with the tale. There have also been more plays, an early Australian feature film, even an opera televised by the Australian Broadcasting Corporation in 1963.

The ghost on old Pinjarrah Bridge

One of Western Australia's earliest recorded ghosts died of an apoplectic fit some time during the 1860s. This account is from the early-1870s journal of settler Thomas Scott.

I had occasion during my stay in Pinjarrah to see Mr. C. on some small business transactions. Mr. C. was a near relation of the nocturnal visitant of which we are about to speak. On the third evening of our stay at Mr. Greenacre's Mr. C. paid me a visit. He was a man of firm resolution and would laugh trifles in the face. And a thorough unbeliever in such things as disembodied spirits. On my remarking how unwell he looked he only shook his hand and said, 'No wonder, Sir, for we have seen her again. And this makes the sixth time of her reappearance, and more distinct she appeared than she has on the former occasions.'

'Seen who? may I ask,' said I.

'Seen who?' reiterated Mr. C. 'Why surely, Mr. Margrave, you have not been in Pinjarrah these three days and heard nothing of the Ghost of the old Bridge?'

'Indeed then I have,' I replied. 'But you really don't mean to tell me that you believe in the story? Why, it was only last night, rather late that I came across the old Bridge and met none save one solitary individual, an elderly lady to all appearance who was attired in a light loose dress.'

'My poor Aunt, Mrs. C.,' exclaimed my friend, 'who has been dead for the last seven years, and this is the anniversary of her mysterious death. Why, Mr. Margrave this is the veritable ghost of the old Bridge of which I was just speaking to you, and which makes its nocturnal appearance on the old Bridge every year about this time. Whether it is the disembodied spirit of my aunt, which carries her feature and is recognised by us all, or whether it is but a phantom of the mind, God only knows, for it is very mysterious.'

'Strange, no doubt, as you say,' I ejaculated, 'but I rather think you are labouring under some illusion.'

'No illusion whatever,' said Mr. C., 'it is too true. She walks that old Bridge towards midnight nine days in each year just before and after the anniversary of her death. She has been recognised by her two sisters, her brother John, and Mr. Koil, my uncle.'

'You say she has been dead for the last seven years. May I ask in what manner she met her death?'

'Certainly, Sir,' answered Mr. C. 'She was found dead seven years ago on the old Bridge. She was supposed to have died from an apoplectic fit, but whatever the cause of death was she was interred next day as the weather was too oppressive to keep her any longer than that short time. On the 1st July, one year from the date of her demise, she, or rather her apparition, for I cannot be convinced to the contrary, was first seen by my uncle at midnight walking the old Bridge like a silent sentinel from the place of departed spirits.

'My uncle came home—I remember the night well—just as he had finished telling us what he had seen, three distinct, loud knocks were heard at our back door. It was a beautiful moonlit starry night—not a cloud was seen in the vast blue firmament; and bewildering stillness seemed to reign supreme. There was no time for anybody to have made off nor was there any place of concealment near at hand, as instantaneously we all ran to the door—but there was nothing to be seen and there was not a breath of air stirring. With palpitating hearts and big drops of perspiration on our foreheads we returned to the house. The door was hardly closed when three more knocks louder than the first was heard again, and at the same time we heard as distinctly as possible my uncle's Christian name repeated two or three times outside the door. The sound or voice was that of my aunt, which was recognised by all present. We all stood looking at each other in mute fear and astonishment—terror seemed to sway every heart now beating thrice three times as fast.

'My uncle was the first to break the spell. He rushed to the door, closely followed by myself, as if ashamed of his momentary fear, to behold a tall stately figure of a female clad in a light loose dress similar to that she had on at the time she was found dead on the old Bridge. 'Yes,' said my uncle, in a tremulous hoarse voice, 'Yes, that is my sister Kate or her apparition which I saw on the old Bridge.' She was walking or rather slowly gliding as it were in the direction of the old Bridge, which is about a quarter of a mile from our farm. My uncle instinctively shouted out 'Kate,' his sister's name. But, as if by magic, on her name being called she immediately disappeared from our view. We all proceeded to the old Bridge with the expectation of seeing the apparition there, for we were all fully convinced now that the figure was nothing else, but we were disappointed. None of us slept that night but kept a vigil till morning.

'On the third night after this the apparition was seen again but could not be approached by my uncle. Finally it disappeared altogether until the following year, about the same time, it made its reappearance again. Each succeeding year to the present one has brought us the ghostly visits of my deceased aunt, and for what purpose is to us as yet a mystery.'

'You say', said I, 'that the apparition is to be seen on the old Bridge but will not be approached; must I understand by that it disappears on your approach to it?'

'Precisely so,' answered Mr. C. 'And', he went on, 'if you, Mr. Margrave, have no objection you are welcome to join our little private party who are going to watch for it to-night.'

'I shall be too glad to accept your offer,' I replied; 'and I only hope I shall have a glimpse of your nocturnal visitant. May I bring a friend?'

'Certainly, with pleasure—half a dozen if you like—the more the merrier.'

The hour appointed by the C. party for apprising the apparition was fixed at midnight, that being the accustomed time of its first appearance. On my informing Mr. M. of our midnight adventure and the object it had in view, he most readily assented to accompany me, saying at the same time, 'And, by my soul, if it were a ghost we'd better be after letting the poor creature rest, faith, or may be it will be giving us a turn as well as its own people, sure. But no matter, go we will and if it should turn out to be some spalpeen night-walking, that wants waking, faith an' we'll give him a good ducking in the river that runs under the old Bridge.'

According to previous arrangements, half-past eleven that night found our small midnight party, comprising five in all, at our respective positions. The night was beautifully starlit with a full moon coursing in the heavens above. To the right of the Bridge was a burying ground and on either side of this lay nothing but the dark, dense forest, that looked in this lonesome hour the very place for a ghost scene. Twelve o'clock came and—no apparition appeared—a quarter-past twelve—half-past—and now five-and-twenty minutes to one and yet no appearance. We were literally counting the minutes after twelve but to no effect.

'Bad luck to it,' exclaimed Mr. M. 'I believe after all it will turn out nothing more than a hoax, sure.'

'Well,' said I, 'never mind, Mr. M., we will keep it up till one o'clock, then we'll give it up as a————.'

'Hist. Look!' interrupted Mr. M. 'By my soul, but there's somebody coming over the Bridge.'

On looking at my watch I found it was just twenty minutes to one. Scarcely had the last word died on Mr. M's lips when from four different quarters we advanced as previously arranged, with stealthy step (like 'stealing a march') toward the Bridge. A slight thrill ran through me as I clearly recognised the same figure I had seen the night previous. The old Bridge was a wooden construction about 50 yards long, with railing on each side as a protection to the dark waters beneath. We were not twenty yards from the apparition when on the deathly stillness of the surrounding dark-looking forest broke the prolonged and mournful howl of a dingo or native dog, causing us to fairly start. But it was only momentarily. Mr. M. and myself arrived at one end of the Bridge whilst at the other end appeared at the same time the C. party.

The apparition was in the centre of the Bridge and seemed to be on the move. It was quite recognisable by all parties and the same that has already been described. We instinctively stopped to watch it for a few minutes. The signal was given by the other party to apprise it, and simultaneously we all rushed to the spot where the apparition stood, visible as plain as day, and—aghast, we stood gaping at each other scarcely believing our own eyes. The figure whether earthly or spiritual had vanished. Five men whom I am in a position to prove were in their sane senses witnessed the mysterious—what shall we call it?—a delusion?—a phenomenon?—or what the world in the nineteenth century laughs at as gross superstition, viz., a ghost or spirit of the departed.

⌐

Although Scott doesn't say, it seems this was the last time that Kate was seen walking the old bridge, which was washed away in a flood some years later.

A Vice-Regal haunting

Yarralumla, the Governor-General's official residence in Canberra, was already said to be haunted when it became government property in the early twentieth century. As the recounter of this chronologically confused version of the tale puts it, 'Here is all the material for a five-reel movie drama.'

*W*hen the Governor-general goes into residence at Yarralumla House, his temporary home at Canberra, he will find that with the old house goes a tale of mystery. According to more or less conflicting versions of the tale, a ghost, a real Australian blackfellow ghost, has been known to walk, but—well, ghosts are rather out of date, anyway.

The story begins with a jewel robbery, tells of a big diamond passed to the robber's friend, and afterwards to the friend's son, and ends with bushrangers, and the murder of a trusty blackfellow. Here is all the material for a five-reel movie drama.

The skeleton of the blackfellow, so the story goes, lies at the foot of a big deodar, nearly a hundred years old, which is the pride of Yarralumla.

The record of the mystery is an old letter or manuscript, unsigned, dated 1881, 'written near Yarralumla', and it was left, no doubt overlooked and forgotten, by the former owners when the place was handed over to the Government. The homestead has been a hostel for members of Parliament, Government officials, and approved visitors, since the Canberra project has been in hand and many visitors have read the tale. It is a rambling story, and you may believe or not, as you like. Here it is :—

'In 1826, a large diamond was stolen from James Cobbity, on

an obscure station in Queensland. The theft was traced to one of the convicts who had run away, probably to New South Wales. The convict was captured in 1858, but the diamond could not be traced; neither would the convict (name unknown) give any information, in spite of frequent floggings. During 1842 he left a statement to a groom, and a map of the hiding-place of the hidden diamond.

'The groom, for a minor offence, was sent to Berrima gaol. He was clever with horses, and one day, when left to his duties, plaited a rope of straw and then escaped by throwing it over the wall, where he caught an iron bar. Passing it over, he swung himself down and escaped. He and his family lived out west for several years, according to the Rev. James Hassall who, seeing him live honestly, did not think it necessary to inform against him. I have no reason to think he tried to sell the diamond. Probably the ownership of a thing so valuable would bring suspicion and lead to his re-arrest.

'After his death his son took possession of the jewel, and with a trusty blackfellow set off for Sydney.

'After leaving Cooma for Queanbeyan they met with, it was afterwards ascertained, a bushranging gang. The blackfellow and his companion became separated, and finally the former was captured and searched, to no avail, for he had swallowed the jewel.

'The gang, in anger, shot him. He was buried in a piece of land belonging to Colonel Gibbes, and later Mr. Campbell. I believe the diamond to be among his bones. It is of great value.

'My hand is enfeebled with age, or I should describe the trouble through which I have passed. My life has been wasted, my money expended, I die almost destitute, and in sight of my goal.

'I believe the grave to be under the large deodar-tree. Being buried by blacks, it would be in a round hole. I enclose my dwindling fortune . . .'

It is said that the ghost of the murdered Aboriginal haunts the grounds of Yarralumla looking for the lost diamond. Some accounts claim that he has been seen digging at the roots of the ancient deodar tree, thought to be the finest example of its type in the country.

The Black Lady of Mount Victoria

In 1841 Caroline Collits, of Little Hartley in the New South Wales Blue Mountains, left her husband William and went to live with John Walsh and his wife. Caroline and Walsh had been lovers before her marriage and, with the apparent blessing of Walsh's wife, resumed their relationship. Early the next year, Caroline and the two men met for a drink at a local tavern in an attempt to reconcile their differences. But the meeting did not go well. The men fought, and William ran off into the night, leaving Walsh and Caroline alone together. The next morning the postman found her battered body by the roadside, her skull smashed in with a large rock. Walsh was arrested and protested his innocence, but he was hanged for the crime at Bathurst a few months later.

Caroline's ghost has since been seen many times near Mount Victoria. She is said to be dressed in black, often with blazing eyes and outstretched arms and is sometimes followed by a hearse drawing four black horses. At least one report claimed the ghost had laid a curse upon the village of Mt Victoria. Today, the ghost is often sighted by truck drivers on the Victoria Pass road.

Henry Lawson became well acquainted with the story of the Black Lady when he lived in the area during the 1880s, and used it in his poem 'The Ghost at the Second Bridge'. His tongue-in-cheek tone, however, suggests he was more than a little sceptical. The 'Second Bridge' refers to a convict-built, stone-lined section of the road through Victoria Pass.

You'd call the man a senseless fool,
    A blockhead or an ass,
Who'd dare to say he saw the ghost
    Of Mount Victoria Pass;
But I believe the ghost is there,
    For, if my eyes are right,
I saw it once upon a ne'er-
    To-be-forgotten night.

'Twas in the year of eighty-nine—
    The day was nearly gone,
The stars were shining, and the moon
    Is mentioned further on;
I'd tramped as far as Hartley Vale,
    Tho' tired at the start,
But coming back I got a lift
    In Johnny Jones's cart.

'Twas winter on the mountains then—
    The air was rather chill,

And so we stopped beside the inn
    That stands below the hill.
A fire was burning in the bar,
    And Johnny thought a glass
Would give the tired horse a spell
    And help us up the Pass.

Then Jimmy Bent came riding up—
    A tidy chap was Jim—
He shouted twice, and so of course
    We had to shout for him.
And when at last we said good-night
    He bet a vulgar quid
That we would see the 'ghost in black',
    And sure enough we did.

And as we climbed the stony pinch
    Below the Camel Bridge,
We talked about the 'Girl in black'
    Who haunts the Second Bridge.
We reached the fence that guards the cliff
    And passed the corner post,
And Johnny like a senseless fool
    Kept harping on the ghost.

'She'll cross the moonlit road in haste
    And vanish down the track;
Her long black hair hangs to her waist
    And she is dressed in black;
Her face is white, a dull dead white—
    Her eyes are opened wide—
She never looks to left or right,
    Or turns to either side.'

I didn't b'lieve in ghosts at all,
    Tho' I was rather young,
But still I wished with all my heart
    That Jack would hold his tongue.
The time and place, as you will say,
    ('Twas twelve o'clock almost)—
Were both historically fa-
    Vourable for a ghost.

But have you seen the Second Bridge
    Beneath the 'Camel's Back'?
It fills a gap that broke the ridge
    When convicts made the track;
And o'er the right old Hartley Vale
    In homely beauty lies,
And o'er the left the mighty walls
    Of Mount Victoria rise.

And there's a spot above the bridge,
    Just where the track is steep,
From which poor Convict Govett rode
    To christen Govett's Leap;
And here a teamster killed his wife—
    For those old days were rough—
And here a dozen others had
    Been murdered, right enough.

The lonely moon was over all
    And she was shining well,
At angles from the sandstone wall
    The shifting moonbeams fell.
In short, the shifting moonbeams beamed,
    The air was still as death,

Save when the listening silence seemed
    To speak beneath its breath.

The tangled bushes were not stirred
    Because there was no wind,
But now and then I thought I heard
    A startling noise behind.
Then Johnny Jones began to quake;
    His face was like the dead.
'Don't look behind, for heaven's sake!
    The ghost is there!' he said.

He stared ahead—his eyes were fixed;
    He whipped the horse like mad.
'You fool!' I cried, 'you're only mixed;
    A drop too much you've had.
I'll never see a ghost, I swear,
    But I will find the cause.'
I turned to see if it was there,
    And sure enough it was!

Its look appeared to plead for aid
    (As far as I could see),
Its hands were on the tailboard laid,
    Its eyes were fixed on me.
The face, it cannot be denied
    Was white, a dull dead white,
The great black eyes were opened wide
    And glistened in the light.

I stared at Jack; he stared ahead
    And madly plied the lash.
To show I wasn't scared, I said—

'Why, Jack, we've made a mash.'
I tried to laugh; 'twas vain to try.
    The try was very lame;
And, tho' I wouldn't show it, I
    Was frightened, all the same.

'She's mashed,' said Jack, 'I do not doubt,
    But 'tis a lonely place;
And then you see it might turn out
    A breach of promise case.'
He flogged the horse until it jibbed
    And stood as one resigned,
And then he struck the road and ran
    And left the cart behind.

Now, Jack and I since infancy
    Had shared our joys and cares,
And so I was resolved that we
    Should share each other's scares.
We raced each other all the way
    And never slept that night,
And when we told the tale next day
    They said that we were—intoxicated.

6
Tales of wonder

...and if they didn't live happy, we may.

Simon McDonald concluding 'The Witches Tale'

WHAT WE NOW call fairy tales did not exist until the seventeenth century, when French writers invented the form for the entertainment of an increasingly literate middle class. Many fairy tales were based on more down-to-earth folk tales, which had generally been told aloud rather than written down.

In an 1852 issue of Charles Dickens' magazine *Household Words*, a writer—clearly of middle-class background—reflected on his experiences as a convict in Australia, including the way he and fellow inmates whiled away the hours after lock-up each night:

> It was a strange thing, and full of matter for reflection, to hear men, in whose rough tones I sometimes recognized the most stolid and hardened of the prisoners, gravely narrating an imperfect version of such childish stories as 'Jack the Giant-Killer', for the amusement of their companions, who with equal gravity, would correct him from their own recollections, or enter into a ridiculous discussion on some of the facts.

By the start of the twentieth century, Australia had its own tales of fairies flitting, often rather unconvincingly, through the bush. More successful were works that invested the country's native plants and animals with magical qualities, such as Ethel Pedley's *Dot and the Kangaroo* and the lovable gumnut babies of *Snugglepot and Cuddlepie*, by May Gibbs, in which the villians were big, bad Banksia Men.

Henny-Penny

Children have always delighted in word play, in stories propelled by repetition and rhyme. The fable of Henny–Penny is a perennial favourite. Australian folklorist Joseph Jacobs transcribed this version he'd heard in Australia during the 1860s. It is still popular today.

One day Henny-penny was picking up corn in the corn-yard when—whack!—something hit her upon the head. 'Goodness gracious me!' said Henny-penny; 'the sky's a-going to fall; I must go and tell the king.'

So she went along, and she went along and she went along, till she met Cocky-locky. 'Where are you going, Henny-penny?' says Cocky-locky. 'Oh! I'm going to tell the king the sky's a-falling,' says Henny-penny. 'May I come with you?' says Cocky-locky. 'Certainly,' says Henny-penny. So Henny-penny and Cocky-locky went to tell the king the sky was falling.

They went along, and they went along, and they went along, till they met Ducky-daddles. 'Where are you going to, Henny-penny and Cocky-locky?' says Ducky-daddles. 'Oh! we're going to tell the king the sky's a-falling,' said Henny-penny and Cocky-locky.

'May I come with you?' says Ducky-daddles. 'Certainly,' said Henny-penny and Cocky-locky. So Henny-penny, Cocky-locky, and Ducky-daddles went to tell the king the sky was a-falling.

So they went along, and they went along, and they went along, till they met Goosey-poosey. 'Where are you going to, Henny-penny, Cocky-locky, and Ducky-daddles?' said Goosey-poosey. 'Oh! we're going to tell the king the sky's a-falling,' said Henny-penny and Cocky-locky and Ducky-daddles. 'May I come with you?' said Goosey-poosey. 'Certainly,' said Henny-penny, Cocky-locky, and Ducky-daddles. So Henny-penny, Cocky-locky, Ducky-daddles, and Goosey-poosey went to tell the king the sky was a-falling.

So they went along, and they went along, and they went along, till they met Turkey-lurkey. 'Where are you going, Henny-penny, Cocky-locky, Ducky-daddles, and Goosey-poosey?' says Turkey-lurkey. 'Oh! we're going to tell the king the sky's a-falling,' said Henny-penny, Cocky-locky, Ducky-daddles, and Goosey-poosey. 'May I come with you, Henny-penny, Cocky-locky, Ducky-daddles, and Goosey-poosey?' said Turkey-lurkey. 'Oh, certainly, Turkey-lurkey,' said Henny-penny, Cocky-locky, Ducky-daddles, and Goosey-poosey. So Henny-penny, Cocky-locky, Ducky-daddles, Goosey-poosey, and Turkey-lurkey all went to tell the king the sky was a-falling.

So they went along, and they went along, and they went along, till they met Foxy-woxy, and Foxy-woxy said to Henny-penny, Cocky-locky, Ducky-daddles, Goosey-poosey, and Turkey-lurkey, 'Where are you going, Henny-penny, Cocky-locky, Ducky-daddles, Goosey-poosey, and Turkey-lurkey?' And Henny-penny, Cocky-locky, Ducky-daddles, Goosey-poosey, and Turkey-lurkey said to Foxy-woxy: 'We're going to tell the king the sky's a-falling.'

'Oh! But this is not the way to the king, Henny-penny, Cocky-locky, Ducky-daddles, Goosey-poosey, and Turkey-lurkey,' says Foxy-woxy; 'I know the proper way; shall I show it you?'

'Oh, certainly, Foxy-woxy,' said Henny-penny, Cocky-locky, Ducky-daddles, Goosey-poosey, and Turkey-lurkey. So Henny-penny, Cocky-locky, Ducky-daddles, Goosey-poosey, Turkey-lurkey, and Foxy-woxy all went to tell the king the sky was a-falling.

So they went along, and they went along, and they went along, till they came to a narrow and dark hole. Now this was the door of Foxy-woxy's cave. But Foxy-woxy said to Henny-penny, Cocky-locky, Ducky-daddles, Goosey-poosey, and Turkey-lurkey, 'This is the short way to the king's palace: you'll soon get there if you follow me. I will go first and you come after, Henny-penny, Cocky-locky, Ducky-daddles, Goosey-poosey, and Turkey-lurkey.' 'Why of course, certainly, without doubt, why not?' said Henny-penny, Cocky-locky, Ducky-daddles, Goosey-poosey, and Turkey-lurkey.

So Foxy-woxy went into his cave, and he didn't go very far, but turned round to wait for Henny-penny, Cocky-locky, Ducky-daddles, Goosey-poosey, and Turkey-lurkey. So at last at first Turkey-lurkey went through the dark hole into the cave. He hadn't got far when 'Hrumph,' Foxy-woxy snapped off Turkey-lurkey's head and threw his body over his left shoulder. Then Goosey-poosey went in, and 'Hrumph,' off went her head and Goosey-poosey was thrown beside Turkey-lurkey. Then Ducky-daddles waddled down, and 'Hrumph,' snapped Foxy-woxy, and Ducky-daddles' head was off and Ducky-daddles was thrown alongside Turkey-lurkey and Goosey-poosey. Then Cocky-locky strutted down into the cave, and he hadn't gone far when 'Snap, Hrumph!' went Foxy-woxy and Cocky-locky was thrown alongside of Turkey-lurkey, Goosey-poosey, and Ducky-daddles.

But Foxy-woxy had made two bites at Cocky-locky, and when the first snap only hurt Cocky-locky, but didn't kill him, he called out to Henny-penny. But she turned tail and off she ran home, so she never told the king the sky was a-falling.

⌒

The witch's tale

Simon McDonald was a bushman-musician who lived in a slab hut in rural Victoria and performed traditional songs and folk tales. In 1967, folklorists Hugh and Dawn Anderson recorded him spinning, from many Irish wonder tales, this magical saga, which he Australianised as he went with bush slang and interspersed comments. By turns serious and tongue-in-cheek, McDonald mixed shape shifting, cannibalism and sorcery to make something entirely new. Stories like this are a hint of what fairy tales were in the days when they were still adult entertainments.

*I*n the Underworld—well, what that means I don't even know, because there was no underworld in those days, but these witches lived underground, that's how it was called, and the underworld these days is a crook business, isn't it? But not those days, and there was a great horse there called Black Entire. He was worth a thousand pounds, and that was a lot of money. And no one could get it and they were all out trying to pinch him.

There was an old woman there—I don't know what her name was, but she had three sons, Pat and Jack and Jim. They lived with her and she used to go out scrubbing and washing every day till she said, 'Well, I can't feed you no longer, you got to go out in the world and earn your own living.' So they said, 'Well, we don't know, Mother, we don't like leaving you.' 'Oh, well,' she said, 'we'll play a game of cards.' Those days you played a game of cards and if you had a wish, whoever had the wish won and you'd have to carry out that wish—oh, yes, it would be disgraceful—whatever the wish was, it had to be carried on.

So they put the cards on the table, and I think Jim won the first wish. 'Right!' he said. 'I won this,' he said. 'Plenty to eat and drink on the table.' That was his wish. The old mother was sitting there with them. Anyhow, the next game of cards they played again, Pat won. 'Plenty to eat and drink on the table' was his wish. Jack won the third and Jack said, 'I'll leave my wish till last, if you don't mind.' There was a law them days that you could leave your wish till last.

Then the fourth one, the old woman won, the mother. She said, 'Look, I wish that you never sleep two nights in the one place or have two feeds on the one spot till you bring back to me the Black Entire from Bryan O'Ville in the Underworld.' It was the most famous horse was ever known in Ireland. It was owned by three witches, and nobody ever come back alive that ever went for it, you see, or tried to get it off them.

So 'Righto, Mother,' they said. Well, Jack said, 'Now I've left my wish till last.' He said, 'Now, what I wish [is] you'd get up on that steeple there in the church and you'd stand there with a sheaf of hay on one side of you and a needle the other side and all you'll eat is what blows through the eye of that needle till we bring back the Black Entire from Bryan O'Ville in the Underworld.' It had to be carried out—all the wishes them days—oh, it was legal.

She got up on the tower saying, 'You bring with you a horse, a hawk and a hound. You'll all have a horse, hawk and a hound, you know, to go with you.' Where they got the horse, hawk and a hound, I don't know. Anyhow, she got up on the tower, and they seen her get up there. And they put a sheaf of hay on the other side of her, and she had a needle in the other hand, and that's the last they seen of her the other side. And they said, 'Well, she's not getting much till we get back.'

They went along the road and they took them, the horse, hawk and hound—and, of course, as far as the hawk, the hawk would perch upon their shoulder in them days; that was part of a man's protection. They didn't have rifles, guns or anything else. And the first man that went along the road was Pat, you see. He went along on his horse with his hawk and his hound, and it went day on and day on, and he hadn't had a bite to eat. And it come towards night and he said, 'I'll camp in this patch of the woods tonight.' There's an old hut there, sort of empty, and he said, 'I'd better camp here anyhow, and I'll tie my horse up.' He got in and he said, 'I'll light a fire. I've got nothing much to eat.' But all of a sudden there was a man come along with a mob of sheep, and as soon as he lay down and went to sleep, Pat said, 'I'll have one of his sheep.'

He come out with his knife and he cut a sheep's throat and he roasted a bit, fair on the fire—there was no cooking pots or anything there. He just got it half roasted when he heard a knock on the door—knock, knock. 'I'm old, cold and feeble, will you let me in?' Anyhow he said, 'Yes. Come in, well, old lady, come in quick, you'll die of the cold.' 'Oh! But I'm frightened of your horse, hawk and hound. Here's three bits of cord to tie them up with.' And she pulled three hairs out of her head. 'Oh,' he said,

'They won't touch you.' 'Well, just tie them up to please me,' she said. So he tied them up, much to his own misfortune after, because they were magic hairs.

Then she said, 'I'm starving with the hunger, will you give me something to eat?' 'Oh, righto,' he said. 'Poor old lady, I've got a sheep on the fire I'm just cooking, and you can have a bit off that.' Anyhow, he could see she was getting a bit restless and as he had it half-cooked he said, 'Well, there's a forequarter, you can have that.' She gulped it down as fast as she could and she said, 'Oh, I feel strong now.' He hadn't time to have a bite, hardly, so he said, 'What did you do with that?' 'Oh, I ate it and I'm still starving with hunger. More meat!'

'Look,' he said, 'I just give you a forequarter, but you can have another one.' So he cut another off the grilled sheep that he's got on the fire still cooking, and he watched her devouring that, and he said, 'Madam, my God! That's awful, I never seen a woman eat like that in my life.' She said, 'More meat!' She was getting stronger and stronger and he got a bit suspicious then. He thought, this is a queer business, this.

'Well,' she said, 'more meat, or else fight.' 'I don't like fighting women,' he said, 'and I've only got one leg left for myself and you're not getting that—you've ate the rest of the sheep.' 'Well,' she said 'more meat, or else fight.' Pat said, 'Fight you must have, then.' And they pulled out their swords—them days they fought with swords—but it wasn't long till she chopped his head off. She was a witch, you see, she had a magic sword and she cut his head clean off. That was the end of poor old Pat.

Jim come along and he met the same fate. The same mob of sheep and everything. But when Jack come along the road the next day, he was looking along and he seen a bit of grass growing like rope, and he thought he'd put these few bits in his pocket, as they might do to tie the horse up and that, you see. He's a wary man, Jack was. He had a look along there and he came to the same place on the same night somehow—you know, days after it. And he slept there and he saw the same man coming with the same mob of sheep, and then he was inside cooking this sheep as usual and he heard a knock at the door.

'I'm old, cold and feeble, will you let me in?' 'Yes,' Jack said, 'come in.' 'No, but I'm frightened of your horse, hawk and hound. Here's three little bits of cord to tie them up with.' 'All right,' he said, 'but they won't touch you.' 'Oh yeah, but just do it to please me.' 'Right,' he said, 'I'll do it to please you.' And he threw the three hairs in the fire—he was a bit suspicious of witches, you see. In them days there were numerous witches in Ireland, hundreds of them perhaps, we don't know. They've died out, I think, to the present day. Anyhow, he threw hers in the fire and he tied them up with his own three bits of rope—the rushes what he brought along the road. He just tied them up to please her, you know.

So while he was cooking his sheep and that, you know, she starts screaming with the hunger and wanting meat and everything. And he says, 'All right.' It come down that she ate three-quarters of the sheep. She said, 'More meat, or else I'll fight you.' Now, you don't often hear an old woman saying that, at her age. Those days, though, they were tough, you see. And he could see her getting stronger and stronger. Jack said to himself, 'That's a witch. I know,' he said. 'That's one of the rottenest witches in this land!' And she screamed out again.

'Look,' he said. 'I've only got one forequarter left for myself, and you're not getting it and that's that.' 'More meat, or else fight,' she said again. 'Well,' he said, 'fight you must have.' 'Right! Take that sword,' she said. 'There's the sword that killed your two brothers, and this'll kill you too.' She thought she had him well tied up. 'You see,' she said, 'I'm the most famous witch in the land. I kill and eat men.' Anyhow, Jack didn't like to do it, but out they went. She flew around in the air and she was hopping about ten feet here and there and coming down on him with the point of the sword, and he was getting beat quick and lively. So he called, 'Help, horse!' 'Ah!' she said, 'hold fast hair.' And the hair said, 'How can I when I burn behind the fire?' 'Ah!' she said, 'you tricked me.'

Out come the horse with his front paws and all, and he come bashing at her, but she was beating the two of them with her sword. Anyhow, Jack said, 'She's doing the two of us, better sing out for the hound. Help, hound!' And she cried, 'Hold fast, hair.' The hair said, 'How can I, when I burn behind the fire?' Out came the hound. She's doing the hound too; she's doing the three of them. And the last thing was the hawk. I don't know where they got the hawk from, but he was always in—one of their famous compatriots them days, you know. 'Help, hawk,' cried Jack. 'This is the last, I'm done.' He's bleeding to death, you see. She's stabbing them in all directions. The horse was done, he was falling down. Anyhow, 'Hold fast, hair' again. The hair said, 'How can I when I burn behind the fire?' And out come the hawk. He picked her two eyes out.

Soon as the eyes went out, Jack up with his sword and he hit a sidelong blow and he cut her head clean off. It flew up in the air about twenty feet. It was coming down again, and he could see it was going to stick on again so he give it a side-swipe with his sword then. 'Ah,' she said, 'if I'd have got me head on again that time you'd have never got it off again'. She said, 'Strike them two stumps there and you'll find your brothers, they'll get up again.' So with the magical sword of hers he struck them two butts of wood, and up jumped Pat and Jim. And they never seen much of the old woman after because she just disappeared in a vanish of smoke.

So they said, 'Well, we might as well all go along the road together'—they were all after the same mission you see—'we've got to bring back that horse.' The mother is still up on the steeple, still waiting there with a sheaf of hay on one side of her and a needle on the other.

They go along the road a bit, and there's a bloke come along on a black horse. And he said, 'Where are you going?' And Pat said, 'Mind your own business, we're not talking to you at all.' He said to Jim, 'Where're you going, what are you doing?' 'Nothing to do with you at all.' And he said to Jack, 'Do you mind telling me where're you going?' And Jack, he was a level-headed sort of fellow and he thought he might even find some information. 'We're going to find the great horse called the Black Entire.' He said, 'I'm just the man that can help you, I'm Gothy Duff.'

Now what that man was like I don't know, but that was his name in Ireland. He said, 'I can turn myself into a rooster. There are three witches own that horse and they're the worst kind of women that ever lived in the underground. Just on account of you being friendly. I'll go along with you.'

So they all tramped along the road and they come into the dark woods and then they went into the deep gullies—one way or another—until they came into what they used to call the underworld. It was all undermined out of the earth, y'know, with caves and everything. [Gothy Duff] says, 'You fellows better stop out here for a minute, and I'll get in and I'll get the horse. I'll get him out, I know the witches that own him. Oh, no,' he said, 'I can turn myself into a rooster anytime and they can't catch me.'

He went down and he was getting in the stable where the horse was, and he just started to put the halter on when the horse give a neigh that shook the world. The witches were inside, and the old mother, she said, 'Go out, there's someone stealing the horse!' When they rushed out, old Gothy just turned himself into a rooster, flew up on the beam, and they couldn't find him. 'Oh, there's nobody there, Mother, at all. Not a soul.'

They went back inside again, and after a while everything was quiet. He thought, 'I'll go back and I'll get this horse out this time,' but he just got the bridle half on him when the horse neighed and shook the world again. The witch said, 'Go out, there's someone stealing the horse.' They went out. Nobody there. He had turned himself into a rooster again. He didn't even crow; he was too cunning to crow. He flapped up on the beam. Anyhow, the third time it happened the old woman put on her thinking cap—she had a thinking cap and once she put that on she could think out anything in the world—and she said to the young witches, 'See if there's a strange rooster in the fowlhouse.'

He was perched up on the roost. They went out and they got him. 'We've got you, Gothy,' they said, 'we've got you at last. Come in, we've got you by the neck!' He was squawk, squawk, squawk. 'Turn yourself back into a man. You've got mates around here.' The old woman said to the young witch, 'Put on the cloak of darkness and the shoes of swiftness and scour the world till you find them.' Out they went. They wasn't long till they came back with Jack and Pat and Jim, bound and gagged. 'We've got them, Mother,' they said. 'You've come stealing our horse.'

As it went on, then they said, 'Well, you're all prisoners, we've got you down.' Gothy said to her, 'Can't you let me and my friends there off? We did come to steal your horse, all right, but we haven't got it.' 'Well,' she said, 'can you tell us a story?'

'Oh yes.' This story goes on and it says: 'One time there was a king. This king was going out every day to the hills and he comes home and he wants to eat meat. He always wanted to eat human meat, and he wanted to cook his own child this day. His wife was living with him, and he said, "I'll have to have the little girl in the pot tomorrow night." His wife didn't like it and said I don't think I can do it. He said, "You got to do it, wife. If I say kill her, kill her and put her in that pot. I've got to eat her." She always knew that he wanted toes first, fingers after. She was just crying along the road one day when she met this Gothy Duff, and he said to her, "What's wrong?" and she said, "Oh, my husband wants to kill the little girl and eat her." "Oh," he says, "it can't be done. You've got a little dog at home, haven't you?"

'"Yes."

'"Well, you cook the little dog. Put him in the pot, don't put in the little girl at all, and when he sings out for the toes, tell him you longed for the toes and you ate them. And when he sings out for the fingers tell him you longed for the fingers and you ate them."

'That night, this king, he was really a giant you know, comes home. "Where's me tucker, wife? I'm longing to eat this little girl." And she said, "All right, husband, I've got her cooked there in the pot in the oven." "Well, dish it out, I want the toes." She said, "I longed for the toes and I ate them." "Well, I want the fingers!"

"I longed for the fingers and I ate them. There you are, you can have the rest of it." The giant was very happy after he ate the little dog, because he thought it was the little girl. And he said, "Thanks, wife, you're a good wife. After that I'll sleep happy."'

When the witch asked for that tale, Gothy said, 'I can't give it while that poor man's all tied up with chains in the corner. If you let him go, he won't run away—it'll be OK.' 'All right,' said the old woman to Gothy. 'I want another tale.' So he said, 'No, you'll have to let one of the other men go every time I tell a story.' Anyhow, he told it, and in the finish she said, 'Do you know who that little girl was? It was my little daughter, she's a big grown-up now. Thanks, Gothy, you saved her life, and I think that youse can have the horse.' And she gave them three girls to go home with and take them for their wives then.

The three horses were found, and they went home leading the black horse along the road. And the old Gothy Duff just disappeared into the bushes the way he come about. But when they were getting near to the town where they lived, and where their poor old mother was still standing on the steeple with a sheaf of hay one side and a needle on the other, she was that overjoyed to see them that she fell off the steeple and broke her neck. Anyhow they stuck three spoons in the wall and they drank tea until they was black in the face, and if they didn't live happy, we may.

7
Bulldust

He's the man who drove the bull through Wagga and
never cracked the whip.

Traditional saying

LYING—IN ITS CREATIVE form—is common in stories told
out loud. Tall tales are staples of the frontier traditions of
Australia and the United States, which have produced some
stupendous liars, boasters and yarn-spinners, among them
Davy Crockett and Mike Fink in the US and Crooked Mick
and Lippy the Liar in Australia.

Tall tales may be told about anyone and anything, of course,
though Australians have tended to focus on unusual animals.
Modern forms of bulldust, such as the urban legend, include
almost-believable tales about sex as well as the dreadful things
that might happen to you on the dunny.

What a hide!

This story is attributed to a famous northwestern yarn-
spinner known as 'Lippy the Liar'. Lippy was a shearer's

cook. He'd grown up, or so he said, living with his mother on a cockatoo farm.

*W*e was so poor we lived on boiled wheat and goannas. The only thing we owned was an old mare. One bitter cold night Mum and me was sittin' in front of the fire tryin' to keep from turnin' into ice blocks, when we hear a tappin' on the door. The old mare was standin' there, shiverin' and shakin'. Mum said, 'It's cruel to make her suffer like this; you'd better put her out of her misery.'

Well, I didn't want to kill the old mare, but I could see it was no good leavin' her like that. So I took her down to the shed. We was too poor to have a gun, so I hit her over the head with a sledgehammer. Then I skinned her and pegged out the hide to dry.

About an hour later, we're back in front of the fire when there's another knock on the door. I open it, and there's the old mare standin' there without her hide. Me mother was superstitious and reckoned that the mare wasn't meant to die and that I'd better do somethin' for her. So I took her back down the shed and wrapped her up in some sheep skins to keep her warm.

And do you know, that old mare lived another six years. We got five fleeces off her and she won first prize in the crossbred ewes section of the local agricultural show five years runnin'.

The split dog

One of Australia's most popular bush tall tales—and one also widely told in Britain and America—involves a hunter and his dog. In the local version, one day, the hunter wounds a kangaroo, and his dog tears off to locate it. The dog either runs through some barbed wire or across an opened tin left by some careless camper, and is cut in half from head to tail. Unperturbed, the hunter puts the two halves of the dog back together. In his haste, however, he connects them the wrong way round, leaving the dog with two legs on the ground and two sticking up in the air. This does not slow down the dog. It continues chasing down the roo until he gets too tired, whereupon he simply rolls over and continues running with the other two legs. When it finally catches the roo, it bites both ends of the animal at once.

Drop bears

Drop bears are mythical creatures of Australian tall-tale tradition that fall from the trees onto unsuspecting bush walkers. They are often described as koala-like, with large heads and sharp teeth. They serve as a peg around which brief yarns can be spontaneously spun, usually cautionary tales for tourists and new migrants. This is not unique to Australia, though Australians do seem to relish giving new arrivals a hard time. This particular drop-bear yarn includes parenthetical comments by the teller on exactly how to tell the tale for maximum effect.

I was working at . . . the hardware shop in 1987 when some Pommy backpackers came in to get some fly screen to cover the bull bar of their Dodge van to stop the insects clogging the radiator. A bit of a slow day, so I helped them attach it. When I was finished, I stood up and stated, 'That'll stop anything from a quokka to a drop bear.'

'A what?'

'Well, a quokka is a small wallaby looking thing from Western Australia.'

'Yeah, but what's a drop bear?' (Made them ask.)

'You guys don't know what a drop bear is?' (Disbelief at their lack of knowledge.) 'OK, they are a carnivorous possum that lives in gum trees but then drops out of the branches, lands on the kangaroo or whatever's back, and rips their throat out with an elongated lower canine tooth. Sort of looks like a feral pig tusk. Then laps the blood up like a vampire bat.' (A couple of references to existing animals with known characteristics.)

'My God. Have you ever seen one?'

'Well, not a live one. During the expansion of the 1930s the farmers organised drives because they were killing stock. There is a stuffed one in the museum in town.' (Offering verification if they want to stay another day. But they had already established they were heading for Mount Isa as soon as I was finished.) 'They're not extinct but endangered; just small isolated groups now.' (More believable that there are only limited numbers as opposed to saying they are everywhere.)

'Really, whereabouts?'

'Here in Queensland; well the western bits at least.' (Which direction are they heading? Townsville to Mt Isa, i.e. west.)

'But how will we know if it's safe to camp?' (Concern now; they can't afford motels.)

'Oh, well, it's a local thing. As you're going through the last town before you're gunna stop for the night, just go into any pub and ask what the drop-bear situation is like. Bye . . . have a nice trip.'

(Jeez, there are some bastards in this world.)

~

In one drop-bear story from Queensland, the creature is said to have size 10 feet, which it uses to kick in the head of its unfortunate victims. There have been a band and an online gaming sports team named the Drop Bears, and the dangerous little beasts also lead a busy life on the internet.

Hoop snakes

Hoop snakes inhabit the same mythical dimension as drop bears and giant mosquitoes. Said to put their tails in their mouths and roll after their intended victims, they have been rolling through Australian tradition since at least the mid nineteenth century. Here's a typical example:

*W*ell, there I was, slogging through this timber country, and just as I gets to the top of the hill I almost steps on this bloody great snake. Of course, I jump backwards pretty smartish-like, but the snake comes straight at me, so off I went back down the hill, fast as I could go. Trouble was, it was a hoop snake. Soon as I took off, the bloody thing put its tail in its mouth and came bowling along after me. And it was gaining on me, too—but just as I reached the bottom of the hill, I jumped up and grabbed an overhanging branch. The hoop snake couldn't stop. It just went bowling along and splashed straight into the creek at the bottom of the hill and drowned. Well, of course it's a true story. I mean—if it weren't true the snake would have got me and I wouldn't be telling you about it, would I?

Hoop snakes are also native to North America, where they sometimes wriggle into tales of Pecos Bill, the superhuman cowboy who bears some resemblance to the Australian shearers' hero Crooked Mick.

Giant mozzies

Australia is also inhabited by mosquitoes that wear hobnailed boots, carry off cows and bullocks, and may be seen later picking their teeth with the beasts' bones. This anonymous twentieth-century ballad tells of a particularly vicious New South Wales variety.

> Now, the Territory has huge crocodiles,
> Queensland the Taipan snake
> Wild scrub bulls are the biggest risk
> Over in the Western state.
> But if you're ever in New South Wales,
> Round Hunter Valley way
> Look out for them giant mozzies,
> The dreaded Hexham Greys.
>
> They're the biggest skeetas in the world,
> And that's the dinkum truth

Why, I've heard the fence wire snappin'
When they land on them to roost.
Be ready to clear out smartly
When you hear the dreaded drone—
They'll suck the blood right out ya' veins
And the marrow from ya' bones.

Now some shooters on the swamp one night,
Waiting for the ducks t' come in,
Loaded their guns in earnest
At the sound of flappin' wings.
As the big mob circled overhead
They aimed and blasted away,
But by mistake they'd gone and shot
At a swarm of Hexham Greys.

And a bullocky in the early days,
Bogged in swampy land,
Left his team to try and find
Someone to lend a hand.
When he returned next morning,
He found to his dismay,
His whole darn team had perished,
Devoured by Hexham Greys.

Oh his swearin' they say was louder
Than any thunderstorm
When he saw a pair of Hexham Greys
Pick their teeth with his leader's horns.
And ya' know, twenty men once disappeared—

To this day they've never been found—
They'd been workin' late on a water tank
By the river at Hexham town.

The skeetas were so savage,
The men climbed in that tank's insides,
Believin' they'd be protected
By the corrugated iron.
When the skeetas bit right through that tank,
Determined to get a meal,
The apprentice grabbed his hammer,
Clinched their beaks onto the steel.
Well, it wasn't long before they felt
That big tank slowly rise,
Them skeetas lifted it clear from the ground
Then carried 'em into the sky.

Well, they're just a few of the facts I've heard,
Concernin' the Hexham Greys
Passed on to me by my dear old dad,
Who would never lie they say.
So if you are in New South Wales,
Round Hunter Valley way
Look out for them giant mozzies,
The dreaded Hexham Greys.

⌒

There is a three-metre-tall statue of a grey mosquito outside the Hexham Bowling Club, near Newcastle. The locals say it is a life-sized model.

Dinkum!

A perennial favourite is the yarn in which an Australian one-ups an American skiter—often quite a feat. This example is from World War I:

*I*n a London café last month a soldier who hailed from the other side of Oodnadatta fell into a friendly argument with an American, as to the relative greatness of the two countries.

'Wal,' said the Yankee, 'that bit o' sunbaked mud yew call Australia ain't a bad bit o' sile in its way, and it'll be worth expectoratin' on when it wakes up and discovers it's alive, but when yew come to compare it with Amurrica, wal, yer might 'swell put a spot o' dust alongside a diamond. Y'see, sonny, we kinder do things in Amurrica; we don't sit round like an egg in its shell waitin' fer someone tew come along and crack it; no, we git hustling' till all Amurrica's one kernormous dust storm kicked up by our citizens raking in their dollars. Why, there's millions of Amurricans who 'ave tew climb to the top of their stack o' dollars on a ladder every morning, so's they ken see the sun rise. We're some people!'

The Australian took a hitch in his belt, put his cigarette behind his ear, and observed:

'Dollars! Do yer only deal in five bobs over there! We deal in nothin' but quids [pounds] in Australia. Anything smaller than a quid we throw away. Too much worry to count, and it spoils the shape of yer pockets. The schoolboys 'ave paperchases with pound notes. Money in Australia! Why, you can see the business blokes comin' outer their offices every day with wads of bank notes like blankets under each arm. I remember before I left Adelaide all the citizens was makin' for the banks with the day's takin's, when a stiff gale sprung up pretty sudden. Them citizens let go their wads ter 'old their 'ats on and immediately the air was full of bank notes—mostly 'undred quidders. Yer couldn't see the sun fer paper. The corporation 'ad to hire a thousand men ter sweep them bank notes in a 'eap and burn 'em. Dinkum!'

The exploding dunny

This is an update of an old bush yarn from the days before septic tanks and sewers. Back then, the dunny was a hole in the ground. Every week or two, as the hole began to fill, kerosene would be poured in to disguise the smell and aid decomposition. As the yarn used to go, one day someone mistakenly poured petrol down the hole and the next person to use the dunny dropped his still-lit cigarette butt. The resulting explosion blew up the dunny, its contents and the smoker too.

In the modern version, the woman of the house is trying to exterminate an insect, often a cockroach. She throws it into the toilet bowl and gives it a good spray of insecticide. Her husband immediately uses the loo, drops his cigarette butt and gets a burned backside when it ignites the flammable mix of gases and chemicals.

With badly burned rear and genitals, the husband is in need of hospitalisation. When the ambulance arrives, the ambulance men are so amused that they cannot stop laughing. They get the husband on to the stretcher, but on the way out their laughter becomes uncontrollable. They drop the stretcher. The burned husband hits the concrete floor and breaks his pelvis.

The continued popularity of this fable is perhaps due to its message that even the most mundane activities can be dangerous.

The well-dressed roo

There are a good many bush yarns about kangaroos mimicking the actions of humans. This one was probably not new when it was published in a 1902 book of humour titled *Aboriginalities*. It was still being told in the 1950s about visiting English cricket sides and in the mid-1980s about an Italian America's Cup team in Western Australia. It has been frequently aired in the Australian press.

A group of tourists is being driven through the Outback. The bus runs down a kangaroo, and the driver stops to assess the damage. The tourists, excited by this bit of authentic Australiana, rush out to have a look. After the cameras have clicked for a while, someone gets the bright idea of standing the dead roo against a tree and putting his sports jacket on the animal for a novel souvenir photo.

Just as the tourist is about to snap his photo, the roo, only stunned by the bus, returns to consciousness and leaps off into the scrub, still wearing the tourist's expensive jacket—with his wallet, money, credit cards and passport in the pocket.

This tale of a supposedly dumb animal meting out poetic justice to a dumb human has many international variations, including the American bear that walks off into Yellowstone Park carrying a tourist's baby, and the deer hunter who loses his rifle after placing it in the antlers of a deer he has just shot. Versions are also told in Germany and Canada. But Australia's is better, of course.

Loaded animals

The ancestry of the 'biter bitten' yarn goes back at least as far as the Middle Ages. It's known in Europe and in India. Probably Australia's best-known version is Henry Lawson's 'The Loaded Dog':

*D*ave Regan, Jim Bently, and Andy Page were sinking a shaft at Stony Creek in search of a rich gold quartz reef which was supposed to exist in the vicinity. There is always a rich reef supposed to exist in the vicinity; the only questions are whether it is ten feet or hundreds beneath the surface, and in which direction. They had struck some pretty solid rock, also water which kept them baling. They used the old-fashioned blasting-powder and time-fuse. They'd make a sausage or cartridge of blasting-powder in a skin of strong calico or canvas, the mouth sewn and bound round the end of the fuse; they'd dip the cartridge in melted tallow to make it water-tight, get the drill-hole as dry as possible, drop in the cartridge with some dry dust, and wad and ram with stiff clay and broken brick. Then they'd light the fuse and get out of the hole and wait. The result was usually an ugly pot-hole in the bottom of the shaft and half a barrow-load of broken rock.

There was plenty of fish in the creek, fresh-water bream, cod, cat-fish, and tailers. The party were fond of fish, and Andy and Dave of fishing.

Andy would fish for three hours at a stretch if encouraged by a 'nibble' or a 'bite' now and then—say once in twenty minutes. The butcher was always willing to give meat in exchange for fish when they caught more than they could eat; but now it was winter, and these fish wouldn't bite. However, the creek was low, just a chain of muddy water-holes, from the hole with a few bucketfuls in it to the sizable pool with an average depth of six or seven feet, and they could get fish by baling out the smaller holes or muddying up the water in the larger ones till the fish rose to the surface. There was the cat-fish, with spikes growing out of the sides of its head, and if you got pricked you'd know it, as Dave said. Andy took off his boots, tucked up his trousers, and went into a hole one day to stir up the mud with his feet, and he knew it. Dave scooped one out with his hand and got pricked, and he knew it too; his arm swelled, and the pain throbbed up into his shoulder, and down into his stomach too, he said, like a toothache he had once, and kept him awake for two nights—only the toothache pain had a 'burred edge', Dave said.

Dave got an idea.

'Why not blow the fish up in the big water-hole with a cartridge?' he said.

'I'll try it.'

He thought the thing out and Andy Page worked it out. Andy usually put Dave's theories into practice if they were practicable, or bore the blame for the failure and the chaffing of his mates if they weren't.

He made a cartridge about three times the size of those they used in the rock. Jim Bently said it was big enough to blow the bottom out of the river. The inner skin was of stout calico; Andy stuck the end of a six-foot piece of fuse well down in the powder and bound the mouth of the bag firmly to it with whipcord. The idea was to sink the cartridge in the water with the open end of the fuse attached to a float on the surface, ready for lighting. Andy dipped the cartridge in melted bees'-wax to make it water-tight. 'We'll have to leave it some time before we light it,' said Dave, 'to give the fish time to get over their scare when we put it in, and come nosing round again; so we'll want it well water-tight.'

Round the cartridge Andy, at Dave's suggestion, bound a strip of sail canvas—that they used for making water-bags—to increase the force of the explosion, and round that he pasted layers of stiff brown paper—on the plan of the sort of fireworks we called 'gun-crackers'. He let the paper dry in the sun, then he sewed a covering of two thicknesses of canvas over it, and bound the thing from end to end with stout fishing-line. Dave's schemes were elaborate, and he often worked his inventions out to nothing. The cartridge was rigid and solid enough now—a formidable bomb; but Andy and Dave wanted to be sure. Andy sewed on another layer of canvas, dipped the cartridge in melted tallow, twisted a length of fencing-wire round it as an afterthought, dipped it in tallow again, and stood it carefully against a tent-peg, where he'd know where to find it, and wound the fuse loosely round it. Then he went to the camp-fire to try some potatoes which were boiling in their jackets in a billy, and to see about frying some chops for dinner. Dave and Jim were at work in the claim that morning.

They had a big black young retriever dog—or rather an overgrown pup, a big, foolish, four-footed mate, who was always slobbering round them and lashing their legs with his heavy tail that swung round like a stock-whip.

Most of his head was usually a red, idiotic, slobbering grin of appreciation of his own silliness. He seemed to take life, the world, his two-legged mates, and his own instinct as a huge joke. He'd retrieve anything: he carted back most of the camp rubbish that Andy threw away. They had a cat that died in hot weather, and Andy threw it a good distance away in the scrub; and early one morning the dog found the cat, after it had been dead a week or so, and carried it back to camp, and laid it just inside the tent-flaps, where it could best make its presence known when the mates should rise and begin to sniff suspiciously in the sickly smothering atmosphere of the summer sunrise. He used to retrieve them when they went in swimming; he'd jump in after them, and take their hands in his mouth, and try to swim out with them, and scratch their naked bodies with his paws.

They loved him for his good-heartedness and his foolishness, but when they wished to enjoy a swim they had to tie him up in camp.

He watched Andy with great interest all the morning making the cartridge, and hindered him considerably, trying to help; but about noon he went off to the claim to see how Dave and Jim were getting on, and to come home to dinner with them. Andy saw them coming, and put a panful of mutton-chops on the fire. Andy was cook to-day; Dave and Jim stood with their backs to the fire, as Bushmen do in all weathers, waiting till dinner should be ready. The retriever went nosing round after something he seemed to have missed.

Andy's brain still worked on the cartridge; his eye was caught by the glare of an empty kerosene-tin lying in the bushes, and it struck him that it wouldn't be a bad idea to sink the cartridge packed with clay, sand, or stones in the tin, to increase the force of the explosion. He may have been all out, from a scientific point of view, but the notion looked all right to him.

Jim Bently, by the way, wasn't interested in their 'damned silliness'. Andy noticed an empty treacle-tin—the sort with the little tin neck or spout soldered on to the top for the convenience of pouring out the treacle—and it struck him that this would have made the best kind of cartridge-case: he would only have had to pour in the powder, stick the fuse in through the neck, and cork and seal it with bees'-wax. He was turning to suggest this to Dave, when Dave glanced over his shoulder to see how the chops were doing—and bolted. He explained afterwards that he thought he heard the pan spluttering extra, and looked to see if the chops were burning.

Jim Bently looked behind and bolted after Dave. Andy stood stock-still, staring after them.

'Run, Andy! Run!' they shouted back at him. 'Run!!! Look behind you, you fool!' Andy turned slowly and looked, and there, close behind him, was the retriever with the cartridge in his mouth—wedged into his broadest and silliest grin. And that wasn't all. The dog had come round the fire to Andy, and the loose end of the fuse had trailed and waggled over the burning sticks into the blaze; Andy had slit and nicked the firing end of the fuse well, and now it was hissing and spitting properly.

Andy's legs started with a jolt; his legs started before his brain did, and he made after Dave and Jim. And the dog followed Andy.

Dave and Jim were good runners—Jim the best—for a short distance; Andy was slow and heavy, but he had the strength and the wind and could last. The dog leapt and capered round him, delighted as a dog could be to find his mates, as he thought, on for a frolic. Dave and Jim kept shouting back, 'Don't foller us! Don't foller us, you coloured fool!' but Andy kept on, no matter how they dodged. They could never explain, any more than the dog, why they followed each other, but so they ran, Dave keeping in Jim's track in all its turnings, Andy after Dave, and the dog circling round Andy—the live fuse swishing in all directions and hissing and spluttering and stinking, Jim yelling to Dave not to follow him, Dave shouting to Andy to go in another direction—to 'spread out', and Andy roaring at the dog to go home.

Then Andy's brain began to work, stimulated by the crisis: he tried to get a running kick at the dog, but the dog dodged; he snatched up sticks and stones and threw them at the dog and ran on again. The retriever saw that he'd made a mistake about Andy, and left him and bounded after Dave. Dave, who had the presence of mind to think that the fuse's time wasn't up yet, made a dive and a grab for the dog, caught him by the tail, and as he swung round snatched the cartridge out of his mouth and flung it as far as he could: the dog immediately bounded after it and retrieved it. Dave roared and cursed at the dog, who seeing that Dave was offended, left him and went after Jim, who was well ahead. Jim swung to a sapling and went up it like a native bear; it was a young sapling, and Jim couldn't safely get more than ten or twelve feet from the ground. The dog laid the cartridge, as carefully as if it was a kitten, at the foot of the sapling, and capered and leaped and whooped joyously round under Jim. The

165

big pup reckoned that this was part of the lark—he was all right now—it was Jim who was out for a spree.

The fuse sounded as if it were going a mile a minute. Jim tried to climb higher and the sapling bent and cracked. Jim fell on his feet and ran. The dog swooped on the cartridge and followed. It all took but a very few moments. Jim ran to a digger's hole, about ten feet deep, and dropped down into it—landing on soft mud—and was safe. The dog grinned sardonically down on him, over the edge, for a moment, as if he thought it would be a good lark to drop the cartridge down on Jim.

'Go away, Tommy,' said Jim feebly, 'go away.'

The dog bounded off after Dave, who was the only one in sight now; Andy had dropped behind a log, where he lay flat on his face, having suddenly remembered a picture of the Russo–Turkish war with a circle of Turks lying flat on their faces (as if they were ashamed) round a newly arrived shell.

There was a small hotel or shanty on the creek, on the main road, not far from the claim. Dave was desperate, the time flew much faster in his stimulated imagination than it did in reality, so he made for the shanty. There were several casual Bushmen on the verandah and in the bar; Dave rushed into the bar, banging the door to behind him. 'My dog!' he gasped, in reply to the astonished stare of the publican, 'the blanky retriever—he's got a live cartridge in his mouth—'

The retriever, finding the front door shut against him, had bounded round and in by the back way, and now stood smiling in the doorway leading from the passage, the cartridge still in his mouth and the fuse spluttering. They burst out of that bar. Tommy bounded first after one and then after another, for, being a young dog, he tried to make friends with everybody.

The Bushmen ran round corners, and some shut themselves in the stable. There was a new weather-board and corrugated-iron kitchen and wash-house on piles in the back-yard, with some women washing clothes inside. Dave and the publican bundled in there and shut the door—the publican cursing Dave and calling him a crimson fool, in hurried tones, and wanting to know what the hell he came here for.

The retriever went in under the kitchen, amongst the piles, but, luckily for those inside, there was a vicious yellow mongrel cattle-dog sulking and nursing his nastiness under there—a sneaking, fighting, thieving canine, whom neighbours had tried for years to shoot or poison. Tommy saw his danger—he'd had experience from this dog—and started out and across the yard, still sticking to the cartridge. Half-way across the yard the yellow dog caught him and nipped him. Tommy dropped the cartridge, gave one terrified yell, and took to the Bush. The yellow dog followed him to the fence and then ran back to see what he had dropped.

Nearly a dozen other dogs came from round all the corners and under the buildings—spidery, thievish, cold-blooded kangaroo-dogs, mongrel sheep- and cattle-dogs, vicious black and yellow dogs—that slip after you in the dark, nip your heels, and vanish without explaining—and yapping, yelping small fry. They kept at a respectable distance round the nasty yellow dog, for it was dangerous to go near him when he thought he had found something which might be good for a dog to eat. He sniffed at the cartridge twice, and was just taking a third cautious sniff when—

It was very good blasting powder—a new brand that Dave had recently got up from Sydney; and the cartridge had been excellently well made. Andy was very patient and painstaking in all he did, and nearly as handy as the average sailor with needles, twine, canvas, and rope.

Bushmen say that that kitchen jumped off its piles and on again. When the smoke and dust cleared away, the remains of the nasty yellow dog were lying against the paling fence of the yard looking as if he had been kicked into a fire by a horse and afterwards rolled in the dust under a barrow, and finally thrown against the fence from a distance. Several saddle-horses, which had been 'hanging-up' round the verandah, were galloping wildly down the road in clouds of dust, with broken bridle-reins flying; and from a circle round the outskirts, from every point of the compass in the scrub, came the yelping of dogs. Two of them went home, to the place where they were born, thirty miles away, and reached it the same night and stayed there; it was not till towards evening that the rest came back cautiously to make inquiries. One was trying to walk on two legs, and most of 'em looked more or less singed; and a little, singed, stumpy-tailed dog, who had been in the habit of hopping the back half of him along on one leg, had reason to be glad that he'd saved up the other leg all those years, for he needed it now. There was one old one-eyed cattle-dog round that shanty for years afterwards, who couldn't stand the smell of a gun being cleaned. He it was who had taken an interest, only second to that of the yellow dog, in the cartridge. Bushmen said that it was amusing to slip up on his blind side and stick a dirty ramrod under his nose: he wouldn't wait to bring his solitary eye to bear—he'd take to the Bush and stay out all night.

For half an hour or so after the explosion there were several Bushmen round behind the stable who crouched, doubled up, against the wall, or rolled gently on the dust, trying to laugh without shrieking. There were two white women in hysterics at the house, and a half-caste rushing aimlessly round with a dipper of cold water. The publican was holding his wife tight and begging her between her squawks, to 'hold up for my sake, Mary, or I'll lam the life out of ye.'

Dave decided to apologise later on, 'when things had settled a bit', and went back to camp. And the dog that had done it all, Tommy, the great, idiotic mongrel retriever, came slobbering round Dave and lashing his legs with his tail, and trotted home after him, smiling his broadest, longest, and reddest smile of amiability, and apparently satisfied for one afternoon with the fun he'd had.

Andy chained the dog up securely, and cooked some more chops, while Dave went to help Jim out of the hole.

And most of this is why, for years afterwards, lanky, easy-going Bushmen, riding lazily past Dave's camp, would cry, in a lazy drawl and with just a hint of the nasal twang—

"El-lo, Da-a-ve! How's the fishin' getting on, Da-a-ve?'

This is a modernised version of Lawson's yarn:

A rabbito, new to the job, was not having much luck. No matter what he did, he couldn't seem to bag a single rabbit. The old hands were doing well, so the new bloke asked them for advice. They told him to get himself a rabbit, tie a stick of gelignite to its tail, light the 'gelly' and send the rabbit down the nearest burrow. This would guarantee a big, if messy, haul.

The new bloke thought this was a fine idea. The only trouble was, he couldn't catch a rabbit in the first place. So he decided to buy one at the pet store in town. Back in the bush, he got the rabbit out of its cage, tied the explosive to it, lit the fuse and pointed the rabbit towards the burrows. Off it went, but, being a pet-shop rabbit, it didn't know what to do in the wild. It circled round, ran back towards the bloke, and scurried, fuse still sputtering, straight under his brand new ute, blowing the whole thing to buggery.

In other recent versions, it is a couple of cruel blokes out hunting who tie the gelignite to the rabbit. The wild rabbit, terrified, does the same thing as the pet-shop one, running under—and duly blowing up—their $50,000 four-wheel drive. There is also an exploding fish—or shark—variant. In Queensland they seem to prefer exploding pigs.

The blackout babies

The subject of sex is often avoided in the lore of the bush. Not so in urban legends, where it's a staple—and where wild exaggeration is the norm (though presented as true, of course).

One such tale is the perennial explanation for an unusual surge in the number of babies born at a certain time of the year. The reason: there was a blackout nine months earlier, and telly-less couples were forced to amuse themselves in more traditional ways. A more inventive reason, as in this story collected by folklorist Bill Scott in Canberra in 1978, is the noisy passing of the night train.

*T*he Census Office was puzzling over the latest figures from Kyogle, New South Wales. The staff couldn't work out why this place had a birth rate three times the national average. They sent an officer to investigate. He found the school crammed with kids and a new wing added to the maternity hospital. After a few days, the officer worked it out.

The Kyogle Mail used to pass through town about 4.30 every morning, blowing its whistle first at the level crossing on the north side of town and waking everyone up. Just as they were dozing off again, the train would cross the crossing on the south side of town and blow its whistle again. By then just about everyone in town was wide awake. It was too early to get up, but . . .

In South Africa the story is so well-known in one particular town that the local offspring are known far and wide as 'train babies'.

The Head

A favourite with teenagers is an urban legend usually called 'The Head' or 'The Escaped Maniac':

*T*his couple went parking in the bush around town one night, and when they went to go home they couldn't get the car started. So the guy went to get help, and the girl waited in the car for him. She waited and waited and waited, but he didn't come back. Then she hears this strange *thump, thump, thump* on the roof of the car. She's terrified. She doesn't move. She sits there all night hearing this weird *thump, thump, thump*. Then suddenly all these bright flashing lights surround the car—it's the police! And they tell her to get out of the car when they count to three, and to run towards them as fast as she can, but not on any account to look back at the car. So they count: one, two, three! And she gets out and runs over, but she looks back to see what was making the thumping noise. And there's this maniac sitting on the roof of the car banging the boyfriend's severed head: *thump, thump, thump.*

An oft-included detail is that while the couple are doing whatever they are doing in the car, a news bulletin comes on the radio, saying that a dangerous maniac has escaped from a local lunatic asylum.

Readers familiar with the Bible will recognise the order to the girl not to turn around as similar to that given to Lot's wife, Sarah. She was told not to look back at the doomed city of Sodom, but she did—and was instantly turned into a pillar of salt.

The sex life of an electron

This tale, a feast of electronics puns and double entendres, is particularly popular with computer geeks. As with urban legends, this story circulates the world in photocopied or email forms and is as popular in Australia as elsewhere.

*O*ne night when his charge was high, Micro Farad decided to seek out a cute coil to let him discharge. He picked up Milli Amp and took her for a ride on his mega cycle. They rode across a Wheatstone bridge, around the sine waves, and stopped in a magnetic field beside a flowing current.

Micro Farad was attracted by Milli Amp's characteristic curve and soon had her fully charged and excited her resistance to a minimum. He laid her on the ground potential and raised her frequency and lowered her inductance. He pulled out his high frequency probe and inserted it into her socket, connecting them in parallel and short-circuiting her resistance shunt so as to cause surges with the utmost intensity. Then, when fully excited, Milli Amp mumbled, 'Ohm, ohm, ohm.' With his tube operating at a maximum and her field vibrating with current flow, it caused her to shunt over and Micro Farad rapidly discharged, drawing every electron. They fluxed all night, trying different connections and sockets until his magnet had a soft core and lost its field strength.

Afterwards, Milli Amp tried self-induction and damaged her solenoids in doing so. With his battery discharged, Micro Farad was unable to excite his field, so they spent the night reversing polarity and blowing each other's fuses . . .

Authorship of this piece is often attributed to one Eddy Current.

Do not break the chain

The chain letter probably existed since postal services were first established. In its standard form, it claims that good luck and riches will be showered on the recipient if only he or she mails the letter to a number of others. Failure to do this will bring disaster. Chain letters have become chain emails, but they've been joined by some playful parodies, including this 'Chain Letter for Women':

*D*ear Friend,
    This letter was started by a woman like yourself, in the hope of bringing relief to the tired and discontented. Unlike most chain letters, this one does not cost anything. Just send a copy to five of your friends who are tired and discontent. Then bundle up your husband or boyfriend and send him to the woman whose name appears at the top of the list.

When your name comes to the top you will receive 16,374 men, and some of them are bound to be a hell of a lot better than the one you already have.

Do not break the chain. Have faith. One woman broke the chain and got her own husband back.

At the time of writing, a friend of mine had already received 184 men. They buried her yesterday, but it took three undertakers 36 hours to get the smile off her face!!!

"Damn yer explosive bullets! You've gone & bust the pocket I 'ad me cigarettes in!"

8
Heroes

'Ave a cup o' tea, Mr Birdwood.

Gallipoli Anzac, on meeting General Birdwood

EVERY COUNTRY HAS its heroes, real and mythic. Australia's include bushrangers, diggers and sportsmen. Even a racehorse can be a hero.

Though most heroes are men, Australia has heroines too, like Grace Bussell, rescuer of shipwreck victims, and Caroline Chisholm, the friend of colonial immigrant women. There are also female heroic types, such as 'the little Irish mother' and military nurses. One of numerous indigenous heroines is Wungala.

Wungala and the wulgaru

The story of Wungala is told by the Waddaman people, whose country is southeast of the Katherine River, in the Northern Territory. This story concerns her encounter with an evil creature known as a wulgaru, which resulted from a botched attempt by a man named Djarapa to make a man from wood, stone, red ochre and magic songs. A little like Frankenstein's monster, it is a shambling mess of twisted limbs, with eyes that blaze like stars. Ever since its misbegotten creation, the wulgaru has menaced Waddaman people as keeper and judge of the dead. Although it is evil, however, the wulgaru is also the caretaker of the spirits and regulator of the rules governing everyday life.

*W*ungala took her young son, Bulla, seed gathering after the wet season. Bulla ran around happily, finding the best mounds of seeds, but when a dark cloud passed across the sun Wungala told him to be quiet. Along with the shadows might come the evil big-eyed one who lived in a cave in the nearby hills. If this being, known as a *wulgaru*, heard Bulla he would come out of his cave and bring evil upon them. But Bulla kept up his chatter, and a *wulgaru* did appear, creeping toward them through the shadows.

Wungala knew that the only way to avoid a *wulgaru*'s power was to ignore it and to show no fear. When Bulla ran to her in terror, pointing at the *wulgaru*, she told him it was only the shadows of the swaying bushes. Trusting his mother, Bulla calmed down and went on gathering seeds. This enraged the *wulgaru*, who gave a fierce yell. Bulla ran to his mother again, saying that he had not only seen the *wulgaru* but heard it. He wanted to run away, but Wungala calmed his fears again, saying that it was just a cockatoo.

She began grinding the seeds on a large flat stone to make flour for bread, as if nothing had happened. This only further angered the *wulgaru*, who began to jump around. He thrust his evil face into Wungala's, but she calmly continued her baking. When the damper, or bush bread, was baked nice and hot, Bulla, who had gone to sleep, awoke and told his mother that the evil one was still there. 'No,' said his mother, 'that is just the smoke from the fire.' Hearing this, the monster pounced, its claws ready to tear Wungala apart. But she jumped straight at him, pushing the hot damper into the *wulgaru*'s face. It screamed in pain and tried to brush the hot mass from its mouth and eyes. That gave Wungala her chance to snatch up Bulla and to run back to camp.

~

Ben Hall

The bushranger is a paradox: a criminal who is seen as a hero. Like Robin Hood, Australian bushrangers are often depicted as helping the poor against the powerful—including the police.

Benjamin Hall (1837–1865), a respected free selector smallholder in the Forbes district of New South Wales, was arrested in early 1862 on suspicion of having participated in a minor highway robbery led by the notorious Frank Gardiner. After a month in prison, Hall was acquitted, but when he returned home he found that his wife had deserted him, taking their baby son with her. The story goes that Hall then joined with the Gardiner gang. He was later arrested over a gold robbery, but soon released for lack of evidence. While he was in jail, the police burned his house and left his cattle to die, penned in the mustering yard.

Hall now became a bushranger, committing highway robbery and attacking wealthy properties. In October 1863 he took part in a raid on Bathurst. Financially it was a failure, but it panicked the population and the colonial government. The bushrangers were officially outlawed and hunted down. Hall was betrayed and shot dead by police—according to legend, while he slept—on 5 May 1865.

The many ballads and stories about Hall portray him as the victim of injustice and unfortunate circumstances. He is shown as courteous to women, even-handed and kind. He robs a wealthy squatter but reportedly gave £5 back to his victim to see him to the end of his journey. One of the ballads about him contains the line: 'He never robbed a needy man', and his local reputation was that of a decent man wronged by circumstances and the law.

In the 1920s, John Gale recalled meeting Hall nearly sixty years earlier, before his bushranging career began:

*I*n the fifties of the last century I was tutor to the children of a squatter on Bland Plains. The sparse population thereabout at the time had never been visited by parson or priest, so in my spare time, from Friday evening to the following Monday morning of each week, I did what in me lay to supply this defect. Amongst the homesteads thus periodically visited was that of Bland Plains. It was here I first became acquainted with Hall, who was the station overseer—of fine physique, courteous bearing, and but newly married. Gardiner's gang of bushrangers were disturbing the country, and had committed some of their most daring raids.

Saddle-swapping was an ordinary practice amongst stockmen in those days. Ben Hall had indulged in this saddle-swapping business. One day the police found in his possession, thus acquired, a saddle which had been stolen by Gardiner's gang from one of their victims. It had without question passed through several hands before it came into Hall's possession. But that possession was enough to justify the police in effecting his arrest. Justices of the peace were then few and far between out in these parts, and consequently Ben was remanded again and again until his case could be heard. This eventually took place, and resulted in his discharge from custody. But that detention was his ruin, and that of his domestic life.

His wife had been seduced during her husband's incarceration, and lived with her paramour, who was well known to me, but whose name for obvious reasons I prefer not to disclose. Ben made it no secret that he would take the life of the betrayer of his wife's honour. From time to time he watched his home, which was also now that of the misguided woman. One day he saw his quarry enter his home, which was on the margin of an extensive plain, overshadowed by large yellow-box trees. Ben followed his quest. He met his wife at the door.

'Where's —?' he queried, 'I've a bullet for him.'

'He saw you coming, Ben, and went out into the bush through the back door-way.'

'Tell him that I'll do for him sooner or later. I don't blame you, Norah, in the least; you are young and foolish, though you ought to have known better.'

Her two-years-old little boy was clinging to his mother's skirts during the colloquy. Turning to the tall fellow conversing with his mother, and clasping him by the knees, 'Don't you shoot my dada,' said he pleadingly, looking up into Hall's face.

That was the determining factor in Ben Hall's career. The pleading child was his own offspring—was clasping his own father's knees—and he had spoken of his mother's seducer as 'my dada'. Then and there Ben broke away from all restraint from all regard for the sanctities of society, saying, 'I've been accused of being in sympathy with the bushrangers: from this out I'll play the game.'

Often and often did I earnestly wish to meet with this deluded man whilst he was operating hereabouts, for I entertained the hope that an interview with him might be productive of some measure of good. But it was a forlorn hope.

Tales of Ben Hall often recount what happened after he died. The wife of the man who betrayed him was pregnant. When she heard that Hall had been shot and that it was her husband who had told the police where to find him, she took it very badly. When her baby (sometimes said to have been Hall's) was born, he was covered in spots on exactly the same places as the shots that had killed Hall. In some versions of the story, the marked child is said to have been that of Hall's estranged wife.

A continuation of this legend has it that the baby grew up to be 'the Leopard Boy', so-called because of the bullet marks on his body, from which he made a living by exhibiting himself in travelling shows.

Thunderbolt

Frederick Ward, who called himself Thunderbolt, began his bushranging exploits in 1865, less than eighteen months after breaking out of the supposedly escape-proof prison on Sydney's Cockatoo Island. He and his fellow escapee, Frederick Britten, were helped by Ward's wife Maryanne, a part-Aboriginal woman. Ward turned to bushranging in New England, but developed a reputation for using minimal violence—he claimed he had been driven to bushranging—and for being kind to women and the poor. On one occasion, he is said to have refrained from stealing a watch when its owner told him it was her only momento of her dead mother, and to have returned gold after stealing it from some children. A verse sometimes attributed to him goes:

> My name is Frederick Ward, I am a native of this isle;
> I rob the rich to feed the poor and make the children smile.

There was a large price on Ward's head, but his bush skills and strong local sympathy kept him at large for nearly seven years, until he was killed by a policeman in May 1870. In an echo of many other outlaw stories, it was long claimed that it was another man—Frederick Britten or a Fred Blake—who had been killed, and that the real Thunderbolt was living safely elsewhere in Australia, or in New Zealand, Canada or even the United States.

Contemporary accounts of Thunderbolt's robberies tend to support his Robin Hood image, as in this letter by one of his victims, hotel manager James Neariah Roper, in May 1867:

*O*n the 3rd May I sent the Hosteler to Tenterfield on business, but he could not find the horse he intended to ride, which at once excited my suspicion that he was stolen, in consequence of a boy the previous evening, purchasing 20 lb of flour with other goods, to go on a journey to Grafton. I wrote a note to Constable Langworthy. He arrived the same evening and has been in and about the neighbourhood till now.

On the 8th (this morning) I sent the mail off to Tenterfield and Constable Langworthy kept it in sight as far as Maidenhead, they had been gone about half an hour (half past 10 o'clock a.m.) when Thunderbolt and boy rode up, both well mounted. I was making up my accounts. Old Dick and Archie Livingstone in my company, immediately recognized the boy that I suspected of stealing my horse. We at once said, that is Thunderbolt. Archie slipped out of the back door and hid his watch under the kitchen bed. I walked into the bar, threw open all the doors and prepared to serve him if he called for grog. When he came in he presented a horse pistol at me and stated his business. I told him I could not resist, being at the moment unarmed, and he then mustered the lot of us, asked for the key of the store and marched us all into it, locked us up and the boy kept guard over us with a small pistol. He then went over the premises and finding a drawer locked, he sent the boy to fetch the key. I went back with the boy and unlocked the drawer, his pistol disagreeably close to my head. I told him he need not be frightened (he appeared to be very nervous) as I did not intend to show fight, the balance of power being against me. He took several cheques and small orders and about £2 worth of silver. I asked him to leave the silver as I could not carry on the business without it, then he gave me back about a dozen shillings, I told him 23 [shillings] belonged to the Hosteler, the price of an accordion I sold for him, he said he would not take the Hosteler's money and left it.

I told him my mates were getting tired of their confinement, he ordered the boy to let them out, and then keeping us in conversation on the verandah whilst the boy selected what ever they fancied in the store. After getting all they wanted, he called for glasses all round and paid me for them. I told him my stock was very low so he only took a couple of bottles of brandy away with him. We had a long conversation after it was over. I tried to persuade him to give over his present calling and take a stockman situation, where he was not known. He thanked me for my advice but said he tried that before but it was no answer.

They left here 10 minutes to 12 a.m. and rode by a few minutes afterwards leading two horses, all in fine condition. Three hours after they left, Constable Langworthy came back from Maidenhead, his horse considerably faded and extremely vexed. He wanted to follow, I told him 'twas no use with the horse he had by him, he went to the station for another, but I don't think he succeeded. I must say Mister Langworthy had exerted himself to the utmost, but will never succeed until he is furnished with better horses. When he borrowed a horse 'tis a 2nd or 3rd rate animal, whereas Thunderbolt is riding the finest horse I have seen in the district. John Macdonald, Esquire is an exception to the rule and furnishes a good horse if one is to be convenient to the place.

May 9th. Thunderbolt and boy went through Ashford today with five horses.

~

Thunderbolt's gentleman-thief image lived on long after his death. It was recalled in 1939 by James Roper's son, then around 90 years old:

*O*f course we often heard of Thunderbolt's doings. It was often rumored that he would stick up Tenterfield, but he never did. Once he was supposed to have paid the town a visit and to have mixed with the people and to have at length been recognized by somebody, but as he was far from being unpopular, he got away from the town without trouble.

My father was stuck up by him when managing a store at Bonshaw for C A Lee. The bushranger took all the cash from the till and made my father have dinner with him. They sat at opposite ends of the table and Thunderbolt had two revolvers and placed one at each side of his plate and watched my father like a cat all the time. My father said to him, 'You need not be afraid of me. I have no gun at all, and you have two. I'm not such a fool as to try anything with you.' The dinner passed off pleasantly enough. Apart from his mission at [that] moment, my father said Thunderbolt was a very nice chap and took a liking to him. Of course, Thunderbolt never took life.

When he was leaving my father said to him. 'Look, you are putting me in a fix, taking all the change. When people come along with only notes or cheques, I won't be able to do business with them.' Thunderbolt agreed it was not quite playing the game and handed him back a good handful of silver, although when he had first taken the money he had said, 'It's not enough.' But my father had been warned that Thunderbolt was about and had previously hidden the bulk of the money in an old boot hidden above the door.

Today, Thunderbolt the gentleman bushranger is like many other bushrangers, proudly advertised by tourism bodies in New England.

Grace Bussell

In September 1838, the steamship *Forfarshire* was wrecked on the Farne Islands, off Britain's northeast coast. The lighthouse keeper William Darling and his daughter, Grace, mounted a heroic rescue effort, rowing a small boat through mountainous seas to save the lives of five passengers. The country was agog with admiration and gratitude. Grace and her father were both awarded gold medals by the Royal Humane Society and an admiring public subscribed 1700 pounds for them. Twenty-three year-old Grace became a national sensation, but she shunned all attempts to turn her into a heroine. She died of tuberculosis at the age of twenty-seven but her story would have a lasting echo in Australia.

Thirty-eight years after the *Forfarshire* was lost, Grace Bussell, a sixteen-year-old living in the Margaret River region of Western Australia, had a strange dream. She saw a smoking sailing ship shattered on jagged rocks, with screaming passengers hanging desperately to the rigging. The following night, the ship *Georgette*, bound for Adelaide with a cargo of jarrah wood, ran aground twenty kilometres from the Bussells' home. With the boiler room flooded, the captain had deliberately wrecked his sinking ship to give its passengers and crew, some sixty people in all, a chance to survive. A lifeboat was launched, but the stormy seas capsized it, drowning five children and two women.

The others in the lifeboat were then rescued by four crewmen, eventually reaching shore after a twelve-hour battle against the wind and waves. The rest of the *Georgette*'s crew and passengers were unable to escape. Any lifeboats they launched capsized in the crashing seas, drowning their occupants.

On shore, an Aboriginal employee of the Bussells' named Sam Isaacs saw the ship and galloped to the homestead with the news. Grace Bussell took a spyglass, ran to the top of a nearby hill and spotted the wreck. She and Sam found some ropes, mounted their horses and rode to the sea.

At a rocky place called Calgardup, they were able to get down a cliff and into the swirling water. They swam the horses out to the ship, and carried or towed the survivors to shore. After four hours, they had saved most of the *Georgette*'s remaining passengers and crew. Grace then rode back to the homestead and alerted her father. He and a rescue party arrived at the scene the following morning. The passengers and sailors were all taken to the family home, where they were cared for by Grace's mother, Ellen.

When news of the rescue reached Perth, and then the world, Grace Bussell was pronounced 'the Grace Darling of the West'. In 1878, she was awarded the silver medal of the Royal Humane Society. Sam received the Society's bronze medal and a grant of 100 acres. Ellen Bussell, already in poor health, died just a few weeks after the disaster. Her last words were supposedly, 'Fetch them all. I can take them in.'

❧

Grace Bussell's legend lives on, though mostly in Western Australia. At Redgate Beach, where the *Georgette* foundered, the rock that brought the ship to disaster is known as Isaacs Rock after Sam Isaacs. Grace is commemorated in the town names Lake Grace and Gracetown, and the city of Busselton is named after the Bussell family. No one seems to have recognised the bravery of the horses.

Diggers

From Gallipoli on, the Australian experience of war has produced a rich trove of anecdotes, legends and yarns, which commonly stress the diggers' wit, lack of pretension, and refusal to kowtow to their presumed betters.

One particularly popular group of stories dealt with Lieutenant-General Sir William Birdwood, the commanding officer at Gallipoli, whom the Anzacs affectionately nicknamed Birdie. One day Birdwood was nearing a dangerous gap in a trench when the sentry called out, 'Duck, Birdie; you'd better —— well duck.' 'What did you do?' asked the outraged generals to whom Birdwood told the story. 'Do? Why, I —— well ducked!'

Most Birdie yarns present the general as a 'digger with stripes', a leader who has—and appreciates—the qualities his men themselves esteem. Set in central London, this story neatly combines Australian anti-authoritarianism with a wariness of the English class system. In it, Birdwood explains to the class-bound English generals that he would be abused by the low-ranking Australian soldiers if he had the temerity to discipline him for failing to observe the military etiquette of saluting officers, thus affirming the egalitarian character of the AIF, as opposed to that of the British army.

*W*hilst General Birdwood was chatting in the Strand with two or three Tommy officers, an Aussie strolled by, characteristically omitting the salute.

'Notice that Digger go by, Birdwood?' asked a Tommy officer.

'Yes, why?'

'Well, he didn't salute. Why didn't you pull him up for it?'

'Look here,' said Birdie, 'if you want to be told off in the Strand, I don't.'

~

A number of the Birdwood yarns play on the general's 'common touch'. When a naive sentry fails to recognise him, for example, Birdwood jovially shakes his hand. At Gallipoli, Birdwood seldom wore his insignia of rank. In one story, a digger addresses him a little too casually. 'Do you know who I am?' asks Birdwood. 'No,' says the digger. 'Who are you?' 'I'm General Birdwood.' 'Struth,' says the digger, springing to attention. 'Why don't you wear your feathers the same as any other bird would?'

There is also the Gallipoli reinforcement who mistakes the general for a cook, and the digger who, when told Birdwood's name, asks him to ''ave a cup o' tea, Mister Birdwood.'

Birdwood sees an Anzac pushing a wheelbarrow, an unusual sight at Gallipoli. 'Did you make it yourself?' he asks. 'No, Mister Birdwood, I bloody-well didn't,' pants the digger, 'but I'd like to find the bastard who did!'

Later, on the Western Front, Birdwood says to a digger, 'Come on, let's go for a run.' 'Too right,' replies the digger, and off they go. After a while, the panting digger draws level with Birdwood. 'Hey, where's that bloody rum you promised me?'

In another tale, Birdwood sees a digger trying to wash from a tin half-full of water. 'Having a good bath?' he asks. 'Yes,' says the digger, 'but I could do much better if I was a blinking canary.'

One digger, flat broke, decides to write to God and ask for a ten-pound note. He addresses the letter 'per General Birdwood, Headquarters'. The general, much amused, takes the letter into the officers' mess. 'We will collect amongst us and raise the tenner for this fellow,' he says. The laughing officers put together seven pounds, and Birdwood sends it to the digger. Next day there arrives a receipt as follows: 'Dear God, Thanks for sending me the tenner; but the next lot you send, don't send it through Headquarters, as Birdie and his mob pinched three quid of it.'

In another anti-authoritarian Aussie tale, Lord Herbert Horatio Kitchener, the British War Minister, visits the Anzacs at Gallipoli and tells them they can be proud of what they've achieved. To which one digger replies: 'My oath we are, Steve.'

Another tale that understood Australians' irreverence towards rank appeared in the *British Australasian* in 1920 under the title 'The Digger and the Colonel':

*a*n 'Aussie' story has to do with a sentry who stopped an English colonel, who was trying to get to his own lines. The officer was without a passport so the sentry would not let him pass.

'But I am an English colonel, and I must get to my lines,' the officer said.

'I don't care a damn,' said the Aussie, as he shouldered his rifle.

The colonel continued his expostulations until he heard a drowsy voice from the trench say: 'Don't argue, Bill; shoot the tinted cow, and let's get to sleep.'

⌒

In a variant on this story, a captain draws the fed-up cry from a nearby tent: 'Don't stand there argufying all night, Dig, shoot the blighter.' Variations of this one were still being told by Australian troops in the Western Desert during World War II.

The toughness and nonchalance of the digger under fire was another common theme. In a typical story, four Aussies have settled down to a game of cards in a quiet corner of the Western Front trenches when a great commotion is heard. One of the players jumps up to the look-out step. 'Hi, you fellows!' he calls to his mates. 'A whole enemy division is coming over!' Another digger gets up, looking bored. 'All right,' he says. 'You get on with the game. I'm dummy this hand; I'll go.'

Similar stories are told of diggers who are so little bothered by enemy fire that they play two-up by the light of the barrage flares, or who are so intent on their game that others think they are praying. Then there are the diggers who blast an enemy position, then, meeting no resistance, run up to it—and find a fellow digger inside, nonchalantly cooking a meal and wondering what all the noise is about.

Other tales underscore the diggers' bravery by gently mocking awards like the Victoria Cross. In one, a soldier is carrying a mate across No Man's Land under heavy fire.

''Ere,' the wounded soldier suddenly exclaims, 'what about turnin' round and walkin' backwards for a spell? You're gettin' the V.C., but I'm gettin' all the blinkin' bullets.'

The same kind of casual iconoclasm features in the yarn in which a digger is taken to see a sacred flame (usually in Bethlehem) that has burned for two thousand years. The puzzled Australian looks at it for a moment, fills his lungs and blows. 'It's about time someone put it out,' he says.

The alleged vulgarity of ordinary Australians—alleged by British visitors, at least—became a popular theme of digger yarns, which often combined a proud use of Aussie vernacular with a tilt at perceived British pretensions.

An officer, inspecting the front lines, calls down, 'What soldiers are in this trench, my man?' 'First Sussex Regiment, Sir.' A few yards on, he repeats, 'What soldiers are in this trench, my man?' 'What the ——— has it got to do with you?' comes the reply. 'Oh, this is the Australian trench,' the officer says.

Or, in another version: 'Halt! Who goes there?' asks a sentry. 'Auckland Mounted Rifles,' or some such. 'Pass, friend.' Next, 'Halt, Who goes there?' 'What the ——— has that got to do with you?' 'Pass, Australian.'

The diggers' egalitarianism and sense of humour went home with them after the war. This tale dates from World War II:

a traveller stopped to chat to a farmer who had a large number of men at work in the fields.

'Are those men ex-soldiers?' he asked.

'Most of them,' the farmer said. 'One was a private; he's a first-class worker. The chap over near the fence was a corporal; he's pretty good. The chap driving the harrow was a major; he's only so-so; and the man over there stacking the weeds used to be a colonel.'

'And how do you find him?'

'Well, I'm not going to say anything against no man who used to be a colonel,' the farmer said; 'but I've made up my mind about one thing—I'm not going to hire no generals.'

Sportsmen

Australia is widely recognised as a sports-loving nation, and one of the largest troves of heroic tales centres on hall-of-famers like Don Bradman, Roy Cazaly, Cathy Freeman, Evonne Goolagong and Dawn Fraser.

In many cases, sporting heroes' life stories are impressive enough to serve as quasi-legends. Les Darcy is just one example.

Born near Maitland, New South Wales, in 1895, Darcy was apprenticed to a blacksmith. As a teenager, he started making money by entering boxing matches, and eventually caught the attention of managers in Sydney. He lost his first three bouts there, but from early 1915 he won twenty-two fights in a row, including thirteen successive Australian middle-weight titles, and seemed well on the way to fame and fortune.

In October 1915, Darcy stowed away on a ship headed for the US. This not only breached the *War Precautions Act* but brought accusations that he was a shirker who was afraid to enlist. When promised American matches did not eventuate, he was reduced to performing in vaudeville. He became a US citizen and joined the army, but his call-up was deferred so he could train for a bout in Memphis, Tennessee. On the eve of the fight, he collapsed from septicaemia, which was later blamed on poor dental work he'd received in Australia. His fiancée flew to his side, but he died at the age of twenty-one.

Already a popular favourite in Australia, Darcy now became a tragic hero. His distant and apparently inexplicable death sparked rumours (still extant) that he had been poisoned by the 'Yanks', who were afraid their own hero would be beaten by an upstart nobody from Down Under, as a contemporary ballad about his death had it:

Way down in Tennessee
There lies poor Les Darcy
His mother's pride and joy
Yes, Maitland's fighting boy.
All I can think of tonight
Is to see Les Darcy fight,
How he beats them,
Simply eats them
Every Saturday night.
And people in galore
Said they had never saw
The likes of Les before
Upon the stadium floor.

> They called him a skiter
> But he proved to them a fighter
> But we lost all hope
> When he got that dope
> Way down in Tennessee.

When his casket was brought back to Sydney, an estimated half a million people turned out to farewell Darcy. Outside sporting circles, his popularity has waned, but on the fiftieth anniversary of his death flags were flown at half-mast in New South Wales and a memorial was built at his birthplace.

~

Racehorses

As might be expected in a country where people are known to enjoy a bet on the 'gee-gees', Australian horseracing is a mine of stories. As well as its own argot ('ring-in', 'mug punter' and so on), the turf boasts legends, yarns and songs about great—and not-so-great—horses, jockeys, punters, trainers and other characters, many with colourful nicknames like Perce 'The Prince' Galea, Harry the Horse and Hollywood George.

Melbourne Cup Day is almost a national holiday: millions of Australians stop work to watch or listen to the race, and many place bets on that day alone.

The country's best-known racing legend by far is the story of Phar Lap. The chestnut gelding was initially thought to be a loser, not even placing in its first four races. But between 1928 and 1932 it won thirty-seven of fifty races, including the 1930 Melbourne Cup. As the hardships of the Great Depression began to weigh on Australians, Phar Lap became a national hero.

On a wave of adulation, Phar Lap travelled to the US, but on the eve of his first race, in April 1932, he suddenly and mysteriously died. People immediately thought of Les Darcy, and rumours quickly spread that the horse too had been poisoned—still a widespread folk belief.

The remains of the fabled horse were parcelled out: the hide to the National Museum of Victoria, the heart initially to the National Institute of Anatomy in Canberra, and the skeleton to the National Museum of New Zealand, where Phar Lap was born. The unusually large heart is the most popular exhibit at the National Museum of Australia, where it now resides, and the expression 'a heart as big as Phar Lap's' has passed into the vernacular.

Phar Lap embodies the culturally powerful image of the battler, the underdog who struggles against adversity—and sometimes triumphs. Such is the popular interest in his story that Australian governments have spent considerable sums investigating the rumours that the horse was poisoned. Tests done in 2006 found abnormal levels of arsenic in Phar Lap's remains. How it got there has yet to be determined.

9
Characters

Mum: Dave's gone and broke his leg, Dad!
Dad: D'yer think we ought to shoot 'im?

Dad and Dave

THE ODD AND the eccentric, those who stand out from the crowd, are popular folk figures in all countries. They might be noted for their stupidity, their idleness, their cleverness or their cheek.

In the idiot category, the French have Jean Sot (Foolish John), the Italians have Bastienelo, and the English have Lazy Jack. Sandy the Shearer is an Australian member of this low-wattage family. When told that some lambs are for sale at five shillings each, he complains bitterly that this is far too expensive. When the seller says he can have them for £3 (sixty shillings) a dozen, Sandy is overjoyed and buys the lot. Interestingly, fools are almost always male.

Tricksters—also mostly male—use their intelligence to hoodwink and manipulate others. Typical examples include the Javanese Pak Dungu, Germany's Till Eulenspiegel, and Turkey's Hodja. Australian Aboriginal tradition has many mythical trickster figures, as well as the more modern character usually known as Jackie Bindi-i.

Dopey or smart, characters are usually humorous figures.

The drongo

The fools of folklore are more than ordinarily dumb, so stupid that they acquire an almost heroic aura. The Australian version of this folk type includes—along with Sandy the Shearer—the ubiquitious drongo. (The name is said to commemorate a racehorse of the 1920s who was famous for losing.) The drongo is a congenitally naive figure who interprets literally whatever he is told. When the boss tells him to hang a new gate, the drongo takes the gate to the nearest tree and puts a noose on it. Asked to dig some turnips about the size of his head, the drongo is found pulling up the entire turnip patch and trying his hat on each uprooted turnip for size.

When the drongo goes fishing, he has no luck. He asks another fisherman who is catching plenty what he uses for bait. 'Magpie,' the man says. The drongo gets his gun, shoots a magpie and returns to the riverside. He hooks the bird to his line and casts it into the water, but still he has no luck. The other fisherman cannot understand it and asks to have a look at the drongo's line. He reels it in, revealing a sodden mess of feathers. 'You didn't pluck the bird!' he says. The drongo replies that he was going to pluck it but thought that if he did the fish would not be able to tell what kind of bird it was.

In another story, the drongo is working for a farmer when the boss decides it is time to build another windmill. The drongo agrees to help but asks the farmer if he thinks it really makes sense to have two windmills. 'What do you mean?' the farmer asks. 'Well,' says the drongo, 'there's barely enough wind to operate the one you already have, so I doubt there'll be enough to work two of them.'

Snuffler Oldfield

Queensland's own drongo is the stockman Snuffler Oldfield, about whom there are said to be thousands of stories. One goes like this:

Snuffler Oldfield was droving one time. He always seemed to be the one who ended up rounding up the cattle each night, while the boss and the jackaroos took it easy or slept back at the camp.

One night the cattle rushed and headed straight through the camp. The drovers had to clamber up trees to avoid being crushed. The boss called out, 'Where are you, Snuffler?'

From just above the boss's head came Snuffler's voice: 'One limb above you.'

Once, when Snuffler's wife was giving birth, the nurse came out to tell Snuffler that he had a child. She returned to the birthing room but returned a short while later saying that he now had a second baby. 'Christ, nurse,' said Snuffler, 'don't touch her again, she must be full of them!'

Tom Doyle

Tom Doyle is said to have been the publican and mayor of Kanowna, in Western Australia's goldfields. An Irishman, he didn't always understand colloquial expressions. In one of the many yarns told about him, he attends a function for a visiting dignitary. For the first time in his life, he is confronted with olives. He gingerly picks one up and is alarmed to discover that it is moist. Just as the dignitary rises to speak, Tom cries out that someone has pissed on the gooseberries.

In Tom's days as a member of the local council, a debate is held on a proposal to enlarge a local dam. Tom declares that the existing dam is so small he can piss halfway across it. When a councillor tells him he is out of order, Tom says, 'Yes, and if I was in order I could piss all the way across it.'

Commenting on a dispute over whether to fence the town cemetery, Tom says, 'Why worry? Them that's in don't want to get out, and them that's out don't want to get in.' He also describes prospectors as 'people who go into the wilderness with a shovel in one hand, a waterbag in the other and their life in their other hand'.

The widow Reilly's pigs

The Irish influence on Australian folklore has been profound. Irish people themselves are almost always portrayed as fools, albeit funny ones. This story first appeared in print in the 1890s, but was probably old by then.

*T*he widow Reilly had eight children. She struggled to provide for them by raising cows and pigs.

One of her sows gave birth to ten piglets. As the piglets grew, the widow's neighbor, whose name was Patrick, would admire them as he passed by on the way to work.

One morning, the widow Reilly discovered that one of the piglets was missing. She informed the local priest, who, based on her suspicions, asked Patrick whether he had seen the pig. Pat, squirming a little, said no. The priest reminded Patrick that on Judgment Day, when all men would stand before the Good Lord, someone would have to answer for the theft of the widow Reilly's piglet.

Pat thought for a moment. 'Will the widow be there on Judgment Day too?' he asked. 'Yes,' said the priest, 'and so will the pig. What will you have to say then?'

Pat replied brightly, 'I'll say to Mrs Reilly, "Here is your pig back, and thanks very much for the lend of it."'

—

Dad, Dave and Mabel

Perhaps the best-known forms of Australian yokel lore are the Dad and Dave yarns. An invention of Australian author 'Steele Rudd' (Arthur Hoey Davis, 1868–1935), Dad, Mum and their foolish son Dave first appeared in *The Bulletin* in 1895. Four years later the sketches appeared in book form under the title *On Our Selection*, which spawned many sequels and subsequent editions. The books were best-sellers, also having stage, film and radio adaptations, and have inspired numerous humorous folktales which concentrate on portraying Dad, Dave and the family as country hicks.

The other important aspect of the Dad and Dave yarns is the portrayal of Dave as a gormless fool, very much in the tradition of the popular 'numbskull' stories. In one typical exchange, Dave is leaving home to join the army. Mum, worried about her son in the big city, prevails on Dad to give him a fatherly lecture about the perils of drink, gambling and women. Dave is at pains to let Dad know that he doesn't have any truck with such things. Dad returns to Mum and says: 'You needn't worry. I don't think the army will take him anyway, the boy's a half-wit!'

In another tale, Dave gets a job driving a truck in the city. On the first day the boss asks him to deliver three bears to the zoo. Hearing nothing from Dave for a very long time the boss decides to find out what has happened to him. He drives along the route that Dave would have taken and sees him buying tickets to the cinema for himself and the bears.

'I told you to take those bears to the zoo,' the angry boss yells at Dave. 'What are you doing at the cinema with them?'

Unperturbed, Dave slowly replies that the truck broke down and as he couldn't take the bears to the zoo he decided to take them to the 'pitchers' instead.

Many Dad and Dave yarns involve Dad, Dave and Dave's mother, but there are also others involving Dave's wife, Mabel. In one of these Dave comes into a bit of extra money and decides to buy Mabel a present. He goes into the dining room, picks up the table and carries it down the street. On the way he meets a mate who asks him if he is moving house.

'Oh no,' Dave replies cheerfully, 'I'm just going out to buy Mabel a new tablecloth.'

The theme of yokel stupidity that lies at the heart of the Dave character continues in a number of stories about Dave and Mabel's escapades in the hospitality business. Dave and Mabel decide to make some money by opening an outback roadhouse. The locals and truckies are quite happy with Mabel's basic but sustaining cooking but the restaurant fails to attract any tourists. Eventually an American comes in. Dave sits him down and asks him what he would like to eat. The American looks around and notices a truckie demolishing a meal of steak, salad, chips and eggs. 'I'll have what he's eating, but eliminate the eggs.'

Dave bustles back to the kitchen to prepare the order but after a few minutes' discussion with Mabel he returns to the American's table. 'Uhh, sorry, but we've had an accident in the kitchen and the 'liminator's broke. Would you like your eggs fried instead?'

In another story from the sequence, Dave and Mabel open a bed and breakfast. The rooms are pretty basic but eventually a couple arrive from the city to stay the night. When they see the room they complain that there is no toilet. Dave assures them that this is just the way things are done in the bush and provides them with a bucket to use if they need to relieve themselves during the night.

Next morning Dave knocks on their door and asks what they would like for breakfast. They order a full bush breakfast and coffee. Dave dashes off but is back in a minute asking if they would like milk in their coffee. 'Yes, please,' chorus the couple. 'Alright,' says Dave, 'but could you give us the bucket back so's the missus can milk the cow?'

When Dave and Mabel finally get married, Dave asks Dad for a quiet word before they leave for their honeymoon. 'Could you do me a favour, Dad?' he asks.

'Of course, Dave,' Dad replies, 'what is it?'

'Would you mind going on the honeymoon for me, you know a lot more about that sort of thing than I do.'

Published Dad and Dave stories are mostly in this style, although there is a considerable number that rarely appear in print due to their overtly sexual nature. By modern standards, the bawdy element is quite mild, although many older Australians consider such tales unsuitable for telling in public or in mixed company. Folklorist Warren Fahey recalls being told 'hundreds' of obscene Dad and Dave jokes in the 1970s and '80s, though believes they are now dying out in oral tradition.

But Dad and Dave are alive and well in the small Queensland town of Nobby. This is 'Dad and Dave Country', where visitors can find 'Rudd's Pub', named after the the author, who allegedly wrote there.

Cousin Jacks

Groups on the periphery of a community are often portrayed as stupid, whether the community is a city or a nation. This mocking of the marginal was perhaps more common before the twentieth century, when such groups were often physically separate from the mainstream. Just as America had its Okies and Canada its Newfoundlanders, Australia had Tasmanians—

and Cousin Jacks, Cornish people who migrated to work in the tin mines of South Australia in the nineteenth century. While Cousin Jacks were not portrayed as inbred like 'Taswegians', they were endowed in folklore with the kind of idiocy city folk have long associated with yokels. Many Cousin Jack yarns poke fun at the Cornishmen's distinctive accent.

A Cornishman hires a carpenter, a fellow Cousin Jack, to erect a fence. When it is done, the boss Cousin Jack complains that it's a bit crooked in the middle.

'It be near enough,' says the carpenter.

'Near enough be not good enough. 'E must be 'zact.'

'Well, 'e be 'zact,' replies the carpenter.

'Oh well, if 'e be 'zact, 'e be near enough,' says the employer, walking away satisfied.

Tom'n'oplas

The central character of a series of tales told around Sydney during the 1980s is an Australian version of the trickster, a staple of folk tradition around the world. The teller in this case acted out the antics he described:

T he bank manager is sitting at his desk, round about lunchtime, when the assistant manager comes in and says, 'Look, he's done it again. Tom'n'Oplas—he's put a thousand dollars in the bank. I can't work it out.'

And the manager says, 'Well, what should we do? Do we have a responsibility to dob this guy in? Is he getting his money legally, or . . . ? What do you think?'

The assistant manager said, 'Well, why don't we call him in and find out?'

So come next Monday Tom'n'Oplas arrives, puts a thousand dollars in the bank. And the assistant manager says, 'Mr Tom'n'Oplas, the manager would like to see you.'

He goes into the office. The manager sits him down, says, 'Mr Tom'n' Oplas, you're one of our best customers, but I can't work out why every Monday morning you put a thousand dollars in the bank.'

Tom'n'Oplas laughs. He says, 'Oh yes. Well, I'm a gambler.'

The manager says, 'What do you mean? Is it something you can let me in on? A thousand dollars a week—that's fifty grand a year. I could retire on that.'

Tom says, 'Well, I tell you what I'll do. I'll bet you a thousand dollars that this time next week you'll have hair growing all over your back.'

And the manager thought, 'Ha, ha, ha. Obviously this fellow's gone off the rails a little bit under a bit of pressure from me.' He said, 'Mr Tom'n'Oplas, that's a bet.'

Next day the manager checks his back. No hair. This is wonderful, he thinks. That night he sleeps on his back so it won't grow because he's putting pressure on it.

Wednesday he wears a sweater because he thinks the only way Tom'n'Oplas can get him is to tape something on his back, or put something on his shirt, or whatever. It's the middle of summer, and all the staff think he's a little bit crazy, but he's thinking 'a thousand dollars'.

Thursday, he doesn't wear a shirt, just a jumper, in case Tom gets to his laundry and puts hairs in his shirt.

Friday he's getting a little bit toey. Saturday and Sunday he just locks himself away in the house.

Monday morning arrives. He checks his back in the mirror and he can't see anything there. 'A thousand dollars,' he thinks.

Tom'n'Oplas arrives at the bank, and he's got a Japanese fellow with him. The manager says 'Mr. Tom'n'Oplas, in here.' Tom says, 'I thought you'd be wanting to see me. I suppose you think you've won your bet.' The manager whips his shirt off and turns around—and the Japanese fellow faints. 'Look, look,' the manager says. 'No hair. But . . . what's happened to your mate?'

Tom says, 'Oh, that's simple, I bet him $2000 that within thirty seconds of getting in here I'd have the shirt off your back.'

❧

Jacky Bindi-i

An Aboriginal stockman or roustabout known as Jacky Bindi-i, Jacky-Jacky or just Jacky, features in a number of bush yarns, and even in song. Jacky is generally distinguished by his sharp retorts, often undercutting the authority of the boss, the policeman or the magistrate. As the folklorist John Meredith points out:

There are literally dozens of these stories, all concerned with situations involving Jacky-Jacky, his lubra Mary, black sheep, white sheep, the white boss and his station-hands and his wife. In this series of folk-tales, 'Jacky-Jacky' generally, but not always, comes out on top, scoring a victory over the white boss.

One day Jacky and his boss needed to cross a flooded river but the only boat was on the far bank. The boss told Jacky to swim across and bring the boat back. Jacky protested, saying that there may be crocodiles in the river. The boss said that he need not worry as crocodiles never touch blackfellas. Jacky replied that the crocodiles might be colour-blind and that it would be better to wait until the flood subsided.

On another occasion Jacky was in a distant part of the property minding a mob of sheep and he needed his rations and other necessities delivered to him by the boss each week. One week the boss forgot to bring Jacky's food. Jacky was not too happy and told the boss that he only had a bone left from last week's rations and that it would be another week before any more meat came. The boss laughed and told him not to worry, saying 'The nearer the bone the sweeter the meat.' When the boss returned the following week the sheep were in a terrible condition as Jacky had kept them where there was no grass to eat. The boss turned on Jacky and angrily asked him what he thought he was doing. Jacky just laughed and said 'The nearer the ground, the sweeter the grass.'

Jacky Bindi-i's other main activity is stealing sheep or cows, for which he is frequently brought before the courts. At one of his hearings the judge gave Jacky three years in prison and asked him if he had anything to say. 'Yes,' said Jacky angrily, 'You're bloody free with other people's time.'

In another court, this time for being drunk and disorderly, the magistrate fined Jacky and gave him twenty days in prison. 'I'll tell you what I'll do, boss,' said Jacky. 'I'll toss you—forty days or nothing.'

Jacky is caught red-handed by a trooper one day as he catches him butchering a stolen bullock. He ties Jacky to his horse and leads the way on the lengthy journey back to town. As they ride, Jacky asks the trooper how he had tracked him down. 'I smelled you out,' replies the trooper proudly.

They ride on and as darkness falls, so does the rain and it is not too long before the trooper loses his way. 'Do you know the way to town, Jacky?' he asks his prisoner at last. Jacky is ready with his answer: 'Why don't you smell the way back to town the same as you smelled out Jacky?'

Jacky-Jacky also features in a modern Aboriginal song sung in many versions around the country:

Jacky Jacky was a smart young fellow
Full of fun and energy.
He was thinkin' of gettin' married
But the lubra run away you see.
Cricketah boobelah will-de-mah
Billa na ja jingeree wah.

Jacky used to chase the emu
With his spears and his waddy too.
He's the only man that can tell you
What the emu told a kangaroo.
Cricketah boobelah will-de-mah
Billa na ja jingeree wah.

Hunting food was Jacky's business
'Til the white man come along.
Put his fences across the country
Now the hunting days are gone.
Cricketah boobelah will-de-mah
Billa na ja jingeree wah.

White fella he now pay all taxes
Keep Jacky Jacky in clothes and food.
He don't care what become of the country
White fella tucker him very good.
Cricketah boobelah will-de-mah
Billa na ja jingeree wah.

Now Australia's short of money
Jacky Jacky sit he laugh all day.
White fella want to give it back to Jacky
No fear Jacky won't have it that way.
Cricketah boobelah will-de-mah
Billa na ja jingeree wah.

Jimmy Ah Foo

A real-life Chinese counterpart to Jacky Bindi-i was Jimmy Ah Foo, a publican in outback Queensland. His great skill was reputed to lie in making himself as agreeable as possible to his customers. In the process, he always seemed to benefit.

During the shearers' strikes of the 1890s, there were serious outbreaks of anti-Chinese violence, since many shearers feared that Chinese workers would be used as strike breakers. A deputation of local shearers visited Jimmy's pub and told him to sack his Chinese cook. They would be returning the next day to see that he did so. Next day the shearers showed up again. 'I've done as you asked,' Jimmy said. 'I'm the cook now.'

Corny Kenna

An Anglo-Saxon version of the jokester is Victoria's Cornelius Kenna (pronounced Ken-*ah!*)

*C*orny, as he is generally called, is served an under-measure whisky in the pub one day. Seeing his frown, the barmaid defensively says the whisky is thirty years old. 'Very small for its age,' says Kenna.

Another time, Corny is taking a lady through the bush in a timber jinker. A storm closes in, and he whips up the horses. Rattling along, the cart hits a tree stump and overturns. Corny's infuriated passenger says, 'I knew this would happen!' Replies Corny: 'Well, why the devil didn't you tell me?'

Corny lends a horse to a man who vows to return it next day. Nearly two weeks later, the horse still unreturned, Corny meets the man at a local auction. 'Oh,' says the embarrassed horse borrower, 'I've meant to bring it back a dozen times.' 'Once will be enough,' says Corny.

On another occasion a city slicker asks Corny for directions to Yaapeet, calling him 'Jack' in the superior manner of many city dwellers when addressing someone from the country. Corny asks the city slicker how he knew that his name was 'Jack'. 'I guessed it,' says the slicker. 'Well guess how to get to Yaapeet, then,' replies Corny.

Three blokes at a pub

Many Australian yarns are not about anyone in particular—just 'a bloke' or 'a couple of blokes', or in this case, three of them.

Three blokes walk into a busy pub. The first one orders a beer, but the barman is too busy to take his money and moves on to serve another customer. Later, he returns to the bloke and asks for the money. 'But I already paid yer,' says the bloke. 'You went and served someone else, came back for my money, took it, and put it in the till with the other money you had.'

The barman, thinking he must have forgotten, says 'OK.' The bloke finishes his drink and leaves.

Then the second orders a beer. The barman serves him without taking the money, serves another customer, then comes back and asks him to pay. 'I already did,' says the bloke. The barman concedes that he must have forgotten and the second bloke leaves.

The third bloke now comes up to the bar. The wary barman tells him, 'Look, two blokes have just ordered beers and I'm pretty sure they didn't pay. Next bloke who tries anything funny like that is going to get it.' And he reaches under the counter and pulls out an iron bar. 'Mate,' says the third bloke, 'I'm sorry for your troubles. All I want is me change, and I'll be out of here.'

～

The smarter soldier

'Working one's nut' was a World War I expression for manipulating the system. Pat, or P.F., of the 3rd Battalion AIF, was especially good at it, as this affectionate trench journal anecdote illustrates.

*T*here are still many old hands left in the Battalion who remember P.F. It is over three years since he went, but his memory is still green in my mind, and his ingenuity still haunts me.

Early on Anzac, he turned down Sergeant's stripes (this fact is not in official records!) and became a batman. As such we speak of him here.

At this time our rations were pure, unadulterated bully beef, hard biscuits, tea and rice; but we had P.F. and his wonderful brains.

The proximity of battleships and hospital ships riding outside Anzac Cove instantly fired his genius. On the former he knew there would be poultry pens; on the latter an ample supply of good provisions. The problem was how to procure them.

A sailor's costume and a few bandages solved the difficulty.

For the rest, he always had plenty of money. Where it came from one cannot say. Perhaps some digger who felt like floating a war loan, ten minutes after pay, can make a shrewd guess.

He has been seen on a lighter in sailor's clothes—hence eggs; and on two occasions live poultry arrived in the 3rd Battalion trenches.

He was probably evacuated through the Beach Clearing Station more than any other man on Anzac.

It is thought that he rather overdid it the day he was evacuated twice onto the same ship, and was, unfortunately, recognised by the M.O. on the gangway. However, he had the cunning of the Scarlet Pimpernel, and got away—his duty nobly done; hence fresh bread and milk in the mess that night.

He would see a fatigue party unloading flour—off with his coat and to work with them for an hour or so. One bag would, sooner or later, be over-carried, and find its way to our dug-out. One day, not content with the flour, he also 'lifted' a mule from a mule train, and arrived at the trenches, mule and flour in good order.

To wait in the queue for water was a waste of time to Pat's inventive mind. Woe betide the new chum he saw with two full tins of water. A conversation for five minutes or so and Pat had the full tins. 'So long mate, I had better get my water'—and he was out of sight. The new chum had the two empty tins and another two or three hours' wait in the queue to fill up again.

Goodness knows what would have become of him had not the General Staff decided Lone Pine. I saw him that day, as full of life as ever—I have not seen him since. Two days later after Lone Pine I saw a neat little bundle marked 'Killed in action'. Contents: one pay-book, one pocket-book, and photos, and one identity disc marked P.F., D. Coy., 3rd Bn. So poor Pat was dead! I believe I shed a genuine tear. The next I heard that he was inspecting one of the military hospitals as a Padre, and tipping the wink to a 3rd Battalion man who recognised him.

How he got away I never heard definitely, but I can imagine someone with a bloodstained bandage round one arm staggering into the clearing station and handing in the dead body on the way down—and P.F., alias Tom Jones was evacuated to the hospital ship. On arrival there I cannot imagine what he would do, but it is quite likely he became a steward or an A.M.C. orderly, or he even may have thrown the skipper of the boat overboard and taken charge.

If ever I want a 'tenner' and P.F. is about, I'll look him up. I know, even if he has not got it—which is not likely—he will know where it is to be got!

⌒

Taken for a ride

An oft-told tale of the turf involves a city bookie taking his horse from the city to a country race meeting.

a bookie decides to get a jockey to run his horse 'dead', meaning that it will lose the race even though it is a good horse. He inflates the odds to 2–1.

A punter then approaches the bookie to make a bet on a three-horse race. Depending on which version of the story is being told, either the punter or the bookie pumps up the odds on the favourite to the point where the punter has laid out a lot of money. The race begins and the favourite, despite being held back by the jockey, still somehow wins against the unbelievably slow two local horses. At this point the bookie, facing a very large payout, snarls at the punter and says something like 'Hey, mate, you think you're pretty bloody clever, don't you? But you didn't know I owned the favourite.'

The punter laughs and says, 'I know, but I own the other two.'

10

Hard cases

How would I be? How would I bloody well be!

The world's greatest whinger

AUSTRALIANS NOTORIOUS FOR miserliness, bloody-minded-ness or a generally contrary nature are often referred to as 'hard cases'. Quite a few of them—named and unnamed—are celebrated in folk stories.

The cocky

Cocky is slang for a small farmer, the kind who scraped a living from marginal land. Cockies' miserliness and dourness make them among the hardest of Australian hard cases, as the poem 'The Cockies of Bungaree' indicates.

We used to go to bed, you know, a little bit after dark,
The room we used to sleep in was just like Noah's Ark.
There was mice and rats and dogs and cats and pigs and poulter-ee,
I'll never forget the work we did down on Bungaree.

A cocky hires a labourer on the basis that work stops at sunset. When the sun goes down, the worker says, 'Time to call it a day.' 'Sun hasn't set yet,' says the cocky. 'You can still see it if you climb up on top of the fence.'

In another, the worker succeeds in getting the upper hand when the farmer wakes up his new labourer well before sunrise and says he needs a hand getting in the oats. 'Are they wild oats?' asks the sleepy labourer. 'No,' says the cocky, taken aback. 'Then why do we have to sneak up on 'em in the dark!'

Another cocky's new labourer asks when he will have a day off. 'Every fourth Sunday's free,' the cocky says. 'Much to do round here on me day off?' asks the worker. 'Plenty,' says the cocky. 'There's cutting the week's firewood, mending the harnesses, tending the vegetables and washing the horses. After that, you can do whatever you like.'

One night in the pub, a local bloke congratulates a cocky on the coming marriage of his daughter. 'That'll be the fourth wedding in your family in the last few years, won't it?'

'Yes,' replies the cocky. 'And the confetti is starting to get awful dirty.'

Other yarns are a little more forgiving of the cocky, stressing the hardships of his situation.

The drought had lasted so long that when a raindrop fell on the local cocky, he fainted clean away. They had to throw two buckets-full of dust into his face to bring him back to consciousness.

Times were so hard that all the cocky had to eat was rabbits. He had them for every meal, week in, week out. He had them stewed, he had them fried, he had them boiled he had them braised.

Feeling rather ill, he decided to give himself a dose of Epsom salts. When that didn't help, he went to the local doctor, who asked him what he'd been eating. 'I've had nothing but rabbits for months,' the cocky said. 'Taken anything for it?' the doctor asked. 'Epsom salts,' said the cocky. 'You don't need Epsom salts,' said the doctor with a laugh, 'you need ferrets.'

Three cocky farmers were chatting over a beer. The first, who came from the Riverina, said he could run three head to an acre all year long. The second cocky, from central New South Wales said that he could run two head to an acre. The third cocky was from out Bourke way. 'Well, we run ninety-five head to an acre,' he says. 'You're bloody kidding,' said the other two. 'It's true,' he insisted, 'I run one head of sheep and ninety-four rabbits.'

Hungry Tyson

James Tyson (1819–1898) was a highly successful pastoralist, or 'squatter', who made a fortune through acquiring rural land during the mid to late nineteenth century. Despite his wealth he lived simply, neither smoking, drinking nor swearing, probably something of a novelty for his time and geography. In folklore, Tyson was renowned for his stinginess and known universally as 'Hungry' Tyson. His Scrooge-like character was even memorialised in folk speech through the saying 'mean as Hungry Tyson'.

Sayings and yarns about Tyson echo his legendary meanness. He is rumoured to have once claimed that he hadn't got rich by 'striking matches when there was a fire to get a light by'.

Once, Hungry Tyson had to cross the Murrumbidgee River. The cost of being ferried across in the punt was one shilling. To save having to pay the money, the tight-fisted grazier swam over.

A rural newspaper of 1891 carried a selection of Tyson yarns in the context of his opposition to the bitter strike of the Queensland shearers:

*T*he name of Mr. James Tyson (or, as he is familiarly called, 'Old Jimmy'), the Queensland millionaire, is so well known throughout this and the other colonies, says the *Narrandera Ensign*, and as he is at present making a most determined stand against the Queensland Union shearers, perhaps the following few anecdotes about the old gentleman may be of some interest. That 'Jimmy' is a very eccentric fellow no one who has ever come in contact with him will deny, and he has made several attempts to perform big public business; attempts which would have brought a less reserved man into prominent notoriety.

The first of these was to offer to construct a line of railway from Rockhampton to the Gulf of Carpentaria, the farthest coastal point in Queensland. The recompense 'James' required from the Government was three miles depth of frontage along the whole route; but the representatives of the people in Bananaland thought the offer was a bit one-sided, and declined to negotiate.

We next find Mr. Tyson in New South Wales, at the recent financial crisis, offering to take up £4,000,000 worth of Government Treasury bills at a moderate rate of interest. As the public well know, this offer was also declined.

A few years back, when the large cathedral that adorns Brisbane was in course of construction, the collector for the building fund called upon a well-known mercantile firm for a subscription, but he was politely told that he should go to the rich people of Queensland, who may be in a better position to 'help the work along'.

'To whom shall I go?' queried the collector.

'Well, go to Jimmy Tyson,' was the answer. 'He has more than any of us.'(I might mention that up to that time 'Jimmy's' name was never seen on any list for more than £1).

'Well,' said the collector, 'as Tyson is a rich man I will go to him for a donation.'

'Do,' said the head of the firm, 'and whatever he gives you we will guarantee you the same amount.'

The collector, a few days after meeting Mr. Tyson, related to him what had taken place, and concluded by saying, 'So, Mr. Tyson, I do not know what amount the firm is going to give until I have your name on my list.' 'Well,' said Tyson in a gruff voice, 'give me yer pen and ink and I'll give yees a bob or two.'

'Jimmy' went into a private room and wrote out a cheque for £5000, and gave it to the astonished collector who in turn presented it to the more astonished merchant, who, however, could not 'ante up' more than a century.

On another occasion the subject of this sketch sent a lady a cheque for £300 towards a 'parsonage fund'. The lady, in a jocular manner, sent the cheque back, and asked Mr. Tyson if he bad not forgotten the other '0' at the end of the figures. It is needless to say Mr. Tyson felt aggrieved, and immediately burnt the cheque—and did not subscribe one shilling.

Meeting a friend on one occasion on the platform at the Orange railway station, the friend expressed surprise at seeing Mr. Tyson riding in a second-class carriage.

'Do you know why I do ride in a second-class compartment?' said Mr. Tyson.

'No, I do not know why,' said the acquaintance.

'Well,' said 'Jimmy', 'it is because there is no third-class', and with a broad smile he resumed his seat, and the friend looked crestfallen, and went and drowned his contempt for the 'old fellow' in a bottle of Bass' ale.

The writer of these lines was at one time engaged by Mr. Tyson for three days to do some clerical work, and when the work was completed, he (Mr. Tyson) reviewed the job, and asked me how much he had to pay me. 'Half-a-guinea a day,' was the reply.

'I wish to goodness I could use the pen as well as you do,' said Mr. Tyson. 'If I could I would be a rich man in a few years.' (He had banked the day before a total of £170,000.)

'You are now a very rich man, Mr. Tyson, are you not?' queried I.

'No, I am not,' said 'Jimmy'. 'No man is rich until he has as much as he wants, and I have not near that yet. However, as you have done your work to my satisfaction, kindly accept my cheque for £35.'

It is not necessary for me to state here that I accepted.

Many people are under the impression that Mr. Tyson is a man devoid of all sense of liberality, but they are, in my opinion, sadly mistaken, for although he has been known to refuse a swagman a match lest he was paid for it, he has, on the other hand, been known to help widows and orphans to the tune of thousands, and when he leaves the scene of his earthly struggles, and his life is recorded, I am sure that his liberality and generosity will overbalance the charge laid against him by a certain section of the community, viz.— parsimony.

'Banjo' Paterson wrote a poem about Tyson and he was said to have frequently dressed as a swagman on his own property, sleeping outside until the manager came back from his duties. In contrast to his miserly image, Tyson was also said to be an anonymous doer of good deeds, as Paterson suggests in his poem 'T.Y.S.O.N.'

Across the Queensland border line
The mobs of cattle go;
They travel down in sun and shine
On dusty stage, and slow.
The drovers, riding slowly on
To let the cattle spread,
Will say: 'Here's one old landmark gone,
For old man Tyson's dead'.
What tales there'll be in every camp
By men that Tyson knew;
The swagmen, meeting on the tramp,
Will yarn the long day through,
And tell of how he passed as 'Brown',
And fooled the local men:
'But not for me—I struck the town,
And passed the message further down;
That's T.Y.S.O.N.!'

There stands a little country town
Beyond the border line,
Where dusty roads go up and down,
And banks with pubs combine.
A stranger came to cash a cheque—
Few were the words he said—

A handkerchief about his neck,
An old hat on his head.

A long grey stranger, eagle-eyed—
'Know me? Of course you do?'
'It's not my work,' the boss replied,
'To know such tramps as you'.
'Well, look here, Mister, don't be flash,'
Replied the stranger then,
'I never care to make a splash,
I'm simple—but I've got the cash,
I'm T.Y.S.O.N.!'

But in that last great drafting-yard,
Where Peter keeps the gate,
And souls of sinners find it barred,
And go to meet their fate,
There's one who ought to enter in,
For good deeds done on earth;
Such deeds as merit ought to win,
Kind deeds of sterling worth.

Not by the strait and narrow gate,
Reserved for wealthy men,
But through the big gate, opened wide,
The grizzled figure, eagle-eyed,
Will travel through—and then
Old Peter'll say: 'We pass him through;
There's many a thing he used to do,
Good-hearted things that no one knew;
That's T.Y.S.O.N.!'

At his death, Tyson's estate was worth two million pounds, a fact that gave further force to an apparently existing outback folk belief that the money was cursed, as a literary-minded contemporary wrote shortly after the pastoralist died:

> Tyson died alone in the night in his lonely bush station, with thousands of stock on it, but with no hand to give him even a drink of water, and no voice to soothe or to console him in his last struggle with death. He was hurriedly buried. No requiem was sung at his grave. He died, and was forgotten. Only his millions, which Bacon calls 'muck', and Shakespeare 'rascally counters', remained for his shoal of relatives to fight for through the law courts. Some of them were but struggling for an overdose of mortal poison, as the gold proved to be to some persons at least.
>
> There is a strange legend regarding this man's money. The old hands out back will tell you that every coin of it is cursed, and if we follow the havoc some of the money has caused, there is much food for the superstitious mind.

Tyson's folktale image is similar to that of another wealthy pastoralist of a slightly later era, Sidney (later Sir) Kidman (1857–1935). Many of the tales of miserliness are told of both men.

Ninety the Glutton

Tasmania's face-stuffing folk hero is said to have got his name when he was set to look after a mob of sheep. After grazing them for three months, he brought them in for shearing, but he was ninety sheep short. What happened? their owner wanted to know. 'Well, I ate one a day for me rations,' said Ninety.

Ninety wandered all over Tasmania in search of work—and food. Smart farmers would give him one large feed and send him on his way. One, however, pointed to a crate of apples. 'You can have some of these,' he told Ninety. The apples were about to go bad, in any case. About an hour later, the owner came back to find Ninety sitting amid a pile of apple cores. 'What time's dinner, boss?' he said.

Queensland's Ninety is Tom the Glutton, who can polish off a crate of bananas, sometimes including the skins, in just ten minutes.

Galloping Jones

Galloping Jones is thought to have lived in northern Queensland and died in 1960. Jones was a bush fighter, a drinker, and a thief, who was not above stealing stock, selling it, and stealing it back again the very same night.

*O*nce, Galloping Jones was arrested by a policeman and an Aboriginal tracker for illegally slaughtering a cow. The evidence was the cow's hide, prominently marked with someone else's brand. On the way back to town, Jones's captors made camp for the night. Jones managed to get them both drunk, and when they fell asleep, he rode away. Instead of escaping, however, he returned a few hours later with a fresh cow hide, substituted it for the evidence, and went to sleep. The party continued to town, and Jones was duly tried. But when the evidence was pulled out, the hide bore his own brand: case dismissed.

Jones was again captured by a young policeman who he fooled into letting him go behind a bush to relieve himself. Of course, Jones escaped and the policeman had to return to town without his captive. When he got to town to report his failure to the sergeant, who was in his usual 'office', the pub, there was Jones, washed and shaved and having a beer. The embarrassed policeman threatened to shoot Jones, but the trickster just said that he felt the need for a cleanup and a drink and that he would now be happy to stroll down to the lockup.

~

The Eulo Queen

Barmaids who may also be prostitutes are not the most likely of heroines, but such was the Eulo Queen or Eulo Belle. The original of the folk figure is thought to have been named Isabel Gray. She is variously said to have been born in England or Mauritius, probably in 1851, and to have been the illegitimate daughter of a British army captain. She apparently reached Australia in her late teens, when she married the first of three husbands. Some twenty years later, she turns up as the owner of the Eulo Hotel (among other establishments) in the small Queensland opal-mining town of that name, west of Cunnamulla. Eulo was on the legendary Paroo Track, a notoriously hot, dry and dusty way described in Henry Lawson's poem 'The Paroo':

> It's plagued with flies, and broiling hot,
> A curse is on it ever;
> I really think that God forgot.
> The country round that river.

She is said to have got her name when, ejecting a drunken patron, she yelled: 'I'm the Eulo queen—now get out!' She was apparently a noted beauty; in any case, there was little competition in that part of the country, and she attracted many admirers, growing wealthy from their gifts. These enabled her to lead a flamboyant lifestyle and acquire another couple of husbands. Estranged from her third, she—and Eulo town—fell on hard times. She died in a Toowoomba psychiatric hospital in 1929, reputedly in her nineties and with only £30 to her name.

Dopers

The racetrack has long been a stamping ground for hard cases of all types. This yarn involves the practice of doping a horse in hopes of making it run faster:

A trainer makes up some dope, soaks a sugar cube in it and slips it to his horse. Along comes the Chief Steward of the track, known as the stipe. 'What are you feeding that horse?' the stipe asks. 'Just a little treat to calm him down,' says the trainer. Seeing that the stipe is still suspicious, he picks up another cube and eats it. 'Give me one,' says the stipe. He apparently finds nothing wrong with it and continues on his way, leaving the trainer free to saddle his horse for the race. As the jockey mounts it, the trainer whispers to him to let the horse simply run the race: 'Give him his head and don't use the whip.'

'But what if someone starts closing on me in the straight?' asks the jockey.

'Don't worry,' replies the trainer. 'It will only be me or the bloody stipe.'

Wheelbarrow Jack

Also known as Russian Jack, Wheelbarrow Jack was a twenty-two-year-old Russian or Finn who arrived in Western Australia in the late 1880s and headed for the Kimberley gold rush. He was said to be tall, well built and extraordinarily strong. A popular mode of transport among the prospectors was the wooden wheelbarrow. Jack built one to carry his goods overland to the diggings. It was unusually large, matching his strength, and said to be able to carry loads of 50 kilograms or more. Jack and his barrow soon became legends. When a fellow would-be digger fell ill along the way, Jack loaded his goods and eventually the man himself onto the barrow and wheeled them far along the track until his ailing passenger died.

The numerous stories about Jack focus on his generosity and unstinting mateship. Most are documented, but there are also less reliable tales; all, however, reflect the esteem in which Jack was held in the frontier country of the northwest.

*W*hen a mate breaks his leg, while they are out hunting, Jack loads him onto his barrow and wheels him into town. The townsfolk gather round, and Jack tells them how many miles of hard country he's covered. 'And you hit every rock along the way,' pipes up his invalid mate.

At the Mount Morgan gold mine, Jack falls down a shaft and lies there for three days before he's found. Badly injured, his first concern is that he's missed his work shift.

Once, while working for a station owner, he is sacked—a move that so angers him that he bends a crowbar with his bare hands. His only weakness is for grog. It's said that a coach driver stopped near his lodgings and offered him a swig of whisky. 'No, I'm off the grog,' Jack said. Prevailed upon to have a small drink, he swallowed the half remaining bottle of whisky in one gulp. 'If this is what you're like when you're not drinking,' said the driver, 'I'd hate to see you when you are.'

Another time, Jack's love of alcohol is almost the ruin of him. After a few beers too many, he loads up his barrow to make the trek back to his camp, a few miles out of town. On it he throws a box of firing caps for the dynamite he is also carrying. Seeing him weave down the street, the local policeman decides to escort Jack out of town—then spots the firing caps and decides to arrest him. Jack's intoxication and strength make this something of a challenge. The imaginative policeman manages to steer Jack, merrily singing, towards the police tents, where other policemen offered him a cup of tea and repacked his wheelbarrow to make it safe.

Jack dozes off, and the police handcuff him to a very large log. They then go off to attend to business. When they return, Jack has vanished—and so has the log. Tracks in the sand lead to the local pub, where the police find Jack drinking a beer with his unchained hand and the log propped up on the bar. Thirsty, he had simply thrown the log onto his shoulder and made for the pub. 'Have a drink with me and I'll go back to jail,' says Jack. Rather than drink on duty, the men follow Jack, still shouldering the giant log, back to the police tents, where they share a billy of tea.

Jack also attracted the interest of many journalists, including Mary Durack and Ernestine Hill. After his death, in 1904, a local newspaper published this obituary:

*A*n old identity, John Fredericks—but a hundred times better known as 'Russian Jack'—died a few days ago. His death came as a surprise, for no one could imagine death in the prime of life to one of such Herculean strength. He was, so far as physical manhood is concerned, a picture, but he combined the strength of a lion with the tenderness of a woman. Though he had a loud-sounding sonorous voice that seemed to come out of his boots, there was no more harm in it than the chirp of a bird. Many instances are known of his uniform good nature, but his extraordinary kindness, some years ago, to a complete stranger—that he picked up on the track in the Kimberley gold rush—exemplified his mateship. The stranger had a wheelbarrow and some food, and the burly Russian picked the stranger up, placed him on his own large wheelbarrow, together with his meagre possessions, and wheeled him nearly 300 miles to a haven of refuge.

It was Ernestine Hill who first suggested that a statue be raised to commemorate Russian Jack. Eventually in 1979, one was erected at Halls Creek. The statue depicts Russian Jack in his Good Samaritan role, carrying a sick digger in his wooden wheelbarrow.

Russian Jack is a Western Australian version of a folktale type known as 'German Charlie' stories. While the heroes of such tales are not always called 'German Charlie', they are usually nicknamed that way because of their national or ethnic origins. These stories tell how some special, unusual or exaggerated skill or attribute is brought to an Australian community.

Using that skill in helpful, often humorous, sometimes absurd ways, German Charlies become accepted members of their communities and feature in commonly told tales of their real and fancied exploits. Russian Jack's wheelbarrow, his assistance to the needy, his strength and his prodigious boozing all combine to make him another example of a type of hard case found all around Australia.

The jilted bride

Eliza Donnithorne is perhaps the most unusual hard case of all, not only because she is a woman, but also because of the rumour that she was the model for the disappointed bride Miss Havisham in Charles Dickens' *Great Expectations*. Miss Havisham spends the rest of her life wearing her wedding dress and sitting among the mouldering ruins of her planned wedding feast.

Eliza Donnithorne arrived in Sydney as a child in the mid-1830s. At the age of thirty, she accepted a proposal of marriage. On the appointed day the guests assembled in St Stephen's Church, Newtown, and the bride in her fine wedding dress awaited the arrival of the groom. He never came. Shattered, she returned to the family home, Camperdown Lodge, put up the shutters and lived ever after in candlelight, attended only by two faithful servants and her pets. She died in 1886, not having set foot outside for thirty years.

In some of the stories about Eliza, she is said to keep the front door permanently ajar on a chain in the hope that her groom would one day return. She orders that her wedding feast is to remain on the table, and refuses to take off her wedding dress. The various reasons given for the groom's failure to arrive at the church include that he was of relatively low status and that her family paid him to disappear, he fell from his horse as he galloped to the wedding, or that he was a military man and suddenly shipped out to India. Yet another variant holds that Eliza was pregnant but the baby was stillborn.

In the late 1880s the bookseller James Tyrrell wrote what may have been the first published account of the legend, recalling that in his boyhood he'd heard Camperdown Lodge was haunted, though it was not until some years later that he heard about its jilted inhabitant.

In my day in Newtown the cemetery was still in use, but it was already a ghostly old graveyard . . . The visitor to the cemetery [today] may see the graves of Judge James Donnithorne and his last surviving daughter, Eliza Emily, who is shown as having died in 1886. In my day the Donnithorne residence, Cambridge Hall [as the house was subsequently renamed], in what is now King Street, came under the wide designation of 'haunted', and I was still young enough to keep to the other side of the road in passing it, especially at night. Still, I would glance fearfully over to its front door, which, by night or day, was always partly open, though fastened with a chain.

Eliza Donnithorne's will included a bequest to the Society for the Prevention of Cruelty to Animals and 'an annuity of £5 for each of my six animals and £5 for all my birds'. She was buried in St Stephen's churchyard and her grave is now a popular tourist destination, the story of her unhappy life and its literary associations, true or not, attracting many visitors.

It is likely that this story is a case of retrospective myth making and that Eliza Donnithorne was not the prototype for Dickens' Miss Havisham. Instead, his story enveloped the Australian tale and partly fused with it. Certainly, although he transported Magwitch to Australia, there is no evidence that Dickens kept up with everyday events in colonial Sydney while he was writing *Great Expectations*.

Long Jack

Another Jack came into legend on the Western Front in World War I. He was said to have been a member of the 3rd Battalion AIF and to have stood out because of a chronic stutter and the speed with which he responded to any perceived slight. Long Jack's exploits were recorded by an anonymous contributor to the *Third Battalion Magazine* some time around 1917:

*T*here are certain characters, which pass through our Battalion life, which are more than worth perpetuating. Such a one was long Jack Dean. In regard to his figure he was an outsider, as he was 6½ feet tall and as slender as a whippet. As a wit he stood alone. A man needed more than ordinary morale to meet him on this ground, and many who purposely or inadvertently engaged him have cause to be sorry for themselves, but glad that they were a party to adding another witty victory to Jack's account. The quickness and smartness of his retorts took the sting from them, and there was no more popular man in the unit than he. This sketch aims at reproducing some stories which came from him, and through which the man himself may be seen.

At the outbreak of war, or soon afterwards, he presented himself before the Recruiting Officers, but his physique was against him. His keenness, however, was proof against his setback, and he came again and again, only to meet with the same result. At last, he asked with his inimitable stutter; 'If you c-c-can't t-take me as a s-s-soldier—s-s-send me-me as a m-m-mascot!'

The Recruiting Officer had become used to his applications, and, recognising the keenness of the man he was dealing with, answered: 'I'll tell you what I shall do. Bring me twelve receipts, and I shall accept you.' 'Done!' said Jack. 'It's a bargain.' He turned up with seventeen fit men and was taken on strength. One can imagine him taking his place among the other recruits at the training depot. His 'length without breadth' immediately singled him out as a butt [of jokes] and one misguided youth was foolish enough to say as he passed him: 'Smell the gum-leaves.' 'Yes,' said Jack, 'feel the branches.' And his long, wiry right shot out with good effect.

He must have been the despair of all that tried to make a smart soldier out of him. Working on the coalface does not keep a long man supple; but in due time he arrived in France, and joined the Battalion—just in time to face the second time 'in' on the Somme. He quickly made himself at home, and in a very short time was known to everybody in the Battalion. It is said that Colonel Howell Price asked him if he had any brothers. 'Y-yes, sir,' he answered: 'one—he's t-t-taller than me, b-but n-not n-n-nearly so well developed.'

Being thin made him appear taller than he actually was, and his height was always the point in question to those who were not used to it. A Tommy saw him ambling along the road very much the worse for wear as a result of a tour in the line and in the mud. 'Reach me down a star, choom,' said the Tommy. 'Take your pick out of these, sonny,' was Jack's answer, together with a very forceful uppercut to the chin. Our late Brigadier never failed to talk to Jack when he met him.

'Good-day, Jack,' was his invariable greeting. 'G-g-g-good day, Brig.,' was always Jack's reply, and it never failed to amuse Brigadier Leslie.

There is one other story which illustrates J.D.' s democratic soul. The Brigadier stopped to have a word with him, and remarked that he wasn't getting any fatter. 'How the hell can a man get fat on 8 [men] to a loaf?' was the response.

Jack's feet were always his worst enemy, and they were the cause of him falling to the rear on one occasion, during a rather stiff route march. He was getting along as best he could when he came up with the Brigadier. 'What Jack! You out!' said the latter. 'Me blanky p-p-p-paddles h-have gone on me, Brig,' replied Jack.

It is only possible to write this sketch because the subject is no longer with us. We hope he is now on his way to Australia, as he has done his bit well, and had come to that stage when he could not effectively carry on. While waiting for the Board which was to examine and determine his future, one of the Sisters, like all who saw him for the first time, said; 'What a lot of disadvantages there must be for such a tall man.' 'Yes,' said Jack. 'The greatest trouble I have is with the rum issue; it dries up before it hits my stomach.'

Jack will remain in our memories and we are grateful to him for these and many other sayings of his which have amused us at all times when we needed the lift of genuine amusement.

The world's greatest whinger

Sometimes said to be as old as the Boer War, this elaborate anecdote probably dates only from World War II. This is one of many versions that have appeared in print:

I struck him first on a shearing station in outback Queensland. He was knocking the fleeces from a four-year-old wether when I asked him the innocent question: 'How are you?'

He didn't answer immediately, but waited till he had carved the last bit of wool from the sheep, allowing it to regain its feet, kicking it through the door, dropping the shears and spitting a stream of what looked like molten metal about three yards. Then he fixed me with a pair of malevolent eyes in which the fires of a deep hatred seemed to burn, and he pierced me with them as he said:

'How would I be? How would you bloody well expect me to be? Get a load of me, will you? Dags on every inch of me bloody hide; drinking me own bloody sweat; swallowing dirt with every breath I breathe; shearing sheep which should have been dogs' meat years ago; working for the lousiest bastard in Australia; and frightened to leave because the old woman has got some bloody hound looking for me with a bloody maintenance order.

'How would I be? I haven't tasted a beer for weeks, and the last glass I had was knocked over by some clumsy bastard before I'd finished it.'

The next time I saw him was in Sydney. He had just joined the A.I.F. He was trying to get into a set of webbing and almost ruptured himself in the process. I said to him: 'How would you be, Dig?'

He almost choked before replying. 'How would I be? How would I bloody well be? Take a gander at me, will you? Get a load of this bloody outfit—look at me bloody hat, size nine and a half and I take six and a half. Get a bloody eyeful of these strides! Why, you could hide a bloody brewery horse in the seat of them and still have room for me! Get on this shirt—just get on the bloody thing, will you? Get on these bloody boots; why, there's enough leather in the bastard to make a full set of harness. And some know-all bastard told me this was a men's outfit!

'How would I be? How would I bloody well be?'

I saw him next in Tobruk. He was seated on an upturned box, tin hat over one eye, cigarette butt hanging from his bottom lip, rifle leaning against one knee, and he was engaged in trying to clean his nails with the tip of his bayonet. I should have known better, but I asked him: 'How would you be, Dig?'

He swallowed the butt and fixed me with a really mad look. 'How would I be? How would I bloody well be! How would you expect me to be? Six months in this bloody place; being shot at by every Fritz in Africa; eating bloody sand with every meal; flies in me hair and eyes; frightened to sleep a bloody wink expecting to die in this bloody place; and copping the bloody crow whenever there's a handout by anybody.

'How would I be? How would I bloody well be?!'

The last time I saw him was in Paradise, and his answer to my question was: 'How would I be? How would I bloody well be! Get an eyeful of this bloody nightgown, will you? A man trips over the bloody thing fifty times a day, and it takes a man ten minutes to lift the bloody thing when he wants to scratch his shin! Get a gander at this bloody right wing—feathers missing everywhere. A man must be bloody well moulting! Get an eyeful of this bloody halo! Only me bloody ears keep the rotten thing on me skull—and look at the bloody dents on the bloody thing!

'How would I be? Cast your eyes on this bloody harp. Five bloody strings missing, and there's a band practice in five minutes!

'How would I be? you ask. How would you expect a bloody man to bloody well be?'

THE BULLOCKY.

11
Working people

*Eventually we will cross the cats with snakes, and they will
skin themselves twice a year, thus saving the men's wages
for skinning and also getting two skins per cat per year ...*

Working on the Dimboola Cat Farm, c. 1920s

TALES ABOUT CO-WORKERS and work-related events are told
in most industries, trades and professions—though they seldom
travel far beyond them. In-group references and jargon can
make such stories all but incomprehensible to outsiders. But
many contain enough of the common stuff of working life to
be told, or adapted for telling, in practically any workplace—as
in the yarn about the boss who scolds an employee for failing
to clean up. 'The dust on that table is so thick I could write
my name in it,' he says. 'Yes,' says the worker, 'but then, you're
an educated man.'

Most tales of working life are humorous, though they often
have a point to make about conditions, management or other
aspects of the working day. They provide a way to carp and
laugh at the same time—a release valve for tensions that might
otherwise cause conflict.

Crooked Mick and the Speewah

Crooked Mick is the legendary occupational hero of Australian shearers and other outback workers. He can shear more sheep, fell more trees, and do anything better and faster than anyone else. Julian Stuart, one of the leaders of the 1891 shearers' strike in Queensland, made the earliest known printed reference to Crooked Mick in *The Australian Worker* during the 1920s:

I first heard of him on the Barcoo in 1889. We were shearing at Northampton Downs, and we musterers brought in a rosy-cheeked young English Johnny who, in riding from Jericho, the nearest railway station to Blackall, where he was going to edit the new paper, had got lost and found himself at the station, where we were busily engaged disrobing about 150,000 jumbucks.

He was treated with the hospitality of the sheds, which is traditional, and after tea we gathered in the hut—dining room and sleeping accommodation all in one in those days—and proceeded to entertain him.

Whistling Dick played 'The British Grenadiers' on his tin whistle; Bungeye Blake sang 'Little Dog Ben'; Piebald Moore and Cabbagetree Capstick told a common lie or two, but when Dusty Bob got the flute I sat up on my bunk and listened, for I knew him to be the most fluent liar that ever crossed the Darling.

His anecdotes about Crooked Mick began and ended nowhere, and made C.M. appear a superman—with feet so big that he had to go outside to turn around.

It took a large-sized bullock's hide to make him a pair of moccasins.

He was a heavy smoker. It took one 'loppy' (rouseabout) all his time cutting tobacco and filling his pipe.

He worked at such a clip that his shears ran hot, and sometimes he had a half a dozen pairs in the water pot to cool.

He had his fads, and would not shear in sheds that faced north. When at his top, it took three pressers to handle the wool from his blades, and they had to work overtime to keep the bins clear.

He ate two merino sheep each meal—that is, if they were small merinos—but only one and a half when the ration sheep were Leicester crossbred wethers.

His main tally was generally cut on the breakfast run. Anyone who tried to follow him usually spent the balance of the day in the hut.

Between sheds he did fencing. When cutting brigalow posts he used an axe in each hand to save time, and when digging post holes a crowbar in one hand and a shovel in the other.

∽

This depiction gives a good idea of the context in which Crooked Mick tales were told and of the (equally legendary) ability of the liar Dusty Bob to string otherwise unconnected fictions into a crude but engaging narrative, a talent not uncommon among real-life bush yarn spinners.

How did Mick come to be called Crooked? As Mick tells it (and there are other versions, of course), he was ploughing one very hot day, and it got so hot that the fence-wire melted. When he took the horses to have a drink, he put one leg in the water bucket. The leg was nearly molten, and when he lifted his other leg, putting his weight on the one in the water, it buckled. It's been that way ever since, which is why Mick walks with a slight limp.

In later life, Mick's escapades included trying to stone the crows by throwing Ayers Rock (Uluru) at them, harnessing willy willies to improve the flow of a water windmill and becoming the ringer of the Speewah shed. Here he set an unbeaten record of 1,847 wethers and twelve lambs, all shorn in just one day using hand blades.

The Speewah is an outback never-never land where every-thing is gigantic: the pumpkins so big they can be used as houses, the trees so tall they have to be hinged to let in the sunlight, and the sheep so large they can't be shorn without climbing a ladder. Many wondrous sights can be witnessed on the Speewah, which is located where the crows fly backwards. The Speewah is so hot in summer that its freezing point is set at 99°F. It is so cold in the winter that the mirages freeze solid and the grasshoppers grow fur coats. Droughts are not over until the people of the Speewah are able to have water in their tea.

The creatures of the Speewah form a weird menagerie that includes the small ker-ker bird, so named from its habit of flying across the Speewah in summer crying 'ker-ker-kripes, it's hot!' Then there is the oozlum bird, which flies tail first in ever-decreasing circles until, moaning, it disappears inside itself head first. Hoop snakes and giant mosquitoes are commonplace on the Speewah, as are giant emus, wombats, crocodiles and boars. The roos are so big they make the emus look like canaries, and the rabbits so thick, large and cunning that Mick had to go off to the war to save himself.

Mick is only one of the Speewah's larger-than-life characters. These include Prickly Pear Pollie, so plain that a cocky farmer hires her as a scarecrow. She's so good at scaring the birds that they start returning the corn they stole two seasons ago. Another is Old Harry, the building worker with one wooden leg. One night he came home and his wife noticed that he only had one leg left. Harry looked down and was amazed to discover she was right. He had no idea how he'd lost it, hadn't even noticed it was gone. Irish Paddy is so good at digging post-holes that he wears his crowbar down to the size of a darning needle. There was Bungeye Bill, the gambler, and Greasy George, the third assistant shearer's cook, who is so greasy that people's eyes slide right off him as they look.

The Speewah shearing shed itself is so large it takes two men and a boy standing on each other's shoulders to see the whole of it, and the boss takes a day or more to ride its length on horseback. Traditions of outsize shearing sheds and stations featuring men of the stamp of Crooked Mick are also found under names like Big Burrawong and Big Burramugga (Western Australia), suggesting that the tales of Mick's doings and those of the mythic stations may have been independent.

Crooked Mick tales have been recounted to many folklorists, but collections of shearer anecdotes made in the past fifty years make no reference to them, suggesting that Crooked Mick may be having a tough time surviving change, despite his prowess.

Crooked Mick has an affinity with other folk heroes of labour. The American lumber worker folk hero, Paul Bunyan, is a superman who performs prodigious deeds of strength and occupational skill. Working conditions on the frontiers of the

New World produced many such fabulous figures, including the American cowboy known as Pecos Bill. Seamen in the days of sail also had a similar unnaturally strong and bold figure known as 'Stormalong John', or just 'Old Stormy', who sailed giant ships blown so fiercely onto the Isthmus of Panama that it cleaved out the Panama Canal.

In some Speewah stories Crooked Mick is the cook and is said to have made pastry so light that it floated into the air when the wind blew. These skills link him with another stock character of bush and, later, digger lore.

Bush cooks were the subject of many humorous anecdotes and yarns especially the shearer's cook, also known as a 'babbling brook', or just a 'babbler', in rhyming slang. Many well-worn bush cook yarns have been collected from around the country. This is probably the most popular:

As the tale usually goes, the shearers or other station workers are fed a monotonous diet of something indigestible for a number of weeks. At first they bring the matter to the attention of the cook, who either refuses to change his menu or, as in the version given by Bill Wannan, claims he is unable to make the custard requested by the shearers because 'there ain't a pound of dripping in the place'. The shearers then begin to abuse the cook on a constant basis until he complains to the boss about the bad language. Fed up with all the irritation, the boss finally calls the shearers together and demands to know 'Who called the cook a bastard?' Quick as a flash came the gun shearer's reply: 'Who called the bastard a cook?'

This tradition of the execrable cook continued into the folklore of World War I diggers. Sometimes known as 'bait-layers' from the poisonous nature of their offerings, the army cook was basically the bush cook in uniform.

I came out of my dugout one morning attracted by a terrible outburst of Aussie slanguage in the trench. The company dag was standing in about three feet of mud, holding his mess tin in front of him and gazing contemptuously at a piece of badly cooked bacon, while he made a few heated remarks concerning one known as Bolo, the babbling brook. He concluded an earnest and powerful address thus:

'An' if the _____ that cooked this bacon ever gets hung for bein' a cook, the poor_____ will be innocent.'

⌀

A variant story piggy-backs on this one.

A digger is being questioned by the officer in charge of his court-martial: 'Did you call the cook a bastard?'

'No,' the digger answers, 'but I could kiss the bastard who did!'

⌀

Historian of the war C.E.W. Bean provided an insight into the dual roles of the cook in digger culture, roles that were also at the base of the cook's bush personality. 'This individual was both a provider of sustenance and the (mostly) willing butt of humour within the military group with which he was affiliated, bearing the "oaths and good-natured sarcasm" of those who had no option but to consume his offerings, with equanimity and humorous forbearance.'

Slow trains

Modern Australia's development was made possible by the railway. After Federation, the various states' railways were linked together via the Transcontinental Railway, or 'the Trans'. The railways' importance, and the armies of workers they employed, gave rise to a large fund of railway yarns, many of which are still told among railway folk. The slow train is a popular theme.

a man jumps off a train as it approaches the platform and rushes up to the station master. 'I need an ambulance!' he cries. 'My wife's about to have a baby.' The station master phones for the ambulance, then says, 'She shouldn't have been travelling in that condition, you know.' The man replies: 'She wasn't in that condition when she got on the train.'

On another slow trip a passenger looks out the window and sees the engine driver throwing seeds onto the sides of the track. All day, as the train crawls along, the driver keeps sowing. Eventually the passenger goes up to the engine and asks, 'Why are you throwing seeds onto the side of the line?'

The driver fixes the passenger with a doleful eye and drawls: 'The guard's picking tomatoes.'

On another journey, a notoriously slow train pulls into the station right on time. An astonished passenger rushes up to the driver and congratulates him for being punctual for a change. 'No chance, mate,' came the laconic reply, 'this is yesterday's train.'

a Texan and an Australian are thrown into each other's company one day on a train. The Texan begins to brag to the Australian about the size of his home state.

'In my state, you can get on a train, travel all day and night but still be in Texas the next morning.'

'Yeah,' drawls the Australian, 'we have slow trains here too.'

Bushies

Anecdotes about real or imagined bush life are a staple of Australian folklore, and many revolve around the itinerant bush workers known as swagmen. In this one, the swaggy is a taciturn loner:

a swaggy is plodding along the dry and dusty track in blazing heat. A solitary car approaches and stops near him. The driver leans out the window and asks, 'Where ya goin', mate?'

'Bourke,' the swaggy says.

'Climb in, then, and I'll give you a lift.'

'No, thanks; you can open and shut your own bloody gates.'

The bullock driver, or bullocky, was an important part of the rural labour force in the era before cars and, in some places, for long after. The ability to control and work a team of sweating, bad-tempered and reluctant beasts was highly prized. A good bullocky could get work just about anywhere. It was a hard job, though, requiring not just strength but a loud voice and special calls, often given in extremely colourful language. A bullocky's ability to swear—creatively and to good effect—was a measure of his status.

Variants of this tale have been well honed over the decades. One was published in the 1940s in Lance Skuthorpe's 'The Champion Bullock Driver', and another, titled 'The Phantom Bullocky', in Bill Wannan's *The Australian* of 1954. The latter version goes like this:

*T*he boss is in need of a bullocky. His eight-yoke team of especially wild beasts has already sent fourteen drivers to their graves. A bushman shows up, looking for a job. 'Can you swear well enough to handle a team?' the boss asks. Assured that the bushman can, the boss decides to give the bloke a trial. He asks him to demonstrate his skills by imagining that eight panels of the wood-and-wire fence are eight bullocks. 'Here's a whip,' says the boss, giving him one eighteen feet long.

The bloke runs the whip through his fingers, then begins to work the fence, swearing, cheering and cracking the whip. Before long there is a blue flame running across the top fence wire. Suddenly, the graves of the fourteen dead bullockies open. They jump out, each with a whip, and, cheering and swearing and cracking their whips along the now fiery fence wire, hail the bloke as King of the Bullockies. Suddenly the fence posts began to move forward, just like a team of reluctant bullocks. The phantom bullockies and the bloke continue exhorting the fence, plying their whips all the while, until the fence strains so hard it rips out a stringybark tree and moves off at a flying pace over the hill with the bloke behind.

The fourteen phantom bullockies give another rousing cheer and disappear back into their graves. The bloke returns with the fence, and the amazed boss says, 'You're the best bullocky I've ever seen. You can have the job.'

The bloke laughs, gives another cheer and jumps into the air. He never comes down again.

~

Later versions of the tale drop the phantom fourteen and simply end with the bloke accepting the job. Another variant has him letting the fence disappear into the back blocks, then asking, 'Can I have the job?' 'Any man who starts up a team an' fergits to stop 'em is no bloody good to me!' says the boss.

Another bullock-driver tale has a bullocky in very trying circumstances cursing his beasts in fine style. The parson happens by. 'Do you know where that sort of language will lead?' asks the reverend. 'Yair,' the irate driver replies. 'To the bloody sawmill—or I'll cut every bastard bullock's bloody throat.'

The bullockies' facility with bad language forms the basis of an oral poem known as 'Holy Dan'.

One bullocky doesn't swear like the rest. When teams die of thirst in the Queensland drought, he tells his fellow drivers it is:

The Lord's all-wise decree,
And if they'd only watch and wait,
A change they'd quickly see.

Eventually even Holy Dan's twenty bullocks begin to die of thirst, and he entreats the Lord to send rain. No matter how hard he prays, the rain fails to fall. Finally there is only one bullock left:

Then Dan broke down—good Holy Dan—
The man who never swore.
He knelt beside the latest corpse,
And here's the prayer he prore:

'That's nineteen Thou hast taken, Lord,
And now you'll plainly see
You'd better take the bloody lot,
One's no damn good to me.'

The other riders laughed so much,
They shook the sky around,
The lightning flashed, the thunder roared,
And Holy Dan was drowned.

The wharfie's reply

Another much-yarned-about worker is the wharfie:

*A*t the end of each shift at the dockyard, the old wharfie would wheel his barrow out for the day. All the wharfies were searched as they left the docks in case they'd pilfered something. But no matter how carefully he frisked the wharfie, the dockyard guard never found any loot on the old bloke.

Eventually, the wharfie retired. A few months later the guard came across him in a waterside pub. 'Howya goin', mate?' said the guard, and bought the wharfie a beer for old time's sake. Conversation turned to working life. After a while, the guard said, 'You're well out of there now, mate, so why don't you tell me the truth? I knew yer were knockin' something off, but we never found anything on you. What were yer stealin'?'

The wharfie, smiling broadly, said: 'Wheelbarrows.'

The union dog

Trade unions' long influence, not only on the railways and docks but in manufacturing and mining, ensure that they feature in many work yarns.

Four union members are discussing how smart their dogs are.

The first, a member of the Vehicle Workers' Union, says his dog can do maths calculations. Its name is T Square, and he tells it to go to the blackboard and draw a square, a circle and a triangle. This the dog does with consummate ease.

The Amalgamated Metalworkers' Union member says his dog, Slide Rule, is even smarter. He tells it to fetch a dozen biscuits and divide them into four piles, which Slide Rule duly does.

The Liquor Trades Union member concedes that both dogs are quite clever, but says his is even cleverer. His dog, named

Measure, is told to go and fetch a stubby of beer and pour seven ounces into a ten-ounce glass. It does this perfectly.

The three men turn to the Waterside Workers' Union member and say, 'What can your mongrel do?' He turns to his dog and says, 'Tea Break, show these bastards what you can do, mate!'

Tea Break eats the biscuits, drinks the beer, pisses on the blackboard, screws the other three dogs, claims he's injured his back, fills out a Workers' Compensation form, and shoots through on sick leave.

~

The Dimboola Cat Farm

This tale began life at least as early as the 1920s, when it circulated in the form of a letter. Since then it has been updated in various ways in photocopied, facsimile and email forms.

Wild Cat Syndicate

Dimboola

Dear Sir,

Knowing that you are always interested and open for an investment in a good live proposition, I take the liberty of presenting to you what appears to be a most wonderful business, in which no doubt you will take a lively interest and subscribe towards the formation of the Company. The objects of the Company are to operate a large cat ranch near Dimboola, where land can be purchased cheap for the purpose.

To start with we want 1,000,000 cats. Each cat will average about 12 kittens per year; the skins from 1/6 [1 shilling, 6 pence] for the white one to 2/6 for the pure black ones. This will give us 12,000,000 skins a year to sell at an average of 2/- each, making our revenue about £2500 per day.

A man can skin about 100 cats a day, at 15/- per day wages, and it will take 100 men to operate the ranch; therefore the net profit per day will be £2425. We feed the cats on rats and will start a rat ranch; the rats multiply four times as fast as the cats.

We start with 1,000,000 rats and will have four rats per cat from which the skins have been taken, giving each rat one quarter of a cat. It will thus be seen that the whole business will be self-acting and automatic throughout. The cats will eat the rats and for the rats' tails we will get the government grant of 4d. [4 pence] per tail. Other by-products are guts for tennis racquets, whiskers for wireless sets, and cat's pyjamas for Glenelg flappers. Eventually we will cross the cats with snakes, and they will skin themselves twice a year, thus saving the men's wages for skinning and also getting two skins per cat per year.

Awaiting your prompt reply, and trusting that you will appreciate this most wonderful opportunity to get rich quick.

Yours faithfully

Babbling Brook,

Promoter

A half-century or so later, the story was still going the rounds in the form of a photocopied page but the 1920s good-time girls known as 'flappers' had disappeared and the figures were in decimal currency. There was also a more modern enticement to invest: 'The offer to participate in this investment opportunity of a lifetime has only been made to a limited number of individuals—so send your cheque now!!' Otherwise, it was the same bizarre tale.

A farmer's lament

The conversion from imperial to metric units that took place in Australia in the 1960s gave rise to this mild satire:

*I*t all started back in 1966, when they changed to dollars and overnight my overdraft doubled.

I was just getting used to this when they brought in kilograms and my wool cheque dropped by half.

Then they started playing around with the weather and brought in Celsius and millimetres, and we haven't had a decent fall of rain since.

As if this wasn't enough, they had to change over to hectares and I end up with less than half the farm I had.

So one day I sat down and had a good think. I reckoned with daylight saving I was working eight days a week, so I decided to sell out.

Then, to cap it all, I had only got the place in the agent's hand when they changed to kilometres and I find I'm too flaming far out of town!

The little red hen

This is one of many tales that turn on tensions between the boss and the workers. Based on a folktale that has itself been around since at least the nineteenth century, this photocopied satire from the 1980s still resonates today with its down-to-earth simplification of industrial politics.

*O*nce upon a time there was a little red hen who scratched around and found some grains of wheat. She called on the other animals to help her plant the wheat.

'Too busy,' said the cow.

'Wrong union,' said the horse.

'Not me,' said the goose.

'Where's the environmental impact study?' asked the duck.

So the hen planted the grain, tended it and reaped the wheat. Then she called for assistance to bake some bread.

'I'll lose my unemployment relief,' said the duck.

'I'll get more from the RED [Royal Employment Development scheme],' said the sheep.

'Out of my classification, and I've already explained the union problem,' said the horse.

'At this hour?' queried the goose.

'I'm preparing a submission to the IAC [Industry Assistance Commission],' said the cow.

So the little red hen baked five lovely loaves of bread and held them up for everyone to see.

'I want some,' said the duck and sheep together.

'I demand my share,' said the horse.

'No,' said the little red hen. 'I have done all the work. I will keep the bread and rest awhile.'

'Excess profit,' snorted the cow.

'Capitalist pig,' screamed the duck.

'Foreign multi-national,' yelled the horse.

'Where's the workers' share?' demanded the pig.

So they hurriedly painted picket signs and paraded around the hen, yelling, 'We shall overcome.' And they did, for the farmer came to see what all the commotion was about.

'You must not be greedy, little red hen,' he admonished. 'Look at the disadvantaged goose, the underprivileged pig, the less fortunate horse, the out-of-work duck. You are guilty of making second-class citizens out of them. You must learn to share.'

'But I have worked to produce my own bread,' said the little red hen.

'Exactly,' said the farmer. 'That is what free enterprise is all about these days. You are free to work as hard as you like. If you were on a Communist farm you would have to give up all the bread. Here you can share it with your needy companions.'

So they lived happily ever after. But the university research team, having obtained a large government grant to study this odd happening, wondered why the little red hen never baked any more bread.

～

The airline steward's revenge

This recent urban legend nicely encapsulates the workplace fantasy of getting one's own back on an especially difficult customer.

a steward was working in First Class on a plane from South Africa to Sydney. On the flight was a very wealthy and snooty elderly couple. A little way into the flight, the steward came along the aisle to where the pair were seated. 'What would you like to drink, Madam?' he asked.

There was no reply. Thinking that the woman might not have heard him, the steward asked again.

Once more she ignored him. But her husband leaned over and said, 'My wife doesn't speak to the help. She would like a bottle of red.'

So the steward went off to get the wine. As he walked away, the man called out 'Boy, boy!' The steward quickly returned to the couple. 'Yes, Sir, how can I help you?'

The man said, 'My wife was wondering about the situation with domestic help in Australia.'

'Oh, Sir,' the steward replied, 'I'm sure Madam will have no trouble at all finding a job.'

The boss

This item, still emailed around, is based on a fable at least as old as Aesop:

W hen the Lord made man, all the parts of the body argued over who would be the BOSS.

The BRAIN explained that since he controlled all the parts of the body, he should be the BOSS.

The LEGS argued that since they took the man wherever he wanted to go, they should be the BOSS.

The STOMACH countered that since he digested all the food, he should be the BOSS.

The EYES said that without them, man would be helpless, so they should be BOSS.

Then the ARSEHOLE applied for the job.

The other parts of the body laughed so hard that the ARSEHOLE got mad and closed up.

After a few days the BRAIN went foggy, the LEGS got wobbly, the STOMACH got ill and the EYES got crossed and unable to see.

They all conceded defeat and made the ARSEHOLE the BOSS.

This proves that you don't have to be a BRAIN to be BOSS . . .

JUST AN ARSEHOLE.

Picture credits

Page 10
Daisy Bates (standing) with Aboriginal women and children
Photograph by A.G. Bolam, 1919–1926
South Australian Museum, Bolam Collection

Page 34
Lost in the Bush
Samuel Calvert (engraver), Nicholas Chevalier (artist), 1864
State Library of Victoria, image no. IMP24/09/64/1

Page 64
The Bunyip
J. Macfarlane (engraver), 1890
State Library of Victoria, image no. IAN01/10/90/12

Page 90
'Inland Sea' from T. J. Maslen, *The Friend of Australia: Or, a Plan for Exploring
the Interior, and for Carrying On a Survey of the Whole Continent of Australia, By
a Retired Officer of the Hon. East India Company's Service*, Hurst, Chance and Co.,
London, 1830.
Battye Library of Western Australian History

Page 110
Fisher's Ghost Creek, Campbelltown, c. 1909
Campbelltown City Library, Local Studies Collection

Page 132
Copy of *Children's Hour*
Photograph of painting by William Ford, 1870
State Library of Victoria, image no. H96.160/1621

Page 148
Captain Hurley spins some yarns, 1929–1931
Commander Blair, W.J. Griggs, Scout Marr, Mr Tyler, Captain Hurley and A.J. Hodgeman
Part of Frank Hurley B.A.N.Z. Antarctic Research Expedition photographs
National Library of Australia, image no. 10932811-95

Page 176
'Damn your explosive bullets' cartoon
From Hartt, C.L, *Humorosities*, Australian Trading & Agencies Co. Ltd., London, 1917

Page 198
'Dad' (character from *On Our Selection*)
Alfred Vincent (artist) from first edition of Arthur H. Davis (Steele Rudd) 'On Our Selection', *Bulletin* newspaper, Sydney, 1899

Page 220
Eulo Queen, 1920
Creator unknown
John Oxley Library, State Library of Queensland, image no. 195153

Page 242
The Bullocky (postcard)
Harry John Weston (artist) 1874–19?
State Library of Victoria, image no. H87.358/15

Sources and selected references

1. STORIES IN THE HEART

Bates, D., *The Passing of the Aborigines: a lifetime spent among the natives of Australia*, John Murray, London, 1938

Berndt, R. & C., *The Speaking Land: myth and story in Aboriginal Australia*, Penguin, Ringwood VIC, 1989

Faurot, J. (editor), *Asian-Pacific Folktales and Legends*, Simon & Schuster, New York, 1995

Hassell, E., revised by Davidson, D., 'Myths and Folktales of the Wheelman Tribe of South-Western Australia', in *Folklore* vol. 45, no. 3, September 1934; vol. 45, no. 4, December 1934; vol. 46, no. 2, June 1935; vol. 46, no. 3, September 1935

Lawrie, M. (collected & translated), *Tales from Torres Strait*, University of Queensland Press, St Lucia QLD, 1972

Mathews, J. (compiler) & White, I. (editor), *The Opal That Turned Into Fire and other stories from the Wangkumara*, Magabala Books, Broome, 1994

McConchie, P. (collected & edited), *Elders: wisdom from Australia's Indigenous leaders*, Cambridge University Press, Melbourne, 2003

Palmer, K., 'Aboriginal Oral Tradition from South-west of Western Australia', in *Folklore*, vol. 87, no. 1, 1976

Parker, K. Langloh (collected & edited), *Australian Legendary Tales*, David Nutt, London, 1896

Rose, D., *Dingo Makes Us Human: life and land in an Aboriginal Australian culture*, Cambridge University Press, Melbourne, 1992

Ryan, J., 'Australia's Best-Known Folkloric Text and its Several Fates', in *Australian Folklore*, vol. 16, 2001

Spencer, B., *The Native Tribes of the Northern Territory of Australia*, Macmillan, London, 1914

2. PIONEER TRADITIONS

Darian-Smith, K., Poignant, R., Schaffer K., *Captive Lives: Australian captivity narratives*, Sir Robert Menzies Centre for Australian Studies, Institute of Commonwealth Studies, University of London, 1993

Moore, G.F., *Diary of Ten Years Eventful Life of an Early Settler in Western Australia*, with an introduction by C.T. Stannage, University of Western Australia Press, Nedlands WA, 1978

Perth Gazette, 5 July 1834, 12 July 1834, 19 July 1834, 26 July 1834, 9 August 1834, 6 September 1834, 4 October 1834

Port Phillip Herald, 10 March 1846

Torney, K., *Babes in the Bush: the making of an Australian image*, Curtin University Books, Fremantle WA, 2005

——'Jane Duff's Heroism: the last great human bush story?' in *La Trobe Journal*, vol. 63, Autumn 1999

3. MAKING MONSTERS

Bauer, N., 'A Mystery Unsolved: the story of the Min Min Light', in *Royal Geographical Society of Australasia (Queensland) Bulletin*, vol. 7, no.1, January 1982

Beatty, B., *A Treasury of Australian Folk Tales and Traditions*, Ure Smith, Sydney, 1960

Birch, R., *Wyndham Yella Fella*, Magabala Books, Broome, 2003

Clarke, P., 'Indigenous Spirit and Ghost Folklore of "settled" Australia', in *Folklore* vol. 118, no. 2, August 2007

Dixon, R., *Oceanic Mythology*, Marshall Jones Co., Boston, 1916

Dunlop, W., 'Australian Folk-Lore Stories', in *Journal of the (Royal) Anthropological Institute of Great Britain and Ireland*, vol. xxviii, 1899

Edwards, R., *Fred's Crab and Other Bush Yarns*, Rams Skull Press, Kuranda QLD, 1990

Farwell, G., *Land of Mirage: the story of men, cattle and camels on the Birdsville Track*, Cassell, London, 1950

Hassell, E., 'My Dusky Friends', undated typescript, Battye Library of Western Australian History

Henry, J., 'Pumas in the Grampians Mountains: a compelling case?', an updated report of the Deakin Puma Society, Deakin University Press, 2001

Holden, R., *Bunyips: Australia's folklore of fear*, National Library of Australia, Canberra, 2001

Journal of the Anthropological Society of South Australia, vol. 29, no. 2, 1991

Journal of the Anthropological-Institute, vol. xxx, 1900

Leeds Mercury, 25 January 1834

Massola, A., *Bunjil's Cave: myths, legends and superstitions of the Aborigines of south-east Australia*, Lansdowne Press, Melbourne, 1968

Morgan, J., *The Life and Adventures of William Buckley*, Archibald Macdougall, London, 1852

North Australian Monthly, January 1961

Parker, K. Langloh, *The Euahlayi Tribe: a study of Aboriginal life in Australia*, Archibald Constable, London, 1905

Praed, Mrs Campbell, 'The Bunyip', in *Coo-ee: tales of Australian life by Australian ladies*, Mrs Patchett Martin (editor), Griffith Farran Okeden & Welsh, London and Sydney, 1891

Robinson, R. (editor), *Aboriginal Myths and Legends*, Sun Books, Melbourne, 1966

Scott, B., *Pelicans and Chihuahuas and Other Urban Legends*, University of Queensland Press, St Lucia QLD, 1996

Short, K., *Echoes of the Clarence*, International Colour Productions, Stanthorpe QLD, 1980

Sorenson, E., *Life in the Australian Backblocks*, Whitcomb & Tombs, Melbourne, 1911

South Australian Gazette and Colonial Register, 28 November 1853, 31 January 1889

Sunday Mail Magazine, 2 March 1941

Unaipon, D., *Legendary Tales of the Australian Aborigines*, Muecke, S. & Shoemaker, A. (editors), The Miegunyah Press, Melbourne, 2001

Walkabout, 1 April 1937

4. LEGENDS ON THE LAND

Anzac Day Commemoration Committee, Queensland, www.anzacday.org.au, February 2009

Australian National Dictionary Centre, www.anu.edu.au/andc/ozwords/April_2000/Anzacs.html, December 2005

Australian War Memorial, www.awm.gov.au, December 2005

Beatty, B., *A Treasury of Australian Folk Tales and Traditions*, Ure Smith, Sydney, 1960

Committee for Geographical Names in Australia, www.icsm.gov.au/icsm/cgna/lesson/story_001.html, September 2008

Department of Defence, www.defence.gov.au/anzacday/history.htm, February 2009

Edwards, R., *Fred's Crab and Other Bush Yarns*, Rams Skull Press, Kuranda QLD, 1989

Idriess, I., *Lasseter's Last Ride: an epic of central Australian gold discovery*, Angus & Robertson, Sydney, 1931

Jack, A., 'I'd had it in mind . . .', in *Wartime*, no. 46, 2009

Marshall-Stoneking, B., *Lasseter: the making of a legend*, G. Allen & Unwin, Australia, 1985

Martin, G., Western Australian Folklore Archive, John Curtin Prime Ministerial Library, Curtin University of Technology

Norledge, M. (editor), *Aboriginal Legends from Eastern Australia: the Richmond–Mary River area*, Reed, Sydney, 1968

Parramatta RSL, www.parramattarsl.com.au/rsl9/DS38.htm, December 2005

Robinson, R., *The Man Who Sold his Dreaming*, Currawong Publishing, Sydney, 1965

Trollope, Anthony, *Australia and New Zealand*, Chapman & Hall, London, 1873

5. THE HAUNTED LAND

Anon., 'Fisher's Ghost: A legend of Campbelltown', in *Tegg's Monthly Magazine*, vol. 1, March 1863

Beatty, B., *A Treasury of Australian Folk Tales and Traditions*, Ure Smith, Sydney, 1960

Beckett, J., 'A Death in the Family: some Torres Strait ghost stories', in Hiatt, L. (editor), *Australian Aboriginal Mythology*, Australian Institute of Aboriginal Studies, Canberra, 1975

Clarke, P., 'Indigenous Spirit and Ghost Folklore of "Settled" Australia', in *Folklore*, vol. 118, no. 2, August 2007

Cusack, F. (editor), *Australian Ghosts*, Angus & Robertson, London, 1975

Davis, R., *The Ghost Guide to Australia*, Bantam Books, Moorebank NSW, 1998

Freeman's Journal, Sydney, 1891

Emberg, B. & J., *Ghostly Tales of Tasmania*, Regal Publications, Launceston, 1991

Gale, J., *Canberra*, A.M. Fallick & Sons, Queanbeyan NSW, 1927

Hasluck, P. 'Travels in Western Australia 1870–74: extracts from the journal of Thomas Scott', in *Early Days*, vol. 2, part 15, 1934

Lang, A., 'The Truth About Fisher's Ghost', in Lang, A., *The Valet's Tragedy and Other Studies*, Longmans, London, 1903

Scott, B., *The Long and the Short and the Tall: a collection of Australian yarns*, Western Plains Publishers, Sydney, 1985

Western Australian Folklore Archive, John Curtin Prime Ministerial Library, Curtin University of Technology

6. TALES OF WONDER

Anderson, H., *Time Out of Mind: the story of Simon McDonald*, National Press, Melbourne, 1974

Bettelheim, B., *The Uses of Enchantment: the meaning and importance of fairy tales*, Knopf, New York, 1976

Briggs, K. (editor), *A Dictionary of British Folk-Tales in the English Language*, vols 1 & 2, Routledge & Kegan Paul, London, 1970–1971

Calvino, I., *Italian Folk Tales: selected and retold by Italo Calvino*, Martin, G. (translator), Harcourt Brace Jovanovich, New York, 1980

Household Words, vol. 5, no. 124, London, August 1852

Jacobs, J. (compiled and annotated), *English Fairy Tales: being the two collections English Fairy Tales and More English Fairy Tales*, Bodley Head, London & Sydney, 1968

Klipple, M., *African Folktales with Foreign Analogues*, Garland, New York & London, 1992

Zipes, J., *Fairy Tales and the Art of Subversion: the classical genre for children and the process of civilization*, Heinemann, London, 1983

7. BULLDUST

Brennan, M., *Reminiscences of the Goldfields, and Elsewhere in New South Wales: covering a period of forty-eight years' service as an officer of police*, William Brooks, Sydney, 1907

Edwards, R., *Fred's Crab and Other Bush Yarns*, Rams Skull Press, Kuranda QLD, 1989

Fields, M., *Dinkum Aussie Yarns*, Southdown Press, Melbourne, nd (early 1990s)

Gammage, W., *The Broken Years: Australian soldiers in the Great War*, Penguin, Ringwood VIC, 1975

Howcroft, W., *Dungarees and Dust*, Hawthorn Press, Melbourne, 1978

Mills, F.J., *Square Dinkum: a volume of original Australian wit and humour / by 'The Twinkler' (Fred J. Mills)*, Melville & Mullen, Melbourne, 1917

Northern Territory News, 18 September 1997

Scott, B., *Complete Book of Australian Folklore*, PR Books, Sydney, 1988

Sydney Morning Herald, 31 August 1988

Wannan, B., *Crooked Mick of the Speewah and Other Tales*, Lansdowne Press, Sydney, 1965

——*A Dictionary of Australian Folklore*, Lansdowne Press, Sydney, 1981

——*Come in Spinner: a treasury of popular Australian humour*, Rigby, Adelaide, 1976

——*The Australian*, Rigby, Adelaide, 1954

Western Australian Folklore Archive, John Curtin Prime Ministerial Library, Curtin University of Technology

8. HEROES

Anon., *Marching On: tales of the diggers*, Petersham, nd (1940s)

Anon., *Digger Aussiosities*, New Century Press, Sydney, 1927

Anzac Bulletin, vol. 64, London, 29 March 1918

Aussie, 15 April 1920, 15 June 1920, 15 October 1920

Australian Corps News Sheet, 6 November 1918

Beatty, B., *A Treasury of Australian Folk Tales and Traditions*, Ure Smith, Sydney, 1960

Bradshaw, J., *The Only True Account of Ned Kelly, Frank Gardiner, Ben Hall and Morgan*, Waverly Press, Sydney, 1911

Bryant, N. & J., 'Captain Thunderbolt', www.halenet.com.au/~jvbryant/thunderb.html#anchor626534, August 2008

Cooper, A.H., *Character Glimpses: Australians on the Somme*, Waverly Press, Sydney, 1920

Cuttriss, G., *Over the Top with the 3rd Australian Division*, Charles H. Kelly, London, 1918

Edwards, R., *The Australian Yarn*, Rigby, Adelaide, 1978

Fair, R., *A Treasury of Anzac Humour*, Jacaranda Press, Brisbane, 1965

Gale, J., *History of and Legends Relating to the Federal Capital Territory of the Commonwealth of Australia*, A.M. Fallick & Sons, Queanbeyan NSW, 1927

Harney, W., *Tales from the Aborigines*, Rigby, Adelaide, 1959

Honk, vol. 11, 7 December 1915

Kennedy, J.J., *The Whale Oil Guards*, J. Duffy, Dublin, 1918

League Post, 1 October 1932

Longmore, C. (editor), *Carry On! The Traditions of the AIF*, Imperial Printing Co., Perth, 1940

——'Digger's Diary', in *Western Mail*, 25 September 1930

Nally, E. (compiler), *Digger Tales 1914–1918, 1939–1942*, np

——*Lest We Forget*, 1941, np

Port Hacking Cough, December 1918–January 1919

Seal, G., *The Outlaw Legend: a cultural tradition in Britain, America and Australia*, Cambridge University Press, Cambridge, 1996

'Semaphore', in *Digger Yarns (and some others) to Laugh At*, E.H. Gibbs & Sons, Melbourne, 1936

Smith's Weekly, 15 August 1925, 29 August 1925, 21 November 1925

Tenterfield Historical Society Archives, Dixon Library, University of New England, Armidale NSW

The Cacolet, journal of the Australian Camel Field Ambulance, Palestine, nd

The Digger, vol. 1, no. 6, 8 September 1918

The Karoolian, April 1919

The Listening Post, 17 August 1923

Wannan, B., *Crooked Mick of the Speewah and Other Tales*, Lansdowne Press, Sydney, 1965

——*A Dictionary of Australian Folklore*, Lansdowne Press, Sydney, 1981

——*Come in Spinner: a treasury of popular Australian humour*, Rigby, Adelaide, 1976

——*The Australian*, Rigby, Adelaide, 1954

Wells, E., *An Anzac's Experiences in Gallipoli, France and Belgium*, W.J. Anderson, Sydney, 1919

9. CHARACTERS

Aussie, 15 December 1920, reprinted from the *Third Battalion Magazine*, nd, (c. 1917)

Bean, C.E.W. (editor), *The Anzac Book*, Cassell, London, 1916

Calvert, A.F., *The Aborigines of Western Australia*, Simpkin, Marshall, Hamilton, Kent, London, 1894

Edwards, R., *The Australian Yarn*, Rigby, Adelaide, 1978

Fields, M., *Dinkum Aussie Yarns*, Southdown Press, Melbourne, nd (early 1990s)

Hardy, F. & Mulley, A., *The Needy and the Greedy: humorous stories of the racetrack*, Libra Books, Canberra, 1975

Howcroft, W., *Dungarees and Dust*, Hawthorn Press, Melbourne, 1978

Papers of Bill Wannan, manuscripts, National Library of Australia, undated (c. 1960s) letter from Mr A.H. Fisher, Camden Park SA

Parker, K.L., (collected and edited), *Australian Legendary Tales*, Melville, Mullen & Slade, London & Melbourne, 1896

Quadrant, vol. 13, Summer 1959–60

Rudd, S., *On Our Selection*, Angus & Robertson, Sydney, 1899

Salt, 8 April 1946

Seal, G., *The Hidden Culture: folklore in Australian society*, Oxford University Press, Melbourne, 1989

Seal, G. & Willis, R. (editors), *Verandah Music: roots of Australian tradition*, Curtin University Books, Fremantle, 2003

Wannan, B., *The Folklore of the Irish in Australia*, Currey O'Neill, Melbourne, 1980

——*Come in Spinner: a treasury of popular Australian humour*, Rigby, Adelaide, 1976

——*The Australian*, Rigby, Adelaide, 1954

Weller, S., *Bastards I Have Met*, Sampal Investments, Charters Towers QLD, 1976

10. HARD CASES

Aussie, 15 December 1920, reprinted from *The Third Battalion* magazine, c. 1917

Australian Pastoralists Review, 16 July 1891

Bridge, P., *Russian Jack*, Hesperian Press, Perth, 2003

Edwards, R., *Fred's Crab and Other Bush Yarns*, Rams Skull Press, Kuranda QLD, 1990

——*The Australian Yarn*, Rigby, Adelaide, 1978

Elliot, I., *Moondyne Joe: the man and the myth*, University of Western Australia Press, Perth, 1978

Fields, M., *Dinkum Aussie Yarns*, Southdown Press, Melbourne, nd (early 1990s)

Hardy, F. & Mulley, A., *The Needy and the Greedy: humorous stories of the racetrack*, Libra Books, Canberra, 1975

Papers of Ian Turner, National Library of Australia

Wannan, B., *Come in Spinner: a treasury of popular Australian humour*, Rigby, Adelaide, 1976

——*My Kind of Country*, Rigby, Adelaide, 1967

Weller, S., *Bastards I Have Met*, Sampal Investments, Charters Towers QLD, 1976

Willis, W N., *The Life of WP Crick*, W.N. Willis, Sydney, 1909

11. WORKING PEOPLE

Adam-Smith, P., *Folklore of the Australian Railwaymen*, Rigby, Adelaide, 1976

Bean, C.E.W., *The Official History of Australia in the War of 1914–1918*, vol. 6, Angus & Robertson, Sydney, 1918

Cooper, A.H., *Character Glimpses: Australians on the Somme*, Waverly Press, Sydney, 1920

Edwards, R., *The Australian Yarn*, Rigby, Adelaide, 1978

Howcroft, W., *Dungarees and Dust*, Hawthorn Press, Melbourne, 1978

Lacy, J., *Off-Shears: the story of shearing sheds in Western Australia*, Black Swan Press, Perth, 2002

Longmore, C., 'Digger's Diary', in *Western Mail*, 2 January 1930, 30 October 1930

Marshall, A., in *Australasian Post*, 18 February 1954

Lest We Forget: digger tales 1914–18, 1939–42, Footscray VIC, nd (c. 1942), np

Scott, W., *Complete Book of Australian Folklore*, PR Books, Sydney, 1980

Seal, G., *The Bare Fax*, Angus & Robertson, Sydney, 1996

Skuthorpe, L., in *The Bulletin*, 4 August 1921

Smith's Weekly, Sydney, 6 June 1925

Stephens, J.B., in *The Australasian*, Melbourne, 8 March 1873

Stuart, Julian, in *Australian Worker*, Sydney, 31 October 1928

Tronson, M (ed.), *Ripping Good Railway Yarns*, IFH Publishing Co., Wallacia NSW, 1991

Wannan, B., *The Australian*, Rigby, Adelaide, 1954

——*Come in Spinner: a treasury of popular Australian humour*, Rigby, Adelaide, 1976

——*Crooked Mick of the Speewah and other tall tales*, Lansdowne Press, Melbourne, 1965

Western Australian Folklore Archive, John Curtin Prime Ministerial Library, Curtin University, Perth